GALAXY'S EDGE
EDITED BY MIKE RESNICK

ISSUE 21: JULY 2016

I0520624

Mike Resnick, Editor
Jean Rabe, Assistant Editor
Shahid Mahmud, Publisher

Published by Arc Manor/Phoenix Pick
P.O. Box 10339
Rockville, MD 20849-0339

Galaxy's Edge is published in January, March, May, July, September, and November.

www.GalaxysEdge.com

Available by subscription (www.GalaxysEdge.com) or through your favorite online store (Amazon.com, BN.com, etc.).

ISBN: 978-1-61242-318-0

FOREIGN LANGUAGE RIGHTS: Please refer all inquiries pertaining to foreign language rights to Spectrum Literary Agency, 320 Central Park West, Suite 1-D, New York, NY 10025. Phone: 1-212-362-4323. Fax 1-212-362-4562

CONTENTS

THE EDITOR'S WORD

by Mike Resnick

Welcome to the twenty-first issue of *Galaxy's Edge*.

We've got new stories by Martin L. Shoemaker, Dantzel Cherry, Steve Pantazis, Laurie Tom, Nathan Dodge, Larry Hodges, and for the first time ever (at your publisher's insistence), your editor. We've also got reprints from old friends such as Nancy Kress, George R. R. Martin, Kij Johnson, and Robert Silverberg. We have our regular columns by Bill Fawcett and Jody Lynn Nye; Gregory Benford; our regular column about literary matters by Barry N. Malzberg; and this issue Joy Ward interviews Robert J. Sawyer. Finally, we have the fourth part of our serialization of Leigh Brackett's *The Long Tomorrow*.

We hope you like it, and that you'll stop by our table to say hello at the upcoming Worldcon.

Last Impressions

I met a young man at a recent convention. He had submitted a story he thought was wonderful, and it had been turned down by me and other editors.

Okay, these things happen. Lots. For every would-be writer who can sell a story, there are dozens who never will.

But let me give you a little hint: if *you* don't have faith in your story, why should anyone else—like, for example, an editor? First impressions are important…but it is last impressions that count. I'm not saying that every rejected story is a misunderstood gem, but a story that remains in a desk drawer or in a computer file never has a chance of being understood *or* misunderstood.

Ever hear of a novel called *Up the Down Staircase*? It spent a year on the *New York Times* bestseller list, and was a major motion picture starring Sandy Dennis, back in the bygone days when she was a major motion picture actress.

That was a last impression. You know how many times the book was turned down?

Eighty-eight.

You know how it finally sold? The author, Bel Kaufman, showed it to her minister's wife, whose brother happened to be peripherally connected to the publishing industry, and one thing led to another, and suddenly the eighty-eight-times-rejected manuscript was the Number One seller in the country. I guess it's lucky that the author didn't burn the damned thing after the fiftieth or so turndown.

You think that just happens in other fields?

Every publisher, major and minor, in the science fiction field turned down Frank Herbert's *Dune*. Every one, without exception. You know how it finally sold? Sterling Lanier, who had written some science fiction in the 1950s, was editing at Chilton, a book company that specialized in, so help me, books on motorcycle maintenance. He had hardly any budget to spend on such a flyer, but Herbert had reached the point where he was happy to take hardly any money for it. And the rest is history: a perennial bestseller, with something like forty million copies sold worldwide, five bestselling sequels by Herbert and a batch more by his son Brian in collaboration with Kevin J. Anderson, two movies already made and a third in pre-production. All because Herbert believed in his book, and despite all those editorial first impressions that it was unsaleable, it was the last impression that counted.

Just one example, you suggest? Not hardly. One of the three or four most prestigious novels since *Dune* has been Joe Haldeman's *The Forever War*. Hugo winner, Nebula winner, bestseller—and, according to Joe, it was turned down by sixteen publishers before he sold it.

It doesn't just happen in novels, and it doesn't just reflect poorly upon some editors.

For example, a single brilliant novelette is sometimes enough to make an author's career. That was certainly the case with Tom Godwin's "The Cold Equations," which fifty-five years after its initial appearance remains the most-discussed novelette on the internet, and was even the basis for a made-for-TV movie. Roger Zelazny became a superstar very early on with the publication of "A Rose for Ecclesiastes." Cyril Kornbluth is remembered (as a solo writer, apart from his collaborations with Fred Pohl) primarily for "The Little Black Bag." A couple of brilliant novellas, Walter M. Miller Jr.'s "A Canticle for Leibowitz" and Orson Scott Card's "Ender's Game" were so stunning and influential that each was expanded into a perennial bestselling novel.

And the same is true of novellas. Harlan Ellison's "A Boy and His Dog" and Thomas M. Disch's "The Brave Little Toaster" were both so well-written and had such universal appeal that they were made into motion pictures.

Speaking of motion pictures, Kurt Vonnegut's *Slaughterhouse-Five* was a major theatrical release with a top-notch cast. They haven't made any movies out of Gene Wolfe's *Book of the New Sun* series or Larry Niven and Jerry Pournelle's *The Moat in God's Eye,* but there's no question that these have entered the realm of universally acknowledged Science Fiction Classics.

And you know something? Every single book and story I named in the preceding three paragraphs lost the Hugo. I don't mean that they were overlooked in obscure publications, or they came out so late in the year that no one had time to read them. Every one of them was a Hugo nominee—and not one impressed enough voters at the time to win.

I have to think that any writer would rather have had any of these stories to his credit than the mostly-forgotten tales that beat them at the time.

I was told a long time ago that if I wrote a good story, and it was rejected, I could give up on the editor and I could give up on the market, but I should never give up on the story. I take that to be an axiom, and I need look no farther than the examples I have just offered you to conclude that last impressions beat the hell out of first ones.

Martin L. Shoemaker is a Writers of the Future winner. He has sold multiple times to Analog, *plus stories to other top markets. This is his third appearance in* Galaxy's Edge. *Martin was a Nebula nominee in 2016.*

THE VAMPIRE'S NEW CLOTHES

by Martin L. Shoemaker
(With acknowledgments to Mike Resnick)

"Repeat your instructions, Renfield."

The Master had a thick accent that the little man to whom he spoke couldn't identify. He was a tall man with dark hair in a widow's peak. He was cultured, powerful, and impeccably dressed in a dark tuxedo, a crisp white shirt, and a crimson bow tie. A small, blood-red rose was pinned to his left lapel. That rose fascinated the other man.

They stood in a luxurious room with marble floors and walls. Unlike the Master, the little man looked completely out of place with his gray sweatshirt, sagging jeans, and sneakers that might once have been red. His brown hair was unkempt, and his face was dirty. He wished *he* had a rose. He reached out a long fingernail but didn't quite touch the flower.

The Master grabbed the short man's shoulder and shook it. "RENFIELD!"

The man cringed, his spray of hair waving as he looked up, down, left, right—anywhere but at the Master. "I'm sorry, I forgot that was my name, Master. Ummm... because it's not."

The Master scowled, revealing long, sharp canine teeth. "So what *is* your name?"

The short man looked down at his left shoe. "I forgot."

The Master stared at the arched ceiling. "Then until you remember a better one, your name is Renfield."

"Yes, Master."

The Master leaned over Renfield, and the little man leaned his head back. "Answer my question!" the Master shouted.

Renfield fell over; but without thinking, he flipped into a handspring and landed in a crouch on a marble-topped table. Renfield liked handsprings, they were fun. But he didn't like upsetting the Master. "Ummm... What was the question?"

"WHAT ARE YOUR INSTRUCTIONS?"

Renfield scurried under the table, but the Master snatched him by the collar, lifted him into the air, and held him so they were face to face. The little man whispered, "I forgot."

The Master sighed—a strange, breathless sound—and set Renfield back on his feet. In a quieter voice, he said, "Write this down."

"But Master... I don't know how to write."

The Master raised one dark eyebrow. "This is the twenty-first century. Who doesn't know how to write?" He counted quietly to ten and tried again. "If I go through this slowly, can you remember it?"

"I'll try."

"Why did I come to Manhattan?" the Master muttered. "London has a better class of lunatics. All right, Renfield, try very hard."

The Master paced. A picture of sunflowers was on the wall behind him, and Renfield found the picture distracting. So pretty. "Soon it will be sunrise," the Master began, "and I must retire to my bed."

Renfield raised his hand and said, "You mean the box of dirt in the coat closet? I planted purple irises in it."

The Master stopped and glared. "In my sacred native soil?"

"They're pretty." Irises were his favorite flowers. And roses. And sunflowers were nice, too.

"You do know flowers need sunlight to grow?"

"Oh." Renfield squinted. "I could haul the box out onto the balcony and open it up for them."

In an instant, Renfield again hung from the Master's grip. The Master's dark eyes peered straight into his own watery blue ones. "Listen to me carefully," the Master said in a quiet tone. "Don't ever say that again. Don't ever *think* that again. And in the name of Darkness, *don't ever do that!* Understood?" Renfield nodded, jiggling in the Master's grip. "All right. I shall let you live."

The Master dropped Renfield, and resumed pacing and talking. "Tomorrow night, I shall confront the Great Detective. So you—"

"But Master," Renfield said. He crouched, ready to race away at any moment. "How do you know you'll confront him?"

"Fate, Renfield, always drives me to confront my one worthy opponent of the era: the Great Vampire Hunter. Once it was the Great Prince. Later it was

the Great Knight or the Great Professor. Always a lonely hunter with but a few companions, fighting the authorities as well as me. Since that fool on Baker Street, it has been Great Detectives. They are the knights of this age."

"Oooh..." Renfield rose, and then bent his legs and held out his arm, imagining holding a sword. "I like knights!" He lunged, thrusting and parrying at his unseen foe. "Avast, knave, defend yourself!"

The Master said slowly, "'Avast' is for pirates. You mean 'Hold, knave!'"

Renfield lowered his arm. "Are you sure?"

The Master shouted, "Does it matter?" Again he counted to ten. The Master liked counting, Renfield thought. He counted a lot. "The sun shall rise soon, so pay attention. Take that garment bag..." He pointed at a large linen bag hanging by the door. "...to the Great Detective's building. Climb up to his office and break in—"

"Which building is that?"

"The one we drove past last night?" The Master paused. "The five-story red brick office building?" Another pause. "The one I told you to remember because the Great Detective's office was in there?"

Renfield remembered... "The one with honeysuckle on the front?" Honeysuckles were his favorite flowers.

"Yes!" The chandelier trembled, and the Master lowered his voice. "The one with honeysuckle. Climb up to his office, break in, and hide that bag in the coat closet near the window. Can you remember that?"

Renfield nodded. "Honeysuckle... Climb up... Garment bag... Closet..." He continued nodding as he recited, because nodding was fun. But then he stopped and asked, "Why, Master? What's in the bag?"

"My spare suit."

Renfield looked at the bag. "You're giving him your suit?"

"No, the suit is for me."

"But you already have a suit. Why should I put one in the closet?"

"Because I said so!" Renfield scurried back under the table, but the Master tried again in a calmer voice. "I am not one of these Hollywood vampires who can do whatever some hack writer wants. I am Lord of the Night, but even I have rules. I can change into a bat, but I cannot change my clothes with me. I must leave those behind. *Now* do you understand?"

Renfield poked his head out. "No, Master."

The Master bent down nose to nose with Renfield. "When I confront the Great Detective, I must do so in my finest style, not stark naked. I have a reputation to maintain! I shall *not* confront him with my three-thousand-year-old *pulă* hanging out!"

Renfield wondered what a *pulă* was, but he thought of a better question, one that might even impress the Master. "But Master, can't you just memorize him to *think* you have clothes?"

"That's *mesmerize!* And no, not unless I can get him to concentrate on my eyes. That won't happen with my *pulă* hanging out, drawing attention. It may be three-thousand years old, but it's still impressive."

The Master sighed. "No, when I arrive as a bat, I must swoop in the window, swiftly change my form and my clothes, and *then* confront my foe. So my trusted ally—" He looked at Renfield and cocked an eyebrow. "—must conceal my clothes on the final battlefield. Can you do that for me, Renfield?"

Renfield nodded again (nodding was *still* fun), and the Master smiled, showing his long fangs in that way that always scared Renfield; but before Renfield could hide again, the Master yanked him back to his feet. "I must rest now, the sun is about to rise. Here is some money so you can take a cab to the office. You have all day to do this one task. Can I trust you, Renfield?"

Renfield feared the Master, and he wanted to do a good job. Doing a good job was important, Mama always said that. Besides, when the Master was satisfied, he was less frightening, so Renfield relaxed and kept nodding.

Then the Master grabbed him by the throat with one knotted hand, stared into his eyes, and whispered, "One more thing: *no irises!*"

✿

Renfield danced through the mortuary lobby, imagining music. He twirled the garment bag like a beautiful lady, through the door and to the Manhattan sidewalk, which was still damp from last night's rain.

He liked dancing almost as much as handstands. And flowers. And knights. And *real* scissors (not *safety* scissors). And staplers. And doing a good job, and pleasing the Master.

Renfield knew he was different. Papa had called him *a failure*, Mama had called him *a burden*, and the police had called him *a dummy*. The woman in the white coat had called him a *deluge* (at least he thought that was the word), and the man in the black robe had called him *a danger to himself*. The attendants in the Home called him *special*. But the Master called him *an ally*. He gave Renfield important work to do, something the attendants had never done. They had let him do small tasks when he had first arrived; but every time he had trouble, they took it away and did it for him. They told him he was special, but they did everything for him. At first they let him make cloth dolls: he couldn't figure out needle and thread, but he could staple the cloth together. Then they took the stapler and safety scissors away. They were nice, but they treated him like a not-very-bright animal, and the Home was his cage. The Master was not a nice person and did not-nice things; but even when the Master was angry, he treated Renfield like a person, and so Renfield had run away from the Home to serve him.

And Renfield knew he saw things that weren't there, or he saw them wrong. That was why white-coat woman called him *a deluge*. He tried to see what he was supposed to, but he couldn't, and it hurt to try. He was comfortable with the world he saw. So when he saw yellow elephants in the street where other people saw cabs, he was okay with that. Either one would take him to the honeysuckle office, right?

Amid the cars that rolled past, splashing water as they went, there was an elephant just down the potholed street. Now what did people say to call an elephant? Renfield was sure he had seen that on TV. Was it...

"Taxes!" Renfield shouted, but the elephant did not budge.

"Toxic!" Neither did the turbaned man who sat atop the elephant.

Renfield paused, frowning; but before he could shout "Ticks!" the elephant rumbled like an out-of-tune engine and ambled forward.

Renfield ran after, but suddenly he saw that the elephant had left behind a big, stinking pile. Or was it motor oil? Either way, he didn't want to step in it. He leaped forward and over the mess, arcing into a handspring and bouncing back to his feet. That was so much fun, he did two more before coming to a halt. He leaned over to catch his breath, resting his hands on his knees.

His left hand was empty.

His right hand was empty, too. Something was missing...

He looked back at the pile of dung and saw the Master's bag laying in it. He took a step toward the bag—just before a truck drove over it, splattering the dung. A big, wet drop landed right in front of his foot.

The garment bag was crumpled in the middle of a wide, stinking mess. Renfield had to retrieve it before another car ran over it, but he didn't want to touch the stink. He searched the nearby bushes and found a long stick. With it, he snagged the hangers and pulled the bag free. Then he used a newspaper from a trash can to scrape the bag clean.

Renfield knew he would never get a cab—or an elephant—so he would walk. He knew the direction, and he had all day. How long could it take to cross Manhattan?

☼

Much later he had his answer: *too long*. He remembered the gardens: park gardens, window gardens, community gardens, even yard gardens. He thought he recognized them from the night before. Gardens—especially flowers—meant more to him than streets. So he let the asters and mums speak to him, leading him... somewhere. Asters were his favorite flowers. Or maybe mums.

Then suddenly he knew where they were leading him, and he broke into a wide grin. In one garden with a high spiked fence, he saw *sunflowers!* Not as many as in the Master's painting, but more than he could count. They stood there in all their golden glory, absorbing the warm autumn sunlight that broke through the remaining clouds! They were taller than him.

He had to touch them. The gate was locked, but Renfield was a good climber. He hung the bag inside the high fence, with the hangers hooked around one spike. Then he clambered over and dropped into the garden. He walked up to the nearest blossom, stuck his face up it, and inhaled deeply. Renfield had never smelled sunflowers before. The scent was green, earthy, and a little sweet, but so faint he might miss it if he wasn't so close.

He smelled another. The plants were in six rows, spaced so a person could just fit between them. He zigzagged from bloom to bloom, smelling and touching and laughing. Their leaves were damp, and he laughed as they showered him with cool droplets. Among all his favorite flowers, sunflowers were his *favorite* favorite flowers! So tall and sheltering and beautiful.

Renfield forgot the bag. He forgot the Master and the Great Detective. He forgot the elephants and the Home and his parents and the city. He forgot time. For this instant, with the tall flowers and their scents surrounding him and hiding him, he was transported to someplace else, someplace he couldn't name. Unless that name was *Happiness*.

But happiness never lasted. He heard a low growl, and he peered between the stalks. A large black Great Dane stood there. Its lips were curled and drool dripped from its jowls to the ground. If the Master were a dog, he would be *that* dog.

"Nice doggie..." Renfield held out his hand to let the dog sniff it.

The dog barked—a deep boom that rattled Renfield's bones—and leaped.

Renfield bounded backward without thinking. He crushed four of the sunflower stalks as he fled, and he moaned for their lost beauty. But he wasted no time springing to the top of the fence and down the other side.

The dog threw itself against the fence, rising up and planting its forepaws near the top of the fence. It barked, and Renfield fell on his butt. Then he realized: the dog was on *that* side of the fence and he was on *this* side. He was safe.

But the garment bag was on *that* side.

Renfield climbed the fence, grabbed the hangers, and lifted... at the same time that the dog grabbed the bottom of the bag and pulled. The dog planted its huge feet in the moist earth of the garden. Renfield got a better hold, while the dog tried to yank the bag from his grip. Renfield pulled for all he was worth, and the Dane was forced to take three steps forward. Maybe it wouldn't win.

The dog lost its grip, and Renfield fell backwards. Before he could catch himself, the bag fell upon the spikes, and he heard a tearing sound. Then the dog leaped up and once more gripped the bag in its teeth, pulling and twisting. Renfield pulled back—and the sound of ripping filled the air, and he and the remnants of the bag tumbled into the street.

And into a mud puddle.

The dog had only an empty bag. And Renfield had... the suit. The muddy, smelly, crumpled, ripped suit.

☼

Mama had taken Renfield to a store like this once, a clothes-cleaning store. He had brought the Master's suit here, and the purple-haired kid behind the counter had taken most of his money, promising the suit would be cleaned and repaired in two hours.

Purple Hair stared at Renfield as he waited, but then he went back to looking at his computer screen, doing something in the back, and talking to customers as they came in.

Renfield didn't want to admit why he waited. He wasn't sure where else to go, and he didn't want to lose track of the Master's suit. And besides, he wasn't sure how long two hours was.

After a long time, Purple Hair brought a box up and set it on the counter. Then without a word he went to the back room.

Renfield fidgeted. Had it been two hours? Was that the suit? Was Purple Hair ashamed to even talk to him anymore?

That had to be it! Many people gave up on talking to Renfield. They didn't like having him around, but the polite ones wouldn't say it. The kid seemed polite, so Renfield could draw only one conclusion: Purple Hair wanted him to take his box and leave.

So he did.

Renfield didn't like making people uncomfortable, and he didn't know how he did it. The Master was never uncomfortable around him, which was another reason he liked the Master. He wanted to like other people, too, if only they would let him. But since he didn't know how, he was glad to leave Purple Hair behind.

Four blocks later, though, he heard shouting. He turned back, and through the crowd he made out a fast-moving spot of purple.

Oh, no... Sometimes people did worse than ignore Renfield: sometimes bad people got angry, and they... hurt him. Not like the Master's threats, they chased him down and really *hurt* him. Purple Hair hadn't *looked* like a bad person. But then, neither had Papa...

Renfield clutched the box and dashed through the crowd. He was small and quick, so he made good time; but when he looked back, Purple Hair was still shouting.

Renfield turned to run again—and collided with a bicycle messenger. The bicyclist crashed to the ground, dazed; but Renfield tumbled and sprang to his feet. He looked around, and the battered box lay under the bicycle. He lifted the bike with his left hand and retrieved the box with his right.

But then he thought... Mama said taking things that weren't yours was wrong. But disappointing the Master was worse. But *paying* for the things you took made it right. So he said, "Sorry," and he held bike and box in one hand as he dropped the last of his money on the cyclist. He climbed onto the bike and pedaled away, clinging to the box as he steered.

The wind in Renfield's face made him smile despite the shouts—which seemed louder, almost as if two people were shouting. But soon they faded, and he was free.

He recognized more plants, and that made him smile even wider. A few blocks further he smelled just the slightest hint of... *honeysuckle!* He rounded a corner, and there was the Great Detective's office building. Renfield knew he wouldn't disappoint the Master: it wasn't even dark yet!

But already the sun was behind the tall buildings. He had no time to waste. Renfield recalled his orders... "Honeysuckle... Climb up... Garment bag... Closet..."

So now he could walk up to the fifth floor. But the Master said *climb up*, not *walk up*. It was important to follow the Master's orders. Did he mean climb the wall? Stairs have steps, so you *step* up those, right? Although Renfield was good at climbing, he didn't like heights. Many times he had climbed trees at the Home, and then the attendants had to get him back down. Climbing was fun, but looking down was not fun.

But he had no choice. "The Master said 'climb up,' so I have to *climb* up!" He dropped the bike, tucked the box under his arm, and walked up to the corner of the wall.

The scent of honeysuckle surrounded him, so powerful when he was so close. Honeysuckles were his favorite flowers! Well, except for sunflowers, of course. The sweet smell made Renfield brave, and he easily scaled the corner, even holding the box. He was careful not to look down; and as the shadows lengthened, he made his way to the fifth floor.

Then he had to climb sideways to reach the office window. The bricks of the corner had offered him many hand and footholds, but the wall was more even. Three times he found no place to put his foot, and he almost lost his grip; but he was a good climber, and patient. He felt with his toe until he found somewhere to put his weight.

At last Renfield stood on his toes on the ledge outside the Great Detective's window. He would make the Master happy! Well, at least he would make the Master not angry, which was pretty good.

Only the window wouldn't open.

It wasn't locked, wasn't even latched, just stuck. He had come so far; he couldn't let that stop him. He clenched the box between his knees, held onto his handhold with his right hand, and pushed up on the frame with the fingers of his left.

He knew that five stories of *down* were right behind him. If the window jerked suddenly open, he could lose his grip and fall.

At last the window budged. Just a little, but Renfield knew he had won. He had beaten the window. But there was no time to celebrate, not until he was inside! Slowly he pulled the window up until his toes slid forward for a more comfortable perch. Then he pulled it all the way open, and he slid inside.

And the box slipped. And fell. Outside. And *down*.

Despite his fear of falling, Renfield leaned out and watched the box fall. It tumbled, almost gracefully, until it struck the cement sidewalk. Then it burst open in a spray of pink.

Pink?

Before Renfield could wonder why the Master had a pink suit, Purple Hair ran up and lifted up a short, puffy pink dress. Renfield was sure the Master would never wear that.

Right behind Purple Hair ran the bicycle messenger. He picked up the fallen bike and inspected it. Then both young men looked up at Renfield and shouted at him, fists raised. Then the messenger mounted the bike and rode away. Purple Hair glared at Renfield and followed.

After the elephant, the wrong turns, the dog, the cleaner, the bike, the wall... After all of that, Renfield had failed. And the shadows told him there was no time to try again. He had let the Master down.

No.

He wasn't going to fail. He wasn't a *deluge*, he was a *person*. And the Master counted on him.

Renfield looked around the office. It was sloppy. Mama would've fainted away at the copies of *Racing Form* and the pictures of not-nice women in not enough clothes. Nearby was a kitchen, with dirty dishes and overstuffed drawers. There had to be something he could work with. He rummaged through the drawers—but very quietly. He thought he heard snoring from the mirror, and he didn't want to wake whatever was in there.

Then Renfield saw it. It had been there all the time, waiting for him to see it: the answer to his problem, right at the window. He would make the Master proud.

He curled up in the closet and waited for the Master. Soon he fell asleep.

Renfield woke instantly when he heard the closet knob turn. The door opened and the Master looked in. Renfield held a finger to his lips, and he tried not to look at the Master's naked body as he whispered, "Quietly, Master. I think the mirror can hear us."

The Master looked at the mirror, and scratched his head. Then he turned back to Renfield and whispered, "What are you doing here? Where's my suit?"

"There was an elephant, and a dog, and a man with Purple Hair... But I have a plan!"

"I don't—" The Master caught himself as his voice rose, and he returned to a whisper. "I don't need a plan, I need a suit!"

"I know, but this is almost as good. At least in the darkness." Renfield brought his loot from the closet: a dingy white tablecloth, the dark gray curtains from the window, and the scissors and stapler from the Great Detective's desk. *Real* scissors, Renfield noted with pride, not *safety* scissors. "Just hold your arms out, and stand with your feet apart. I have to work fast."

The Master looked nervously at the clock. "Do I have a choice?"

Renfield held up the tablecloth and cut a front piece, a back, and sleeves. They were too big, but no one would notice in the dark. He held the pieces up to the Master and pinched the edges together, stapling him into the shirt.

The Master flexed and raised his arms, frowning at the gaps that showed, so Renfield stapled some more. The Master flexed again, and nodded.

Then he smiled, and Renfield knew he had done a *very* good thing.

Next Renfield stapled the Master into pants (being careful not to look at the Master's *pulă*—good boys didn't look there, Mama had said). The pants sagged, so Renfield stapled them to the shirt. There were also no shoes, so Renfield cut out black slippers, stapled the Master's feet into them, and stapled them to the pant cuffs.

That left the suit coat, but Renfield frowned. The Master's coat should look perfect, and Renfield wasn't perfect. So he settled for a long cape, cutting it from one complete curtain and stapling the hem. When he draped it around the Master's shoulders and stapled the collar, the look was close enough to frighten Renfield.

"How does it look?" the Master whispered. He could never check his appearance, even in a normal mirror, so Renfield was used to this job.

He looked at the Master. "*Almost* perfect." Renfield tiptoed to the open window, plucked a honeysuckle blossom, held it up to the Master's chest, and stapled it in place.

"Ouch!"

"Sorry, Master. But now... perfect!"

"This had better work, Renfield..."

"It will, Master, it will!"

The Master twirled, holding his arms out so his cape flowed. "All right, now leave. I can't protect you from the Great Detective and his henchmen." And he headed toward the bedroom at the far side of the office.

But Renfield couldn't help himself. He had never seen a Great Detective before, and he had never seen the Master confront his arch nemesis. He had to know how the battle would play out, so he crept close to the open door, hid under a table, and peered through the door. "Get him, Master!" he whispered very quietly.

But they didn't fight, they... talked. Renfield didn't understand most of the words, but it sounded bad for the Master. The Great Detective wasn't intimidated by him. How could *anyone* not be intimidated by the Master?

Maybe the Master was right: the Great Detective *was* a knight. Renfield had never seen a knight before, but he knew they were real. They did the right thing and treated everyone fairly. Could this man be one? Maybe his knight's armor and sword were in the bedroom.

At one point, a woman snuck into the office, closed the window, and sprayed it with some solution. The Master and the Great Detective kept talking as the woman snuck back out. Renfield wondered if he should warn the Master, but he didn't know how.

Later the Master stormed out of the bedroom and to the window; but before he could touch it, he recoiled so quickly and roared so loudly that Renfield feared the staples would give out. The Master ran back into the bedroom, and they argued more. Renfield couldn't follow all the words, all the things unsaid, but he could tell from the tone: somehow, impossible as the idea was, the Master had lost, and was simply reluctant to admit it.

Finally the Great Detective and the Master walked out of the bedroom. The Master's shoulders slumped. He was defeated.

Yet even in victory, the Great Detective was cautious. He walked behind the Master, keeping his guard up to the last as they discussed shipping schedules and the Master leaving the country for good.

Leaving... Leaving Renfield!

Then, when it seemed to be over, the Great Detective stepped toward the door; but he accidentally stepped on the hem of the Master's cape, pulling it to the side. The Master jerked away, but that made matters worse: the detective also stood on one of the slippers. Renfield heard staples pop loose and ping against the wall.

Just like that, the makeshift trousers let go. The Master stood before the Great Detective, half naked, with his three-thousand-year-old *pulă* hanging out.

The Master glanced down. The Great Detective glanced down as well. Then both men looked up, not quite looking into each other's eyes. The Master spoke in a low, clenched tone. "When you tell this story, detective, will you do me the honor of leaving this part out?"

The Great Detective nodded. "Not. A. Word. But..." He whistled as he opened the door. "Impressive!"

"Indeed." And with that, the Master turned into a bat, leaving behind the last of his stapled clothing. As he flew out the door, Renfield knew that was the last he would ever see of the Master.

The little man felt a touch of panic at that. *Who will I serve now?* But the panic was brief. Renfield had triumphed over adversity many times today. Against all odds, he had succeeded in his quest. He was a person, no matter what the Home said, and he would find someone who would appreciate that.

Maybe... Maybe a knight needed a squire...

Copyright © 2016 by Martin L. Shoemaker

Larry Hodges has sold more than seventy stories, including three to Galaxy's Edge. *His third novel,* Campaign 2100: Game of Scorpions, *was recently published by World Weaver Press.*

PENGUINS OF NOAH'S ARK

by Larry Hodges

The new U.S. president's fist slammed into his desk, his response to the realization that things are a lot harder to get done in the White House than they are to say on the campaign trail. Unknown to him, he was about to become the fist driving history. The vibrations caused the wooden bust of George W. Bush on a nearby shelf to fall off and disappear into the time vortex that suddenly appeared just below it.

The Bush bust passed through the vortex, catching fire through friction as it shot through time. It came out in 2348 BC in the Larsen Ice Shelf in Antarctic, near a waddle of penguins, for that is what a group of penguins would someday be called.

Two penguins from the waddle waddled over, never realizing that their doing so saved their lives while dooming all other penguins to a watery death. They were a husband and wife, with a baby penguin left behind as they came over to examine the burning Bush. The baby bleeped over and over, very much like the son of Job when he was about to be killed by his father in the interests of righteousness, and it has been hypothesized that this willingness to doom their baby because of a persuasive burning Bush might be why these two were selected for survival.

The burning Bush spoke to them. "You must go to Babylonia and board a great ark so that you may survive a great flood and then procreate penguins afterwards so that your species may survive despite the scientifically insolvable problem of genetic diversity."

The mother penguin, who was known as Bleep, said, "Bleep," by which she meant, "How do we get there?"

"You must swim and walk there," said the burning Bush. "And now, if you will excuse me, I have to give a pep talk to some dinosaurs, and then sit around for a thousand years so I can talk to Moses."

The father penguin, who was known as Bleep-Bleep, said, "Bleep Bleep," by which he meant, "Is he fudging kidding us?" by which he also proved that even under duress, penguins don't cuss. The two bleeped back and forth for a time, arguing over the merits of abandoning their baby and leaving their home behind to save all penguinhood at the behest of a burning piece of organic material.

The two finally shrugged their non-existent shoulders and stretched their non-existent knees (ignoring the evolutionary skeletal ones inside their bodies), waved goodbye to their doomed baby, and jumped into the icy water. After many tribulations and the resulting discovery that penguins truly can cuss, the two completed the six hundred-mile swim to Cape Horn. They waddled north, avoiding Panthera atrox *lions* and saber tooth *tigers* and Arctotherium *bears*.

However, they became disheartened as they would have to swim the Atlantic Ocean to get to Babylonia. Bleep-Bleep tried to dig his way through the center of the Earth, but after a worthy attempt, he gave up, leaving behind a large hole in Arizona. Then they discovered the Garden of Eden, which turns out to be in New Jersey, and decided to retire there. However, when they disobediently ate the fish of knowledge, a herring full of omega-3 fatty acids, they realized they were naked and so they put on suits, and were also asked to leave.

The frustrated penguins stared out over the Atlantic. Then Bleep stretched her flippers out over the ocean, and it divided into two, leaving a clear trail down the middle all the way across, and oh, by the way, beaching huge numbers of poor whales, dolphins, and fish. The two penguins feasted on the fish as they waddled across the ocean floor, into Europe, and south to the Middle East.

They finally arrived at Babylonia, and there it was—the wondrous ark and its architect, Noah himself, though they could not see him as he was moving at light speed, thereby making it possible for him to both build the huge ark by himself as well as to live to a grand old age of nine hundred and fifty, due to relativistic effects.

However, the ark was surrounded by a pair of Tyrannosaurus Rexes, a pair of Spinosauruses, a pair of Allosauruses, a pair of...well, you get the idea, a pair of every major dinosaurian predator. They were feasting on the incoming pairs of animals, many of whom had made long journeys from all over the world to the ark at the urging of the burning Bush—Mastodons, Paraceratheriums, unicorns, and many other species, now doomed to extinction by the jaws of dinosaurs.

Unable to board the ark, all land life on Earth would have died in the flood if not for the noble sacrifice of the plant-eaters. At the urging of the burning Bush, which declared that they would not be misunderestimated, roving pairs of Apatosaurus, Diplodocus, Brachiosaurs, and all other plant-eating dinosaurs charged the flesh-eating dinosaurs in the greatest dinosaur battle in, like, ever. A few cowardly dinosaurs hid in the bushes, and their distant descendants became birds, though strangely and retroactively many of those descendants would time travel back and become extinct in the great flood, such as Archaeopteryx, Giant Moas, and Argentavis magnificens.

The plant-eaters cried, "BLEEP," by which they meant, "Save yourselves all you little animals! We'll sacrifice ourselves for you!" The penguins and the ancestors of all surviving land creatures charged onto the ark, rationalizing it was survival of the fittest as they uncaringly left the dinosaurs to their doom as they fought to the death. Soon all that was left of the dinosaurs were their bones, which would soon be radioactively adjusted by Satan to make them seem much older.

And so it was that Bleep and Bleep-Bleep survived the Great Flood. After waddling and swimming their way back from Mount Ararat they finally returned to Antarctica only to discover that all the penguins were still alive since penguins are primarily aquatic.

Copyright © 2016 by Larry Hodges

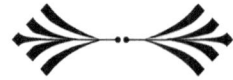

Kij Johnson won Nebulas in 2010, 2011, and 2012, as well as a Hugo in 2012. Her first collection, At the Mouth of the River of Bees, *features this as the title story.*

AT THE MOUTH OF THE RIVER OF BEES

by Kij Johnson

It starts with a bee sting. Linna exclaims at the sudden sharp pain; at her voice, her dog Sam lifts his head where he has settled his aging body on the sidewalk in front of the flower stand.

Sucking at the burning place, Linna looks down at the bouquet in her hand, a messy arrangement of anemones and something loose-jointed with tiny white flowers, dill maybe. The flowers are days from anywhere that might have bees. But she sees one, dead or dying on the yellow petal of one of the flowers.

She tips the bouquet to the side. The bee slides from the petal to the ground. Sam leans his dark head over and eats it.

Back in her apartment, she plucks the stinger from her hand with tweezers. It's clear that she's not going to die of the sting or even swell up much, though there's a white spot that weeps clear fluid and still hurts, still burns. She looks out the windows of her apartment: a gray sky, gray pavement and sidewalks and buildings, trees so dark they might as well be black. The only colors are those on signs and cars.

"Let's go, Sam," she says to the German shepherd. "Let's take a road trip. We need a change, don't we?"

Linna really only intended to cross the Cascades—go to Leavenworth, maybe as far as Ellensburg and then home—but now it's Montana. She drives as fast as the Subaru will go, the purple highway drawing her east. Late sun floods the car. The honey-colored light flattens the brush and rock of the badlands into abrupt gold and violet shapes as unreal as a hallucination. It's late May and the air is hot and dry during the day, the nights cold with the memory of winter. She hates the air conditioner so she doesn't use it, and the air thrumming in the open window smells like hot dust and metal and, distant as a dream, ozone and rain. Her hand still burns. She absently sucks on the sting as she drives.

There are thunderheads ahead, perhaps as far away as North Dakota. Lightning flashes through the gold-and-indigo clouds, a sudden silent flicker of white so bright that it is lilac. Linna eyes the clouds. She wants to drive through the night, wonders whether she will drive through rain, or scurry untouched beneath their pregnant weight.

The distance between Seattle and her present location is measured in time, not miles. It has been two days since she left Seattle, hours since she left Billings. Glendive is still half an hour ahead. Linna thinks she might stop there, get something to eat, let Sam stretch his legs. She's not sure where she's going or why. Her mind whispers *east, toward sunrise*, and then *my folks live in Wisconsin; that's where I'm going*, but she knows neither are the real answer. Still, the road feels good. Sam sleeping in the back seat is good.

A report would say traffic is light, but that is an overstatement. In the past twenty minutes, she has seen exactly two vehicles going her way on the interstate. Ten minutes ago she passed a semi with the word covenant on the side. And just a moment ago, a rangy Montana State Patrol SUV swept past with its lights flashing at a hundred miles an hour to her eighty-five. As the siren Dopplered past, Sam heaved upright and barked once. Linna glances into her mirror: he's asleep again, loose-boned across the back seat.

Linna comes over a small hill to see emergency lights far ahead: red, blue, a lilac-white bright as lightning. The patrol SUV blocks the freeway. There are six cars stopped in the lanes behind it, patient as cows lined up at the door of the barn. The sun is too low behind her to light the dip in the highway ahead of the cars. The air collected there seems dark.

Sam wakes up and whines when the car slows. Linna stops next to a night-blue Ford, an Explorer. The other drivers and the state trooper are out of their cars, so she turns off the Subaru's engine. It has run, with occasional stops for gas and food and dog walks and a half-night of sleep snatched at a Day's Inn outside of Missoula, for two days. The silence is deafening. The wind that parched Linna's skin and hair is gone. The air is still and warm as dust, and spicy with asphalt and sage.

Linna lifts Sam from the back seat, places him on the scrub grass of the median. He would have been too heavy to carry last year, but his muscles atrophy as his spine fuses, and he's lost weight. Sam stretches painfully, a little urine dribbling. He can't help this; the nerves are being pinched. Linna has covered the back seat of the Subaru with a waterproof tarp and a washable blanket. She's careful when she takes corners, not wanting him to slide.

Whatever else he is (in pain; old; dying), Sam is still a dog. He hobbles to a shrub with tiny flowers pale as ghosts against the leaves, and sniffs it carefully before marking. He can no longer lift his leg so he squats.

The only sunlight that Linna can still see fades on the storm clouds to the east, honey to rust. The rest of the world is already dim with twilight: ragged outlines of naked rock, grass, and brush stained imperfect grays. A pickup pulls up behind her car and, a moment later, the Covenant truck beside it. Another patrol vehicle blocks the westbound lanes, but its light bar seems much too faint, perhaps a reflection of the sky's dying light. If time is the measure for distance, then dusk can be a strange place.

Linna clips Sam onto his leash and loops it over her wrist. She rubs at her sore hand as she walks to the patrol SUV. The people standing there stare at the road to the east, but there's nothing to see.

Linna knows suddenly that this is not twilight or shadows. The air over the road truly *is* flowing darkness, like ink dropped in moving water. "What *is* that?" she asks the patrolman, who is tall with very white skin and black hair. Sam pulls to the end of his leash, ears and nose aimed at the darkness.

"The Bee River is currently flooding east- and westbound lanes of Ninety-four, ma'am," the patrolman says. Linna nods. All the rivers here seem to have strange names: Tongue River, Automatic Creek. "We'll keep the road closed until it is safe to pass again, which—"

"The *freeway's* closed?" A man holds a cell phone. "You can't do that! They *never* close."

"They do for floods and blizzards and ice storms," the patrolman says. "And the Bee River."

"But I have to get to Bismarck tonight!" The man's voice shakes; he's younger than he looks.

"That's not going to be possible," the trooper says. "Your options would be Twelve and Twenty, and they're blocked, too. Ninety's okay, but you'll have

to backtrack. It's going to be a day or two before anyone can head east here. Town of Terry's just a couple of miles back and you might be able to find lodging there. Otherwise, Miles City is about half an hour back."

Linna watches the seething darkness, finally hears what her engine-numbed ears had not noticed before: the hum, reminding her of summers growing up in Iowa, hives hot in the sun. "Wait," she says: "It's all bees. That is a river of *bees*."

A woman in a green farm coat laughs. "Of course it is. Where you from?"

"Seattle," Linna says. "How can there be a river of bees?" Someone new arrives and the patrolman turns to him, so the woman in the green coat answers.

"Same way there's a river of anything else, I suppose. It happens sometimes in June, July. Late May sometimes, like now. The river wells up, floods some roads, runs through some ranch yards."

"But it's *not* water," Linna says. Sam pushes against her knees. His aching spine stiffens up quickly; he wants to move around.

"Nope. Nice dog." The woman waggles her fingers at Sam, who pushes his head beneath them. "What's wrong with him? Spinal fusion?"

"Yeah," Linna says. "Arthritis, other stuff."

"That's not good. Not much they can do, is there? We used to raise shepherds. Lot of medical problems."

"He's old." Linna stoops to wrap an arm around his ribcage, to feel his warmth and the steady thumping of his heart.

The woman pats him again. "Well, he's a sweetie. Me and Jeff are going to turn back to Miles City, try and get a room and call Shelly—that's our daughter—from there. You?"

"I'm not sure."

"Don't wait too long to decide, hon. The rooms fill fast."

Linna thanks her and watches her return to their pickup. Headlights plunge as it feels its cautious way across the median to the other lanes. Other cars are doing the same, and a straggling row of taillights heads west.

Some vehicles stay. "Might as well," says the man with the Covenant truck. He is homely, heavyset; but his eyes are nice as he smiles at Linna and Sam. "Can't turn the rig around anyhow, and I want to see what a river of bees looks like with the light on it. Something to tell the wife." Linna smiles back. "Nice pup," he adds, and scratches Sam's head. Leaning heavily against Linna's leg, Sam stands patiently through it, like a tired but polite child.

She walks Sam back to the Subaru and feeds him on the grass, pouring fresh water into a plastic bowl and offering food and a Rimadyl for the pain. He drinks the water thirstily while she plays with his ears. When he's done, she lifts him carefully onto the back seat, lays her face against his head. He's dozing when she rolls his window down and returns to the river of bees.

A patrol car has rolled up the outside shoulder to park beside the SUV, and a second officer has joined the first. Lit by their headlights, the young man with the cell phone still pleads. "I don't have a *choice*, officers."

"I'm sorry, sir." The patrolman shakes his head.

The man turns to the other officer, a small woman with dark hair in an unruly braid stretching halfway down her back. "I have a Ford Explorer. This—river—is only twenty, thirty feet wide, right? *Please.*"

The patrolwoman shrugs, says, "Your call, Luke."

The patrolman sighs. "Fine. Sir, if you insist on trying this—"

"Thank you," the man says.

"—I have a winch on the patrol vehicle. We'll attach it to your rear axle, so I can pull you out of trouble if you stall partway. Otherwise unhook it on the other side and I'll drag it back. Keep all vents and windows closed, parking lights only. Tap your brakes if you need a pull. As slow as the truck will go. And I am serious, sir: the river is dangerous."

"Yes, of course," the man says. "I'm really grateful, Officer Tabor."

"All right then," the patrolman, Tabor, says, and sighs again. He talks into the radio on his shoulder. "Tim, I've got someone who's going to try and crawl through. I've warned him of the dangers, but his wife's in the hospital in Bismarck, he really wants to try. If he gets through, can you make sure he's okay?" Indecipherable squawks. "Right, then."

Linna and the Covenant driver (his name is John, he tells her as they wait, John Backus, from Iowa City originally, now near Nashville, trucking for twelve years, his wife Jo usually comes along but

she's neck-deep in preparations for the oldest's wedding, on and on) watch the huge Ford roll forward, trailing cable like a dog on an inertia-reel leash. Barely lit by its parking lights, the truck inches onto, into, the dark patch of highway. Blackness curls like smoke, drifts over the truck. It revs its engine for a moment and then dies. Brake lights tap on, and Tabor sighs a third time, sets the winch in motion, and pulls the truck back.

The air is cold, the sky moonless but bright with stars. To warm herself, Linna walks along the line of cars and trucks. People sleep across their front seats, or read or talk or play cards under dome lights. Engines purr, running heaters. The air is sweet with exhaust, an oddly comforting smell. An older couple sit in lawn chairs by their parked RV; the woman offers Linna a Styrofoam cup of coffee and the chance to use their bathroom. Linna accepts both gratefully, but refuses their offer to sleep on the couch.

She does not think she'll be able to sleep. Stars pace across the sky, their dim light somehow deeper than blackness and yet too bright to sleep through. A coyote or perhaps a dog barks once, a long way away. Back at the car, Linna watches Sam chase something in his sleep, paws twitching in the rhythm of running. *Live forever*, she thinks, and wills his twisted spine and legs straight and well.

It is very cold and the sky through the windshield is the color of freshwater pearls when Linna wakes, blinks, and remembers. There is half a cup of coffee on the floor of the passenger seat. It's cold and acidic, but the familiar bitterness anchors her. Sam is still sleeping. He never liked morning, and they moved to Mountain Time as they drove yesterday, so whatever local time it is (4:53, the dashboard clock tells her when she looks), it is actually an hour earlier for them. Once out of the car, she stretches. Her eyes are sticky and her back aches, but the time before dawn is a strange land to her, and she finds herself surprisingly happy.

She walks to the patrol SUV. Tabor sits with the door open, drinking directly from a thermos. "Coffee," he says. "Still hot. Want some? I lost the cup, though."

She takes the steel cylinder. The smaller patrol car and its driver are gone, as are the big Ford and the distraught young man. "What happened to the guy who had to get to his wife?"

"We scraped all the bees off the air intakes and got the truck running again. He drove back to Ninety. It's adding three, four hundred miles, but he's going to try and go around."

Linna nods and drinks. The coffee *is* hot, and it warms her to her toes. "Oh," she says with delight: "That's good." She returns the thermos.

"You get stung last night?" Tabor has seen the white spot on her hand.

She rubs it and laughs a little, oddly embarrassed. "No, right before I left Seattle. And now here's a river of them. Small world," she says and looks toward the fog collected in the dip.

"Hmm." Tabor drinks off some of the coffee. Then: "Listen for it," he says.

Linna listens. The SUV's idling engine throbs. A car door clicks open, far back in the line. There's no wind, no whispering grass or rubbing leaves—but there is a humming, barely audible. "That's *them*." She whispers, as though her voice might disturb them.

"Yeah. The fog is clearing. Look."

She walks a little toward where the river should be, will be. "No closer," Tabor behind her warns and she stops. A tiny breeze brushes her cheek. Mist recoils, and patches of darkness show through: asphalt black with sleeping bees. The sky lightens, turns from pearl to lavender to blue. The clouds are gone and the eastern horizon glows. The fog retreats. There is the river.

The river is a dark changeable mist like the shifting of a flock of flying starlings, like a pillar of gnats over a highway in hot August dusk, like a million herring turning. South to north, the river runs like cooling lava, like warm molasses. It might be six feet deep, though in places it is much less, in others much more. It alters as she watches.

The river of bees streams as far as she can see. It flows from the south, down a butte beside the freeway and across the road and into the river bed of the Yellowstone, then pours up over the side of a gully to the northwest. As she watches, more sleeping bees wake and lift to join the deepening river. The buzz grows louder.

Tabor stands beside her now but she cannot look away. "Where does it begin?" she says at last. "Where does it end?"

He is slow answering and she knows he is as trapped in its weird beauty as she. "No one knows," he says: "Or no one says. My dad used to tell me tales, but I don't know that he knew, either. Maybe there's a spring of bees somewhere, and it sinks underground somewhere else. Maybe the bees gather, do this thing, and then go home. There's no ocean of bees, anyway."

Others join them, talking in loud and then hushed voices; there are snapshots, videos—"not that the pictures ever come out," a voice grumbles. This is peripheral. Linna watches the bees. The sun rises, a cherry ovoid blur that shrinks and resolves as it pulls away from the horizon. Pink-gold light fills the hollow. The river quickens and grows. People watch for a time and then walk back to their cars. Their voices grow louder as they move away, conversations full of longing for coffee and breakfast and hot showers and flush toilets. They reassure themselves with the ordinary.

Linna does not move until she hears Sam bark once, the want-to-go-out-*now* bark. Even then, she walks backward.

"This is going to sound strange," Linna says to Tabor.

She walked Sam until his joints loosened and he no longer dragged his hind legs. She exchanged pleasantries with the man from the Covenant truck, though now she remembers nothing but his expression, oddly distant and sad as he watched her rub her hand. She drank orange spice tea and ate a fried-egg sandwich when the woman at the RV offered them, and used the little stainless steel bathroom again. The woman's husband was cooking. He flipped an egg to the ground between Sam's feet. Sam ate it tidily and then smiled up at the cook. Linna spoke at random, listening for the bees' hum. "Excuse me," she remembers saying to the couple, interrupting something. "I have to go now." She has led Sam back to the patrol SUV, and says:

"This is going to sound strange."

"Not as strange as you probably think," Tabor says. He's typing something into the computer in his vehicle. "Let me guess. You're going to follow the river."

"Can I?" she says, her heart leaping. She knows he shouldn't know this, shouldn't have guessed; knows she won't be allowed, but she asks anyway.

"Can't stop you. There's the river, and then I saw the sting and I knew. My dad—he was a trooper, back twenty and more years ago. He told me it happens like this sometimes. There's always a bee sting, he said. Let me see your car."

She leads Tabor back to the Subaru, lifts Sam into the back seat. The trooper makes her open the back hatch, sees the four gallon jugs of water there. "Good, but could be better. What about food?" She shows him what she has, forty pounds of dog food (she bought it two weeks ago, as though it were a charm to make Sam live long enough to eat it all) and two boxes of granola bars. "Gas?" She has half a tank: just under two hundred miles' worth maybe. "Get some, next time you're near a road," Tabor says. "Subaru, that's good," he adds, "but you don't have much clearance in a Forester. Be careful when you're off-road."

"I won't go off-road," Linna says. "There's just too much that can go wrong."

"Yes, you will," Tabor says. "You'll follow the river to its mouth, whatever and wherever that is. I can't stop you, but at least I can make sure you don't get into trouble on the way."

Tabor brings her a heavy canvas bag from his SUV. "This is sort of an emergency kit," he says. "My dad put it together before he retired. We've been keeping it at the base ever since. Got the report and hauled it down with me, figuring someone might show up needing it. Heavy gloves, snakebite kit, wire, some other stuff."

"Do people get back?" Linna says.

Tabor unzips the bag a few inches, drops a business card in. "Don't know. But when you get wherever it is, you're going to send all this gear back to me. Or leave it. Or—" he pauses, looks again at the river.

She laughs, suddenly ashamed. "How can you be so calm about this? I know this is all insane and I'm *still* doing it, but you—"

"This is Montana, ma'am," Tabor says. "Good luck."

The aqua clock says 6:08 and the sun is two hands above the horizon when Linna puts the Subaru into gear and eases across the median.

Linna is lucky at first. The exit to Terry and its bridge across the Yellowstone are only a couple of miles back, and she learns her first lesson about following the river: she doesn't have to *see* the river of bees because she can taste its current in the air. Terry is a couple of gas stations and fast-food places, a handful of trailers and farmhouses, everything shaded by cottonwoods, their leaves a harsh silver-green when the wind moves through them.

Her second lesson: the river tells her where to go. There is only one road out of Terry, but there is no chance she might make a mistake and take another. She stops long enough to buy gas and road food and breakfast, and eats in the car on her way out of town. Sam is interested, of course, so she feeds him a hash-brown cake by holding it over her shoulder. Soft lips lift the cake from her hand. The vet would not be pleased, but she's not here and Linna and Sam are.

The road is two empty lanes of worn pavement following a dry streambed through soft-edged badlands. She knows the bees are a mile or two to the east. Gravel roads branch off to the north from time to time. She longs to take one, to see the bees again, but she knows the roads will taper off, end in a farmyard, or turn abruptly in the wrong direction. It will be many miles before she reaches the river's mouth. These roads will not take her there.

The road changes from worn to worse, and then decays to gravel. Linna slows and slows again. The sun that pours in the passenger windows loses its rosy glow as it climbs, turns flat and hot. The only traffic she sees is a single ancient tractor that might once have been orange, heading into town. The old man driving it wears a red hat. He salutes her with a thermos. She salutes with her own cup of fast-food coffee. The dust he's raised pours into the car until she rolls the windows closed.

Once, when she crosses the mouth of a little valley, Linna can see the bees at a distance. She stops there to walk and water Sam and to drink stale water from one of the jugs. The cooling engine ticks a few times, then leaves her in the tiny hissing of the wind in the grasses. The river of bees cannot be heard from here, but she feels the humming in her bones, like true love or cancer.

She opens the bag that Tabor gave her. There are all the things he mentioned, and others besides: wire-cutters and instructions for mending barbed wire; a Boy Scout manual from the '50s; flares; a spade; a roll of toilet paper that smells of powder; tweezers and a magnifying glass and rubbing alcohol; stained, folded geological survey maps of eastern Montana; a spare pair of socks; bars of chocolate and water purification tablets; a plastic star map of the northern hemisphere in summer—and a note. *Do not damage anything permanently. Close any gates you open—mend any fences you cut—Cattle, tractors and local vehicles receive right of way—Residents mostly know about the river. They'll allow you to pass through their property so long as you don't break the fences.* It was signed: *Richard Tabor.* Officer Luke Tabor's father, then.

In another small town—the sign says Brockway—the road tees into another dusty two-lane, this one going east-west. She finds a gravel road heading northwest, but it turns unexpectedly and eventually leaves her in a ranch yard in an eddy of barking dogs, Sam yelling back. The next road she tries turns east, then north, then east again. The gravel that once covered it is long gone. The Subaru humps its way through gullies and potholes. She drives over a rise, and the river streams in front of her, blocking off the road.

She's close enough to see individual bees but only for an instant before they drop back into the texture of the river. Brownian motion: she can see the bee but she cannot see the river; or she sees the current but not the bees.

What am I doing? she asks herself. She is fifty miles off the freeway, following hypothetical roads through an empty land in pursuit of something beautiful but impossible and so very dangerous. This is when she learns the third lesson: she cannot help doing this. She backtracks to find a better road, but she keeps slewing around to look behind her as though she has left something behind, and she cries as she drives.

So she threads her way across eastern Montana, gravel to dirt to cracked tar to dirt, always north, always west. Sometimes she's in sight of the river. More often it's only a nagging in her mind: *this way.* She drives past ranches and ruined lonely barns, past a church of silver wood with daylight shining through its walls. She drives across an earthen dam, a narrow paved ridge between afternoon sunlight on water and a small town straggling under cottonwoods, far below what would be water level if it weren't for the dam. She crosses streams and dry runs with strange names: Powder Creek, Milk River. When she slows on the narrow bridges to look down, she does not see powder or milk, just

water or nothing. Only the river of bees is what it claims to be.

When she crosses U.S. Highway 2, Linna stops for a while in Nashua. Sam is asleep, adrift in Rimadyl. She parks in the shade and leaves her windows open, and sits under the glare of fluorescent lights in a McDonald's, stirring crushed ice in a waxed cup. Conversations wash over her. The words are as strange as a foreign language after the hours alone: the river of bees (which blocks Highway 2 less than a mile east of town), but also feline asthma, rubber flip-flops for the twins, and Jake's summer job canning salmon in Alaska.

The bees pour north. The roads Linna follows grow sketchier. The Subaru is all-wheel drive and set fairly high, but it lurches through potholes and washouts, and scrapes its undercarriage. Sam pants in her ear until Linna slows to a crawl. He relaxes a little, lies back down. The sun crawls northwest, scalding Linna's arm and neck and cheek. She thinks sometimes of using the air conditioner but finds she cannot. The dust, the heat, the sun: they are all part of driving to the river's mouth. Sam seems not to mind the heat, though he drinks almost a gallon of water.

Linna is able to stay close enough to the river that individual bees sometimes stray into an open window. Black against sun-gold and dust-white, they inscribe intricate calligraphy in the air. Linna cannot read their messages.

Linna stops when the violet twilight starts to hide things from her. She parks on a ridge beside a single ragged tree that makes the air sharp with juniper. Thinking of snakes, she walks Sam carefully, but it is growing dark and cold and only the hot-blooded creatures remain awake. A bat or perhaps a swift or a small owl veers overhead with the almost inaudible whirring of wings. A coyote barks. Sam pricks his ears but does not respond, except to urinate on a shrub he has been smelling.

She does not sleep well that night. At one point, great snorting animals surround the Subaru for what seem hours, occasionally bumping into it as they pass. Sam is as awake as she. At first she thinks they're bears, that she has stumbled somehow upon a river of bears, but starlight shows they are steers. For some reason they are not asleep but travel under the spinning sky, toward water or away from some-thing or out of simple restlessness. Still, she cannot sleep until they are long gone, no more than a mem-ory of shuffling and grunts.

It is past dawn when Linna brings herself to ad-mit she won't be sleeping anymore. After the steers passed she couldn't stop shivering, so she crawled awkwardly over the front seats to curl up with Sam, and pulled his soft blanket over them both. Now his spine presses against her thigh. Each bone is sharp as a juniper knurl. He smells of stale urine and sick-ness, but behind that is the sweetness that has al-ways been his. She presses her face to his shoulder and inhales deeply. His muskiness works its way into her lungs, her blood and bones.

People have smells like this, smells that she has collected to herself and stored in the memory of her body; but Sam has been part of her life for lon-ger than anyone but parents and siblings. For the first time, she thinks that perhaps she should have stayed on the road, closer to where veterinarians and their bright clean buildings live; but she has enough Rimadyl to kill Sam if he needs it, and she thinks that death is the only gift she or anyone can give him now.

At last she climbs from the car, stretches in the surprising simultaneous sensations of cold air and sun's warmth. "Come on, pup," she says aloud. Her voice startles her. It's the first she's heard since Nash-ua—yesterday, was it? It seems longer. Sam staggers upright and she lifts him to the ground. He creeps a few steps and then urinates, creeps a few more and pauses to smell a tuft of something yellow-green. She doesn't bother with the leash.

Perhaps a hundred yards away, the river hums along, broader and slower now. Linna can see indi-vidual straying bees as she squats to urinate, grateful again for the toilet paper in the kit the officer, Tabor, gave her. Something wild and sweet-smelling grows all around her. It might be lavender, though she thinks of lavender as something polite and domes-ticated, all about freshly ironed sheets and bath salts and tussie-mussies. Bath salts: she sniffs her armpits as she squats and then recoils. Well, dogs like stink.

The wandering bees explore the flowers around her, spiraling and arrowing like electrons in a cloud chamber. One lands on her stung hand as it rests on her knee. The slight touch of its legs might be no more than an imagined tickle if she did not also see its stocky, velvety bulk. It's the Classic bee: yellow-and-black striped, small-bodied, dark transparent wings folded tidily. It strokes the air with tiny feel-ers, then leans its head over and touches its mouth to the white spot on her hand, as though tasting her. For a dizzying moment she wonders if it's going to snap her up the way Sam snapped up the bee that gave her the sting back in Seattle.

Behind her, Sam gives a yelp, all surprise and pain. Linna whirls around and feels a drop of her urine splash against her knee as she stands. There is a hot sharp shock to her hand. A bee sting.

"Sam?" she shouts and stumbles forward, dragging her pants up, feverish with panic or the sting. She knows he's going to die, *but not yet*, her mind tells her. *Too soon.*

Sam limps to her, a comical look of distress on his face. She's reassured, as she's seen this expression before and it doesn't mesh with her fears. She folds to her knees beside him (lightheaded or concerned) and looks at the paw he's lifting. A tiny barb against a pale patch of skin on his pad. She finds herself laughing hysterically as she removes the stingers, first from his paw and then from her hand. Officer Tabor's father knew what he was doing.

Linna has not driven more than five miles an hour since awakening, though these terms—mile, hour—seem irrelevant. It might be better or more accurate to say she has driven down forty little canyons and up thirty-nine of them, and crossed twelve ridges and two surprising meadows, softly sloped as any Iowa cornfield and spangled with flowers that are small and very blue: time measured as distance. She thinks perhaps she's crossed into Canada, but there's been nothing to indicate this. She's running low on water and is tired of granola bars, but she hasn't seen anything that looked like a town since Nashua.

The trail she follows is a winding cow or deer path. She keeps one set of tires on the track and hopes for the best, which works well so long as she goes slowly enough. She keeps inspecting where the bee stung her earlier. There is an angry swelling across her hand, centered on a weeping white spot, half an inch from the first. What is half an inch, if measured in time? Linna doesn't know but she worries over the question, as though there might be an answer.

Since the sting the light has seemed very bright, and she is by turns hot and cold. She wonders whether she should turn around and try to find a hospital (where? how can she know when she measures distance by event?). But the calligraphy of the bees hovers; she is just on the edge of making sense of it; she is reluctant to give this up.

The Subaru grinds to a stop in a gully that is too deep to cross. Linna feels the river: *close*, it says, *so close*; so she lifts Sam out and they walk on. He is very slow. There are bees everywhere, like spray thrown from a mountain stream. They rest on her hands and tickle her face with their feather-tip feet, but she is not stung again. Sam watches them, puffs air at one that clings to the silver-furred leaves of a plant. They cross a little ridge and then a second one. There is the mouth of the river of bees.

The bees pool in a grassy basin. As she watches, the river empties a thousand—a million—more into the basin, but the level never changes and she never sees bees leave. It is as though they sink into the ground, into some secret ocean.

She knows she is hallucinating, because at the bank of the lake of bees is an unwalled tent hung with tassels and fringe. Six posts hold a white silk roof. The sunlight through it is intimate, friendly. And because this is a hallucination Linna approaches without fear, Sam beside her, his ears pricked forward.

Linna cannot later say whether the creature under the tent was a woman or a bee, though she is sure this is the queen of the bees, as sure as she is of death and sunlight. She knows that—if the creature was a woman—she had honey-colored eyes and black hair, with silver streaks glinting in both. And if the creature was a bee, her faceted eyes were deep as Victorian jet, and her voice held a thousand tones at once.

But it's easier to think of the queen of the bees as a woman. The woman's gold skin glows against her white gown. Her hands are very long and slender, with almond-shaped nails. They pour tea and arrange cakes on plates ornamented with pink roses. For a disconcerting moment, Linna sees slim black legs arrange the cakes and blinks the image back to hands. Yes, better to think of her as a woman. "Please," the queen of the bees says. "Join me."

In the shade of the awning are folding teakwood chairs draped with white fringed shawls. Linna sinks into one, takes a cup that is as thin as eggshell, and sips. Its contents are warm and clearly tea, but they are also cooling and sweet and fill her with a sudden happiness. She watches the queen of the bees place a saucer filled with tea on the ground beside Sam (a thousand dark facets reflect his face. No. Simple gold eyes, caught in a mesh of laugh-lines fine as thread that smile down at him). He drinks it thirstily, grins up at the woman.

"What is his name?" she says. "And yours?"

"Sam," says Linna. "I'm Linna."

The woman gives no name for herself but gestures to her skirts as they swirl around her ankles. A small cat with long gray-and-white fur and startling blue eyes sits against one foot. "This is Belle."

"You have a cat," Linna says. Of all the things she has seen today, this seems the strangest somehow.

The woman reaches down a hand. Belle walks over to sniff her fingers. Her fur is thick but it doesn't conceal how thin she is. Linna can see the bumps of her spine in sharp outline. "She's very old now."

"I understand," Linna says softly. She meets the woman's eyes, sees herself reflected in their gold, their black depths.

Silence between them stretches, defined by the eternal unchanging humming of the river of bees, the scent of sage and grass in the sun. Linna drinks her tea and eats a cake. Across from her the bee's body glows brilliantly in the silk-muted sun.

Linna holds out the injured hand. "Did you do this?"

The woman touches Linna's hand where the two stings burn. The pain is there, under fingers that flicker soft as antennae, and then it is not. Linna inspects her hand. The white spots are gone. Linna's mind is as clear as the dry air, so she knows this is an illusion. She must still be having some sort of reaction, or everything—the tent, the woman, the lake of bees—would be gone. "Can you heal your cat like this?"

"No." The woman bends to pick up Belle, who curls up in her thin black insect's legs. Belle's blue eyes blink up at the face of the queen of the bees. "I cannot stop death, only postpone it for a time."

Linna's mouth is dry. "Can you do that for Sam? Make him run again?" She leans over to touch Sam's ruff. The blood rushing to her head turns everything red for a moment.

"I cannot say. I hope that you and I will talk a while. It's been many years since I had someone to talk to, since the man who brought me Belle. She couldn't eat. Her jaw—" the cat purrs against the bee's thorax "—it was ruined, a cancer. He walked the last day after his car gave up, carrying her. We talked for a time, and then he gave her to me and left. So long ago now."

"What was his name?" Linna thinks of a canvas bag back in the Subaru, filled with all the right things.

"Tabor," she says. "Richard Tabor."

And so they talk, eating cakes and drinking tea under the silk awning of the queen of the bees. Linna recalls certain things, but cannot later say whether they are hallucinations; or stories she was told or told herself; or things she did not speak of but knew. She remembers the taste of sage pollen, bright and smoky on what might be her tongue or might be her imagination. They talk of (or visit, or dream of) countless infants, creamy smooth and packed safe in their close cribs; small towns in the middle of nowhere; great cities; towers and highways seething with urgent activity. They talk of (or visit, or dream of) great tragedies—disaster, whole races destroyed by disease or cruelty or misfortune—and small ones, drizzly days and mislaid directions and dirt and vermin. Later, Linna cannot recall which stories or visions or dreams were about people and which were about bees.

The sun eases into the west. Its light crawls onto the table. It touches the black forefoot of the queen of the bees. She stands and stretches, then gathers Belle into her arms. "I must go."

Linna stands as well and notices for the first time that the river is gone, leaving only the lake of bees, and even this is smaller than it was. "Can you heal Sam?" she says suddenly.

"He cannot stay with you and stay alive." The woman pauses, as though choosing her words. "If you and Sam chose, he could stay with me."

"Sam?" Linna puts down her cup carefully, trying to conceal her shaking hands. "I can't give him to anyone. He's old, he's too sick. He needs pills." She slips from her seat to the dry grass beside Sam. He struggles to his feet and presses his face against her chest, as he has since he was a puppy.

The queen of the bees looks down at them both, stroking Belle absently. The cat purrs and presses against her black-velvet thorax. Faceted eyes reflect a thousand images back to Linna, her arms around a thousand Sams.

"He's mine. I love him, and he's *mine*." Linna's chest hurts.

"He's Death's now," the woman says. "Unless he stays with me."

Linna bends her face to his ruff, smells the warm living scent of him. "Let me stay with him then. With you." She looks up at the queen of the bees. "You miss company. You said so."

The black heart-shaped head tips back. "No. To be with me is to have no one."

"There'd be Sam. And the bees."

"Would they be enough for you? A million million subjects? Ten thousand lovers, all as interchangeable and mindless as gloves? No friends, no family, no one to pull the sting from your hand?"

Linna's eyes drop. She cannot bear to look into that fierce face, proud and searingly alone.

"I will love Sam with all my heart," the queen of the bees continues in a voice soft as a hum. "Because I will have no one else."

Sam has rolled to his side, waiting patiently for Linna to remember to scratch him. *Live forever*, she thinks, and wills his twisted spine and legs straight and well.

"All right then," she whispers.

The queen of the bees exhales sweet air. Belle makes a tired cranky noise, a sort of question. "Yes, Belle," she says, and touches her with what might be a long white hand. Belle sighs once and is still.

"Will you—?" the queen of the bees asks.

"Yes." Linna stands, takes the cat from her black arms. The body is light as wind. "I will bury her."

"Thank you." The queen of the bees kneels and places her long hands on either side of the dog's muzzle. "Sam? Would you like to be with me for a while?"

He says nothing, of course, but he licks the soft black face. The woman touches him and he stretches lavishly, like a puppy awakening after a long afternoon's sleep. When he is done, his legs are straight and his eyes are very bright. Sam dances to Linna, bounces onto his hind legs to lick the tears from her face. She buries her face in his fur a last time. The smell of sickness is gone, leaving only Sam. *Live*, she thinks. When she releases him, he races once around the little field before he returns to sit beside the queen of the bees, smiling up at her.

Linna's heart twists inside her but it's the price of knowing he will live. She pays it, but cannot stop herself from asking, "Will he forget me?"

"I will remind him every day." The queen rests her hand on his head. "And there will be many days. He will live a long time, and he will run and chase what might as well be rabbits, in my world."

The queen of the bees salutes Linna, kissing her wet cheeks, and then she turns and walks toward the rising darkness that is the last of the lake of bees and also the dusk. Linna watches hungrily. Sam looks back once, confused, and she nearly calls out to him, but what would she be calling him back to? She smiles as best she can and he returns the smile, as dogs do. And then he and the queen of the bees are gone.

Linna buries Belle using the spade in the canvas bag. It is almost dark before she is done, and she sleeps in her car again, too tired to hear or see or feel anything. In the morning she finds a road and turns west. When she gets to Seattle (no longer gray, but green and blue and white with summer), she sends the canvas bag back to Officer Tabor—Luke, she remembers—along with a letter explaining everything she has learned of the river of bees.

She is never stung again. Her dreams are visited by bees, but they bring her no messages; the calligraphy of their flights remain mysterious. Once she dreams of Sam, who smiles at her and dances on young straight legs, just out of reach.

—for Sid and Helen

Copyright © 2004 by Kij Johnson

Laurie Tom has been entranced by science fiction and fantasy since childhood and has never been able to stop visiting other worlds. Her work has also appeared in venues such as Strange Horizons, Galaxy's Edge, *and the* Mammoth Book of Dieselpunk. *This is her fifth appearance in* Galaxy's Edge.

THE WORLD THAT YOU WANT

by Laurie Tom

I was fifteen when the world ended, on schedule, as predicted, by a man no one important took seriously. The world convulsed, the sky bled red, and hell came to earth. It is the cycle, the demons tell us. Our time is past and they will feast on the leavings.

Brandon and I spend most of our days scavenging and talking to ghosts who forget the world they knew no longer exists. They still wander the old community garden, inquiring about the crops and complaining about the hole in the maintenance shed that Brandon patched months ago.

The water situation is particularly bad. Plumbing no longer works and southern California is naturally a desert. I have to barter with a crow spirit who guards the nearest well, a magic one dug by no human hands. He is not hostile to humans so long as they pay. He takes avocados, potatoes, carrots, and other produce from our garden.

"Listen," the crow calls to me. "The cycle is moving."

Death and rebirth. I know. Our world is gone, and a new one will come. I set my bucket on the ground and take out today's payment. The fruits and vegetables pile beside the well where the crow can see them.

"What tells you this?" I ask.

I don't really expect an answer. Demons only reply if it suits, and their words don't always address what was asked.

"The light shines from the peak. Soon there will be fighting."

The crow cocks his head to the southeast as though he can see something great in the distance. I see only old buildings bathed in the light of the afternoon sun. Empty.

"The Bank Tower," says the crow. "It will be there. A human will have to make a decision."

"What kind of a decision?"

"An important one." The crow pecks at his payment. "Take the water," he says, before snapping a carrot in his beak and flying to his nest.

I fill the bucket and it is heavy. It's the big kind a person uses when mopping floors. Now it carries clean water. The crow is not cheap, but his water is good. The rain is acid when it comes. We try not to drink it and the stores have been looted long ago.

When I get back to the house, I find the front door open and Brandon's backpack on the patio. It is stuffed thicker than I've seen in months and his canteen hangs from one side. His baseball bat sits beside it. Brandon emerges from inside the house. He eyes the water.

"You can put it down," he says, and I do.

"Are you going somewhere?" I ask, though the answer is obvious.

"Downtown."

Downtown Los Angeles is miles from here. Before the world ended it was a half hour drive through city traffic. On foot it would take several hours. I can't imagine why he would go there. Then I remember the crow spoke of the US Bank Tower. It is the tallest building in downtown.

"Did you decide—"

He cuts me off. "I don't feel like talking about it." His voice is surly as he snatches the canteen from his pack and dunks it in the bucket. It fills quickly as the air escapes. Glub. Glub.

When are you coming back? I want to ask, but instead I say, "Can I come too?"

He eyes me. "If you hurry."

I sprint to my bedroom in the back of the house. This wasn't my house originally, or Brandon's, but our homes still sheltered the ghosts of our families. My mother couldn't know that it was no longer 4 p.m. on a particular Wednesday of last year, so she would always nag me: "Eun Hee, why aren't you at tutoring? Eun Hee you need to study harder to get into a good university." She never called me Joan like my American-born friends.

The house I share with Brandon has no ghosts. Either no one had died here or the demons had eaten them. Either way, it isn't as though the owners still needed it. Brandon was the one who suggested we take it, and I had to agree it was a good decision.

I grab my backpack, check that I still have a change of clothes and my first aid kit inside, then dash for the kitchen where we keep our dried fruit and demon bread. The bread is not evil, at least not in any way we can tell, but without flour we can only obtain bread through bartering with the demons. Brandon always leaves that to me. He won't talk to them.

I put both bread and fruit in my backpack and jog through the living room to the front door. To my relief, Brandon is still waiting outside, though at the end of the walk by the street.

I close the door behind me. We don't have the key so I can't lock it, and I worry that we will come back to a ransacked home, but Brandon does not seem concerned. He looks to the southeast. It's the direction of downtown.

"Do you know how to get there?" I ask.

"Yeah." He has a faded street map with him, something he found in a desk of one the homes we stayed in.

We set off with him in the lead and me following close behind. Brandon carries his bat, sometimes over his shoulder, sometimes by his side. Some demons are congenial, even if they are not inclined to be friends. Some demons ignore us. But other demons frown on humans and would leave us as so much blood smeared on the walls and sidewalks in front of buildings. We find people like that sometimes, so Brandon carries the bat. He knows demons can be killed. He's the only person I know who's killed one. But still, some are better to hide from.

Brandon and I were classmates in geometry, and until the world ended we'd barely said two words to each other. But when the world heaved and most people became ghosts we were the only two left in the school.

We've seen other people since; living ones. They're furtive, scurrying like we scurry. They rarely talk to us, as if by banding together in a larger group we would draw unwanted attention—and we would, the same way a single feral dog is a nuisance and a pack must be put down.

We do not reach the Bank Tower by sunset, having left too late in the day, so we spend the night huddled in two layers of clothing on the eight lanes of the 101 freeway. There are still cars parked, bumper to bumper, frozen in early rush hour traffic. Uneaten ghosts linger in them, usually in the driver's seat, sometimes in the passenger's.

Brandon finds a gap between the cars where we're unlikely to be seen by hungry demons. I can hear a ghost mutter, "I'm gonna miss the game. I'm gonna miss the game." It stops now and then, but the words don't change.

"What's downtown?" I ask, hoping he won't rebuff me a second time. We've just eaten dinner and he's usually nicer after some food.

"The tower," he says, and though I'm sure he means the US Bank Tower, I can't help but ask for confirmation.

The moon is full tonight and I can see his face. He glares at me as though I'm stupid.

"Of course the US Bank Tower," he mutters. "You'd have to be deaf not to have heard all the demons ranting about the Decision. Everyone's going there."

"Including the demons?"

"Everyone *human*. It takes a human soul. Haven't you been paying attention? You're always talking to demons. More than you should."

I talk because I don't know how to fight and I'm not good at hiding. If the demons think I'm harmless, they might not hurt me and I won't be a blood smear on the side of a building. I know talking won't always work, but if the demon is willing to hear me, then it's at least worth a shot.

"I've made my Decision," he says, with an air of finality. "If you haven't made one, that's fine by me. It's probably better that you don't."

"Can you at least tell me so I know whether I should?"

He rolls over and settles his head on his backpack. He intends to sleep. End conversation. "Better that you don't," he says. "You'll thank me later."

I wake the next morning and do not see him. His backpack is gone and when I look around there are only empty cars and ghosts. Maybe he's scouting ahead, I tell myself, and there's nothing to do but put one foot in front of the other and walk down the freeway. The downtown area is in sight.

My stomach rumbles, reminding me of breakfast, but I don't touch the bread in my backpack. Eating will slow me down and I can't be a burden to Brandon.

He's the only other human being I have in the world. Even if we don't always get along, even if he's abrasive, at least he's company.

When the world ended he was the one who figured out how to store food now that refrigerators no longer had power. He was the one who could pick out the quickest escape route when demons were near. He broke into homes, stores, getting us food, shelter, and supplies. He might listen to a demon, but he would never trust one.

At first he seemed to like caring for me, and I tried to repay him by being a good housekeeper, so I wouldn't have to rely on his charity, but there was no denying that I needed him more than he needed me.

The US Bank Tower rises above the rest of downtown. It is a distinctive building not only for its height, but its cylindrical shape. I'd never been there before. Downtown L.A. was always crowded and there was no reason to visit what was really an office building.

There is an off-ramp from the 110 to 4th Street, and while I have no idea if this is the closest one, it looks close enough.

That's when it hits me. Brandon really did leave me behind. I'm not going to catch up with him. I don't even know if he went this way. I've spent all morning, walking as fast as I can, but he's nowhere in sight and the demons didn't get him or I would have been taken as well and we'd both be piles of bone and gore.

I stumble to the bottom of the off-ramp and blunder into an SUV halted in the intersection. There's no ghost in this one. I don't hear muttering, but I don't care anymore.

I curl up and sob, because now I'm alone.

After a time I become aware of the sound of wings beating above me. Something is circling. There are no normal birds anymore so it can only be a demon. I am probably dead, lying out in the open like this, and I find I almost don't care. Almost.

I raise my head and through puffy eyes I see a winged serpent silhouetted against the morning sun. The demon sails lower, sweeping to the ground.

"Why do you cry?" he asks. "There are no plants here for you to nourish."

He is a splendid creature, with feathers like the rainbow and teeth like a shark. His eyes are shiny and black, like obsidian. I call him Quetzalcoatl after the Aztec god. Whether he is or not he puffs his chest with pride and I think he won't eat me.

"A human's tears aren't enough to nourish a flower," I say.

He tilts his head. "No? But they are enough to feed a new world."

"The Decision," I say. "What is it?"

"The birth, the coming. As it was, as it has been, as it continues to be. Worlds and then worlds in an endless cycle." He pauses, perhaps reflecting. "You should make yours soon."

"But what am I deciding?"

"What else? Time in this timeless world is running out. Already the cycle draws to a close."

Brandon was in a hurry to get to the US Bank Tower. He said everyone is going there. I look to its peak and it shines with a blue light that comes from no lamp.

"Will you nourish a new world?" asks the serpent.

"What will happen to this one?"

"Does it matter?"

The buildings downtown are worn and tired at the street level. Doors and windows have been broken by scavengers and there are dull smears where the unfortunate have died. I see no ghosts anywhere. The demons have eaten them all.

I say, "It matters to you, doesn't it?"

"It does."

The serpent spreads his wings and lies down before me. His torso is as wide as a small horse. "I will carry you as high as I can," he says, "for you are already very late."

I climb on and cling tight to his neck, knees bent to keep from scraping the ground as he takes off. Then we are flying, soaring upward on his beautiful feathered wings. Other demons soar around the peak of the Bank Tower. Though I can see the skyscraper's helipad through the wild throng, none of them approach it. A few attempt, but are rebuffed by an unseen force. They are watching something. I see small figures, humans, moving on the rooftop and I don't know why. Aren't they afraid of the demons?

The demons pay us no mind. Even below the peak, all eyes are looking in through the windows. I catch a flutter of movement. Black feathers? But the important thing is I see an open window. Shattered.

"Over there!" I shout, and I point though I realize the serpent probably can't see me.

He spots the opening regardless and sails close.

"Beware the glass," says the serpent, as I dismount and watch where I step.

"Thank you," I tell him, and I bow once I'm safely inside.

The serpent nods and flies away.

I look up at the ceiling as though I could somehow gauge how much higher I had to go. The very structure is humming and I'm at least few floors down. I need to find the stairs.

The exit signs in the hall are no longer lit, but they point the way regardless. The stairs are on the other side of a heavy door which I push open as hard as I can. There is resistance on the other side that suddenly gives way. The air of the stairwell smells thickly of blood; sweet and full of iron.

I see the source of the resistance, a man on his hands and knees. His white collared shirt is splotched with dirt and blood. He's been shot, multiple times. In his hand is a broken ruler—sharpened plastic. It's a poor weapon, but he clutches it to him like a rosary. It's all that keeps him from death. Well, a quicker death.

"I can't make a Decision anymore," he breathes. "Please, just leave me alone."

I nod, and carefully step around him to go up the stairs.

"But if you would, if you like my Decision..."

I look back at him. It is taking so much for him to talk.

"I wanted a world where people had to respect each other, a world where everyone was civil and cared about others..."

I nod again, to show I've heard, but I don't think he sees me anymore.

There are more bodies and dying people as I climb the tower. Those still living plead their cases for the new world.

A world without sickness and death.

A world with only one god.

A world where no child is unwanted.

But I come to realize that no one world can satisfy everyone, and what disturbs me the most is that none of these people died to demons. The wounds are from guns, from knives, or blunt trauma. There are no claws, no fire, no teeth, or unholy elements.

Others must have realized before me that there can be only one new world, and they'd fought to ensure the one created was the one they wanted.

"Please," says a woman, "there can't be more than two or three ahead of me. I don't want anything special—just the old world back. It wasn't so bad, was it?"

I step over her and reach for a battered door, held shut only by its natural resting position, and not by its busted latch. It's the door to the roof. Heart pounding, I can only think of Brandon. He hasn't been among the bodies I crossed.

The roof is bathed with the blue light I'd spotted while riding the serpent. Oddly it is dimmer now, and seems to be coming from still higher above me. The helipad is nearby, chain link surrounding its base should anyone fall. I find the steps up. There is another corpse along the way. This one's skull has been beaten.

I draw eye level with the helipad and the sight is horrible. The helipad's number 12, painted in red, blends with the blood from the myriad bodies crowded around the base of a clear obelisk. It is from the obelisk that the blue light shines. Even as I approach, it continues to dim, and I can look at it without blinding myself.

There are two figures still on their feet. No. Only one. Brandon. The other man is being stood on his toes, his collar snug around his neck, as Brandon holds him fast. Brandon has his baseball bat, stained a terrible red. The other man is unarmed, but there is a gun by his feet.

"Brandon!" I shout.

He does not take his eyes off the writhing man he holds. "Why are you here, Joan? Did you actually make a Decision?"

"No, I—" I just didn't want to be left behind.

"Then you can help me make mine."

"What is it? What is the world that you want?"

It occurs to me that though Brandon and I have lived together for almost a year, we never talked of any hopes or desires, unless they pertained to food, shelter, or demons.

"Even you'll like this one." He glares contemptuously at the man he holds and shakes his captive when the other man tries to speak. "Even this guy would too."

"Can't you let him go?" I ask. "He doesn't have a gun anymore."

"My world," says Brandon, undeterred, "is one where no one ever needs another person. You won't have to rely on anyone to take care of you. I won't be obligated to help. Everyone would be self-sufficient. Wouldn't you like that? To not need other people?"

I'd never considered such a thing, and I can't quite believe such a world could exist. If we didn't need each other for anything, not even companionship, would we all live alone?

Brandon takes my silence for acceptance. It has always been this way when we made decisions that I didn't like.

"Finish this guy then, while I hold him. Pick up his gun."

I hesitate.

"It's not that hard to use. Just point and shoot."

The man babbles. He doesn't care about making a new world anymore. He just doesn't want to die.

"It's not that," I say. "Why do we need to kill him?"

"Each person who dies in this tower weakens the barrier withholding the rebirth. Have you notice they leave no ghosts?"

Now that he mentions it, I haven't seen any, nor any demons who would have eaten them.

"Their spirits are filling the obelisk, and when there are enough the walls will be weak enough to release the rebirth."

"The rebirth is powered by human souls?"

That's not the kind of world I want...

Brandon scoffs. "They're already dead. It'll get us and any remaining humans out of this hellhole and into a new world where there won't be any demons."

The other man suddenly twists and kicks. Brandon swears, releasing him as he grabs his baseball bat in both hands. Before I know what I'm doing, I throw myself at Brandon, arms outstretched. I don't want him to kill someone.

We collide, and he stumbles mid-swing. He wasn't expecting me. I feel myself falling and I try to correct myself, but my feet and legs aren't responding. I spin to one side, trying to get an arm out, when I slam against the concrete. It hurts and the wind is knocked from my lungs.

Brandon is screaming. It takes me a while to recognize his voice. I've never heard him scream like this before, so obviously in pain. Nothing ever hurts Brandon enough for him to scream.

But this... This is nothing he's expected.

I lift my head, trying to see him.

I had pushed him into the obelisk and it had broken like so much glass. I hadn't realized it was so thin.

Beware the glass. I remember.

The shards bury themselves in his body, digging in like maggots, and he is bleeding from so many places his skin is slick and red. He flails, kicking, and I watch as he grows weak, his movements less vigorous, less frantic. Not once does he look to me. He has never wanted my help.

The light, dimly shining, even after the destruction of the obelisk, goes out as Brandon ceases to move.

So much for the new world.

The other man stares in disbelief, then staggers away, back to the stairs. I see a familiar crow flying overhead, weaving in and out among the other demons. They are all watching.

I have never liked Brandon, but at least he was company, and at times, in his own way, he'd been kind. I remember our early days, when there had still been hope, and he killed a demon to save me. I'd been a blubbering mess and he told me, "Don't worry. I've got you."

Now Brandon is just one of many bodies lying by the remains of the obelisk.

"It is time for the new world."

I look up and through blurry eyes I see the crow, standing before me.

"But the obelisk was destroyed."

"As it was meant to be, and the final soul that was needed was captured atop this tower. Have you made your Decision?"

A world where people don't need each other. It was a promising world, but I realize I like needing and being needed. I would not exist in a world such as Brandon envisioned.

There is a touch at my shoulder, and I turn to see the feathered serpent I called Quetzalcoatl. He says nothing, but licks beneath my eyes, taking away the tears.

"Does there have to be a new world?" I ask.

The helipad around me is covered with so much death. This tower is a mausoleum of worlds that did not agree.

"No," says the crow.

The conflict between people would not be erased with the creation of a new world. I had only to lift my head to see the pain and destruction that the want of one had caused. For a brief moment, I consider a world where I am never alone, where I am appreciated, but I realize I could never force others to befriend me.

I place my hand on the wing of the feathered serpent. His eyes glitter bright and a loud thrum issues from his throat.

"I don't want a new world," I tell the crow. "Let this one remain."

"So it is done!"

The crow's voice thunders from atop the skyscraper and the demons wheel in the sky like flocks of birds before scattering. I am not certain, but I think a few of them bow to me before they leave.

The feathered serpent extends himself before me, beckoning me to mount, and the crow hops on to my shoulder. My life will be different now, but I find myself unafraid. However strange my new companions are, I am not alone.

Copyright © 2016 by Laurie Tom

HEINLEIN PRIZE TRUST
Dedicated to advancing Robert and Virginia Heinlein's dream of securing humanities future in space.

www.HeinleinPrize.com

Robert Silverberg is one of the true giants of science fiction. He is a multiple Hugo winner, a multiple Nebula winner, has been a Worldcon Guest of Honor, and is a Nebula Grand Master and the author of numerous acknowledged classics in the field.

CAPRICORN GAMES

by Robert Silverberg

Nikki stepped into the conical field of the ultrasonic cleanser, wriggling so that the unheard droning out of the machine's stubby snout could more effectively shear her skin of dead epidermal tissue, globules of dried sweat, dabs of yesterday's scents, and other debris; after three minutes she emerged clean, bouncy, ready for the party. She programmed her party outfit: green buskins, lemon-yellow tunic of gauzy film, pale orange cape soft as a clam's mantle, and nothing underneath but Nikki—smooth, glistening, satiny Nikki. Her body was tuned and fit. The party was in her honor, though she was the only one who knew that. Today was her birthday, the seventh of January, 2029, twenty-four years old, no sign yet of bodily decay. Old Steiner had gathered an extraordinary assortment of guests: he promised to display a reader of minds, a billionaire, an authentic Byzantine duke, an Arab rabbi, a man who had married his own daughter, and other marvels. All of these, of course, subordinate to the true guest of honor, the evening's prize, the real birthday boy, the lion of the season—the celebrated Nicholson, who had lived a thousand years and who said he could help others to do the same. Nikki…Nicholson. Happy assonance, portending close harmony. You will show me, dear Nicholson, how I can live forever and never grow old. A cozy soothing idea.

The sky beyond the sleek curve of her window was black, snow-dappled; she imagined she could hear the rusty howl of the wind and feel the sway of the frost-gripped building, ninety stories high. This was the worst winter she had ever known. Snow fell almost every day, a planetary snow, a global shiver, not even sparing the tropics. Ice hard as iron bands bound the streets of New York. Walls were slippery,

the air had a cutting edge. Tonight Jupiter gleamed fiercely in the blackness like a diamond in a raven's forehead. Thank God she didn't have to go outside. She could wait out the winter within this tower. The mail came by pneumatic tube. The penthouse restaurant fed her. She had friends on a dozen floors. The building was a world, warm, snug. Let it snow. Let the sour gales come. Nikki checked herself in the all-around mirror: very nice, very very nice. Sweet filmy yellow folds. Hint of thigh, hint of breasts. More than a hint when there's a light-source behind her. She glowed. Fluffed her short glossy black hair. Dab of scent. Everyone loved her. Beauty is a magnet: repels some, attracts many, leaves no one unmoved. It was nine o'clock.

"Upstairs," she said to the elevator. "Steiner's place."

"Eighty-eighth floor," the elevator said.

"I know that. You're so sweet."

Music in the hallway: Mozart, crystalline and sinuous. The door to Steiner's apartment was a half-barrel of chromed steel, like the entrance to a bank vault. Nikki smiled into the scanner. The barrel revolved. Steiner held his hands like cups, centimeters from her chest, by way of greeting. "Beautiful," he murmured.

"So glad you asked me to come."

"Practically everybody's here already. It's a wonderful party, love."

She kissed his shaggy cheek. In October they had met in the elevator. He was past sixty and looked less than forty. When she touched his body she perceived it as an object encased in milky ice, like a mammoth fresh out of the Siberian permafrost. They had been lovers for two weeks. Autumn had given way to winter and Nikki had passed out of his life, but he had kept his word about the parties: here she was, invited.

"Alexius Ducas," said a short, wide man with a dense black beard, parted in the middle. He bowed. A good flourish. Steiner evaporated and she was in the keeping of the Byzantine duke. He maneuvered her at once across the thick white carpet to a place where clusters of spotlights, sprouting like angry fungi from the wall, revealed the contours of her body. Others turned to look. Duke Alexius favored her with a heavy stare. But she felt no excitement. Byzantium had been over for a long time.

He brought her a goblet of chilled green wine and said, "Are you ever in the Aegean Sea? My family has its ancestral castle on an island eighteen kilometers east of—"

"Excuse me, but which is the man named Nicholson?"

"Nicholson is merely the name he currently uses. He claims to have had a shop in Constantinople during the reign of my ancestor the Basileus Manuel Comnenus." A patronizing click, tongue on teeth. "Only a shopkeeper." The Byzantine eyes sparkled ferociously. "How beautiful you are!"

"Which one is he?"

"There. By the couch."

Nikki saw only a wall of backs. She tilted to the left and peered. No use. She would get to him later. Alexius Ducas continued to offer her his body with his eyes. She whispered languidly, "Tell me all about Byzantium."

He got as far as Constantine the Great before he bored her. She finished her wine, and, coyly extending the glass, persuaded a smooth young man passing by to refill it for her. The Byzantine looked sad. "The empire then was divided," he said, "among—"

"This is my birthday," she announced.

"Yours also? My congratulations. Are you as old as—"

"Not nearly. Not by half. I won't even be five hundred for some time," she said, and turned to take her glass. The smooth young man did not wait to be captured. The party engulfed him like an avalanche. Sixty, eighty guests, all in motion. The draperies were pulled back, revealing the full fury of the snowstorm. No one was watching it. Steiner's apartment was like a movie set: great porcelain garden stools, Ming or even Sung; walls painted with flat sheets of bronze and scarlet; pre-Columbian artefacts in spotlit niches; sculptures like aluminum spiderwebs; Dürer etchings—the loot of the ages. Squat shaven-headed servants, Mayans or Khmers or perhaps Olmecs, circulated impassively offering trays of delicacies: caviar, sea urchins, bits of roasted meat, tiny sausages, burritos in startling chili sauce. Hands darted unceasingly from trays to lips. This was a gathering of life-eaters, world-swallowers. Duke Alexius was stroking her arm. "I will leave at midnight," he said gently. "It would be a delight if you left with me."

"I have other plans," she told him.

"Even so." He bowed courteously, outwardly undisappointed. "Possibly another time. My card?" It appeared as if by magic in his hand: a sliver of tawny cardboard, elaborately engraved. She put it in her purse and the room swallowed him. Instantly a big, wild-eyed man took his place before her. "You've never heard of me," he began.

"Is that a boast or an apology?"

"I'm quite ordinary. I work for Steiner. He thought it would be amusing to invite me to one of his parties."

"What do you do?"

"Invoices and debarkations. Isn't this an amazing place?"

"What's your sign?" Nikki asked him.

"Libra."

"I'm Capricorn. Tonight's my birthday as well as *his*. If you're really Libra, you're wasting your time with me. Do you have a name?"

"Martin Bliss."

"Nikki."

"There isn't any Mrs. Bliss, hah-hah."

Nikki licked her lips. "I'm hungry. Would you get me some canapés?"

She was gone as soon as he moved toward the food. Circumnavigating the long room—past the string quintet, past the bartender's throne, past the window—until she had a good view of the man called Nicholson. He didn't disappoint her. He was slender, supple, not tall, strong in the shoulders. A man of presence and authority. She wanted to put her lips to him and suck immortality out. His head was a flat triangle, brutal cheekbones, thin lips, dark mat of curly hair, no beard, no moustache. His eyes were keen, electric, intolerably wise. He must have seen everything twice, at the very least. Nikki had read his book. Everyone had. He had been a king, a lama, a slave trader, a slave. Always taking pains to conceal his implausible longevity, now offering his terrible secret freely to the members of the Book-of-the-Month Club. Why had he chosen to surface and reveal himself? Because this is the necessary moment of revelation, he had said. When he must stand forth as what he is, so that he might impart his gift to others, lest he lose it. Lest he lose it. At the stroke of the new century he must share his prize of life. A dozen people surrounded him, catching his glow. He glanced through a palisade of shoulders and locked his eyes on hers; Nikki felt impaled, exalted, chosen. Warmth spread through her loins like a river of molten tungsten, like a stream of hot honey. She started to go to him. A corpse got in her way. Death's-head parchment skin, nightmare eyes. A scaly hand brushed her bare biceps. A frightful eroded voice croaked, "How old do you think I am?"

"Oh, God!"

"How old?"

"Two thousand?"

"I'm fifty-eight. I won't live to see fifty-nine. Here, smoke one of these."

With trembling hands he offered her a tiny ivory tube. There was a Gothic monogram near one end—FXB—and a translucent green capsule at the other. She pressed the capsule, and a flickering blue flame sprouted. She inhaled. "What is it?" she asked.

"My own mixture. Soma Number Five. You like it?"

"I'm smeared," she said. "Absolutely smeared. Oh, God!" The walls were flowing. The snow had turned to tinfoil. An instant hit. The corpse had a golden halo. Dollar signs rose into view like stigmata on his furrowed forehead. She heard the crash of the surf, the roar of the waves. The deck was heaving. The masts were cracking. *Woman overboard!* she cried, and heard her inaudible voice disappearing down a tunnel of echoes, boingg boingg boingg. She clutched at his frail wrists. "You bastard, what did you *do* to me?"

"I'm Francis Xavier Byrne."

Oh. The billionaire. Byrne Industries, the great conglomerate. Steiner had promised her a billionaire tonight.

"Are you going to die soon?" she asked.

"No later than Easter. Money can't help me now. I'm a walking metastasis." He opened his ruffled shirt. Something bright and metallic, like chain mail, covered his chest. "Life-support system," he confided. "It operates me. Take it off for half an hour and I'd be finished. Are you a Capricorn?"

"How did you know?"

"I may be dying, but I'm not stupid. You have the Capricorn gleam in your eyes. What am I?"

She hesitated. His eyes were gleaming too. Self-made man, fantastic business sense, energy, arrogance. Capricorn, of course. No, too easy. "Leo," she said.

"No. Try again." He pressed another monogrammed tube into her hand and strode away. She hadn't yet come down from the last one, although the most flamboyant effects had ebbed. Party guests swirled and flowed around her. She no longer could see Nicholson. The snow seemed to be turning to hail, little hard particles spattering the vast windows and leaving white abraded tracks: or were her perceptions merely sharper? The roar of conversation seemed to rise and fall as if someone were adjusting a volume control. The lights fluctuated in a counterpointed rhythm. She felt dizzy. A tray of golden cocktails went past her and she hissed, "Where's the bathroom?"

Down the hall. Five strangers clustered outside it, talking in scaly whispers. She floated through them, grabbed the sink's cold edge, thrust her face to the oval concave mirror. A death's-head. Parchment skin, nightmare eyes. No! No! She blinked and her own features reappeared. Shivering, she made an effort to pull herself together. The medicine cabinet held a tempting collection of drugs, Steiner's all-purpose remedies. Without looking at labels Nikki seized a handful of vials and gobbled pills at random. A flat red one, a tapering green one, a succulent yellow gelatin capsule. Maybe headache remedies, maybe hallucinogens. Who knows, who cares? We Capricorns are not always as cautious as you think.

Someone knocked at the bathroom door. She answered and found the bland, hopeful face of Martin Bliss hovering near the ceiling. Eyes protruding faintly, cheeks florid. "They said you were sick. Can I do anything for you?" So kind, so sweet. She touched his arm, grazed his cheek with her lips. Beyond him in the hall stood a broad-bodied man with close-cropped blond hair, glacial blue eyes, a plump perfect face. His smile was intense and brilliant. "That's easy," he said. "Capricorn."

"You can guess my—" She stopped, stunned. "Sign?" she finished, voice very small. "How did you do that? Oh."

"Yes. I'm that one."

She felt more than naked, stripped down to the ganglia, to the synapses. "What's the trick?"

"No trick. I listen. I hear."

"You hear people thinking?"

"More or less. Do you think it's a party game?" He was beautiful but terrifying, like a Samurai sword in motion. She wanted him but she didn't dare. He's got my number, she thought. I would never have any secrets from him. He said sadly, "I don't mind that. I know I frighten a lot of people. Some don't care."

"What's your name?"

"Tom," he said. "Hello, Nikki."

"I feel very sorry for you."

"Not really. You can kid yourself if you need to. But you can't kid me. Anyway, you don't sleep with men you feel sorry for."

"I don't sleep with you."

"You will," he said.

"I thought you were just a mind-reader. They didn't tell me you did prophecies too."

He leaned close and smiled. The smile demolished her. She had to fight to keep from falling. "I've got your number, all right," he said in a low, harsh voice. "I'll call you next Tuesday." As he walked away he said, "You're wrong. I'm a Virgo. Believe it or not."

Nikki returned, numb, to the living room. "…the figure of the mandala," Nicholson was saying. His voice was dark, focused, a pure basso cantante. "The essential thing that every mandala has is a center—the place where everything is born, the eye of God's mind, the heart of darkness and of light, the core of the storm. All right. You must move toward the center, find the vortex at the boundary of Yang and Yin, place yourself right at the mandala's midpoint. *Center yourself.* Do you follow the metaphor? Center yourself at *now*, the eternal *now*. To move off center is to move forward toward death, backward toward birth, always the fatal polar swings. But if you're capable of positioning yourself constantly at the focus of the mandala, right on center, you have access to the fountain of renewal, you become an organism capable of constant self-healing, constant self-replenishment, constant expansion into regions beyond self. Do you follow? The power of…"

Steiner, at her elbow, said tenderly, "How beautiful you are in the first moments of erotic fixation."

"It's a marvelous party."

"Are you meeting interesting people?"

"Is there any other kind?" she asked.

Nicholson abruptly detached himself from the circle of his audience and strode across the room, alone, in a quick decisive knight's move toward the bar. Nikki, hurrying to intercept him, collided with a shaven-headed tray-bearing servant. The tray slid smoothly from the man's thick fingertips and launched itself into the air like a spinning shield; a rainfall of skewered meat in an oily green curry sauce spattered the white carpet. The servant was utterly motionless. He stood frozen like some sort of Mexican stone idol, thick-necked, flat-nosed, for a long painful moment; then he turned his head slowly to the left and regretfully contemplated his rigid outspread hand, shorn of its tray; finally he swung his head toward Nikki, and his normally expressionless granite face took on for a quick flickering instant a look of total hatred, a coruscating emanation of contempt and disgust that faded immediately. He laughed: hu-hu-hu, a neighing snicker. His superiority was overwhelming. Nikki floundered in quicksands of humiliation. Hastily she escaped, a zig and a zag, around the tumbled goodies and across to the bar. Nicholson, still by himself. Her face went crimson. She felt short of breath. Hunting for words, tongue all thumbs. Finally, in a catapulting blurt: "Happy birthday!"

"Thank you," he said solemnly.

"Are you enjoying your birthday?"

"Very much."

"I'm amazed that they don't bore you. I mean, having had so many of them."

"I don't bore easily." He was awesomely calm, drawing on some bottomless reservoir of patience. He gave her a look that was at the same time warm and impersonal. "I find everything interesting," he said.

"That's curious. I said more or less the same thing to Steiner just a few minutes ago. You know, it's my birthday too."

"Really?"

"The seventh of January, 2005 for me."

"Hello, 2005. I'm—" He laughed. "It sounds absolutely absurd, doesn't it?"

"The seventh of January, 982."

"You've been doing your homework."

"I've read your book," she said. "Can I make a silly remark? My God, you don't *look* like you're a thousand and seventeen years old."

"How should I look?"

"More like him," she said, indicating Francis Xavier Byrne.

Nicholson chuckled. She wondered if he liked her. Maybe. Maybe. Nikki risked some eye contact. He was hardly a centimeter taller than she was, which made it a terrifyingly intimate experience. He regarded her steadily, centerdly; she imagined a throbbing mandala surrounding him, luminous turquoise spokes emanating from his heart, radiant red and green spiderweb rings connecting them. Reaching from her loins, she threw a loop of desire around him. Her eyes were explicit. His were veiled. She felt him calmly retreating. Take me inside, she pleaded, take me to one of the back rooms. Pour life into me. She said, "How will you choose the people you're going to instruct in the secret?"

"Intuitively."

"Refusing anybody who asks directly, of course."

"Refusing anybody who asks."

"Did *you* ask?"

"You said you read my book."

"Oh. Yes. I remember—you didn't know what was happening, you didn't understand anything until it was over."

"I was a simple lad," he said. "That was a long time ago." His eyes were alive again. He's drawn to me. He sees that I'm his kind, that I deserve him. Capricorn, Capricorn, Capricorn you and me, he-goat and she-goat. Play my game, Cap. "How are you named?" he asked.

"Nikki."

"A beautiful name. A beautiful woman."

The emptiness of the compliments devastated her. She realized she had arrived with mysterious suddenness at a necessary point of tactical withdrawal; retreat was obligatory, lest she push too hard and destroy the tenuous contact so tensely established. She thanked him with a glance and gracefully slipped away, pivoting toward Martin Bliss, slipping her arm through his. Bliss quivered at the gesture, glowed, leaped into a higher energy state. She resonated to his vibrations, going up and up. She was at the heart of the party, the center of the mandala: standing flat-footed, legs slightly apart, making her body a polar axis, with lines of force zooming up out of the earth, up through the basement levels of this building, up the eighty-eight stories of it, up through her sex, her heart, her head. This is how it must feel, she thought, when undyingness is conferred on you. A moment of spontaneous grace, the kindling of an inner light. She looked love at poor sappy Bliss. You dear heart, you dumb walking pun. The string quintet made molten sounds. "What is that?" she asked. "Brahms?" Bliss offered to find out. Alone, she was vulnerable to Francis Xavier Byrne, who brought her down with a single cadaverous glance.

"Have you guessed it yet?" he asked. "The sign."

She stared through his ragged cancerous body, blazing with decomposition. "Scorpio," she told him hoarsely.

"Right! Right!" He pulled a pendant from his breast and draped its golden chain over her head. "For you," he rasped, and fled. She fondled it. A smooth green stone. Jade? Emerald? Lightly engraved on its domed face was the looped cross, the crux ansata. Beautiful. The gift of life, from the dying man. She waved fondly to him across a forest of heads and winked. Bliss returned.

"They're playing something by Schönberg," he reported. *"Ver klärte Nacht."*

"How lovely." She flipped the pendant and let it fall back against her breasts. "Do you like it?"

"I'm sure you didn't have it a moment ago."

"It sprouted," she told him. She felt high, but not as high as she had been just after leaving Nicholson. That sense of herself as focal point had departed. The party seemed chaotic. Couples were forming, dissolving, reforming; shadowy figures were stealing away in twos and threes toward the bedrooms; the servants were more obsessively thrusting their trays of drinks and snacks at the remaining guests; the hail had reverted to snow, and feathery masses silently struck the windows, sticking there, revealing their glistening mandalic structures for painfully brief moments before they deliquesced. Nikki struggled to regain her centered position. She indulged in a cheering fantasy: Nicholson coming to her, formally touching her cheek, telling her, "You will be one of the elect." In less than twelve months the time would come for him to gather with his seven still unnamed disciples to see in the new century, and he would take their hands into his hands, he would pump the vitality of the undying into their bodies, sharing with them the secret that had been shared with him a thousand years ago. Who? Who? Who? Me. Me. Me. But where had Nicholson gone? His aura, his glow, that cone of imaginary light that had appeared to surround him—nowhere.

A man in a lacquered orange wig began furiously to quarrel, almost under Nikki's nose, with a much younger woman wearing festoons of bioluminescent pearls. Man and wife, evidently. They were both sharp-featured, with glossy, protuberant eyes, rigid faces, cheek muscles working intensely. Live together long enough, come to look alike. Their dispute had a stale, ritualistic flavor, as though they had staged it all too many times before. They were explaining to each other the events that had caused the quarrel, interpreting them, recapitulating them, shading them, justifying, attacking, defending—you said this because and that led me to respond that way because…no, on the contrary, I said this because you said that—all of it in a quiet screechy tone, sickening, agonizing, pure death.

"He's her biological father," a man next to Nikki said. "She was one of the first of the in vitro babies, and he was the donor, and five years ago he tracked her down and married her. A loophole in the law." Five years? They sounded as if they had been married for fifty. Walls of pain and boredom encased them. Only their eyes were alive. Nikki found it impossible to imagine those two in bed, bodies entwined in the act of love. Act of love, she thought, and laughed. Where was Nicholson? Duke Alexius, flushed and sweat-beaded, bowed to her. "I will leave soon," he announced, and she received the announcement gravely but without reacting, as though he had merely commented on the fluctuations of the storm, or had spoken in Greek. He bowed again and went away. Nicholson? Nicholson? She grew calm again, finding her center. He will come to me when he is ready. There was contact between us, and it was real and good.

Bliss, beside her, gestured and said, "A rabbi of Syrian birth, formerly Muslim, highly regarded among Jewish theologians."

She nodded but didn't look.

"An astronaut just back from Mars. I've never seen anyone's skin tanned quite that color."

The astronaut held no interest for her. She worked at kicking herself back into high. The party was approaching a climactic moment, she felt, a time when commitments were being made and decisions taken. The clink of ice in glasses, the foggy vapors of psychedelic inhalants, the press of warm flesh all about her—she was wired into everything, she was alive and receptive, she was entering into the twitching hour, the hour of galvanic jerks. She grew wild and reckless. Impulsively she kissed Bliss, straining on tiptoes, jabbing her tongue deep into his startled mouth. Then she broke free. Someone was playing with the lights: they grew redder, then gained force and zoomed to blue-white ferocity. Far across the room a crowd was surging and billowing around the fallen figure of Francis Xavier Byrne, slumped loose-jointedly against the base of the bar. His eyes were open but glassy. Nicholson crouched over him, reaching into his shirt, making delicate adjustments of the controls of the chain mail beneath. "It's all right," Steiner was saying. "Give him some air. It's all right!" Confusion. Hubbub. A torrent of tangled input.

"—they say there's been a permanent change in the weather patterns. Colder winters from now on, because of accumulations of dust in the atmosphere that screen the sun's rays. Until we freeze altogether by around the year 2200—"

"—but the carbon dioxide is supposed to start a greenhouse effect that's causing *warmer* weather, I thought, and—"

"—the proposal to generate electric power from—"

"—the San Andreas fault—"

"—financed by debentures convertible into—"

"—capsules of botulism toxin—"

"—to be distributed at a ratio of one per thousand families, throughout Greenland and the Kamchatka Metropolitan Area—"

"—in the sixteenth century, when you could actually hope to found your own empire in some unknown part of the—"

"—unresolved conflicts of Capricorn personality—"

"—intense concentration and meditation upon the completed mandala so that the contents of the work are transferred to and identified with the mind and body of the beholder. I mean, technically what occurs is the reabsorption of cosmic forces. In the process of construction these forces—"

"—butterflies, which are no longer to be found anywhere in—"

"—were projected out from the chaos of the unconscious; in the process of absorption, the powers are drawn back in again—"

"—reflecting transformations of the DNA in the light-collecting organ, which—"

"—the snow—"

"—a thousand years, can you imagine that? And—"

"—her body—"

"—formerly a toad—"

"—just back from Mars, and there's that *look* in his eye—"

"Hold me," Nikki said. "Just hold me. I'm very dizzy."

"Would you like a drink?"

"Just hold me." She pressed against cool sweet-smelling fabric. His chest unyielding beneath it. Steiner. Very male. He steadied her, but only for a moment. Other responsibilities summoned him. When he released her, she swayed. He beckoned to someone else, blond, soft-faced. The mind-reader, Tom. Passing her along the chain from man to man.

"You feel better now," the telepath told her.

"Are you positive of that?"

"Very."

"Can you read any mind in the room?" she asked.

He nodded.

"Even *his*?"

Again a nod. "He's the clearest of all. He's been using it so long, all the channels are worn deep."

"Then he really is a thousand years old?"

"You didn't believe it?"

Nikki shrugged. "Sometimes I don't know what I believe."

"He's *old*."

"You'd be the one to know."

"He's a phenomenon. He's absolutely extraordinary." A pause—quick, stabbing. "Would you like to see into his mind?"

"How can I?"

"I'll patch you right in, if you'd like me to." The glacial eyes flashed sudden mischievous warmth. "Yes?"

"I'm not sure I want to."

"You're very sure. You're curious as hell. Don't kid me. Don't play games, Nikki. You want to see into him."

"Maybe." Grudgingly.

"You do. Believe me, you do. Here. Relax, let your shoulders slump a little, loosen up, make yourself receptive, and I'll establish the link."

"Wait," she said.

But it was too late. The mind-reader serenely parted her consciousness like Moses doing the Red Sea and rammed something into her forehead, something thick but insubstantial, a truncheon of fog. She quivered and recoiled. She felt violated. It was like her first time in bed, in that moment when all the fooling around at last was over, the kissing and the nibbling and the stroking, and suddenly there was this object deep inside her body. She had never forgotten that sense of being impaled. But of course it had been not only an intrusion but also a source of ecstasy. As was this. The object within her was the consciousness of Nicholson. In wonder she explored its surface, rigid and weathered, pitted with the myriad ablations of reentry. Ran her trembling hands over its bronzy roughness. Remained outside it. Tom, the mind-reader, gave her a nudge. Go on, go on. Deeper. Don't hold back. She folded herself around Nicholson and drifted into him like ectoplasm seeping into sand. Suddenly she lost her bearings. The discrete and impermeable boundary marking the end of her self and the beginning of his became indistinct. It was impossible to distinguish between her experiences and his, nor could she separate the pulsations of her nervous system from the impulses traveling along his. Phantom memories assailed and engulfed her. She was transformed into a node of pure perception: a steady, cool, isolated eye, surveying and recording. Images flashed. She was toiling upward along a dazzling snowy crest, with jagged Himalayan fangs hanging above her in the white sky and a warm-muzzled yak snuffling wearily at her side.

A platoon of swarthy little men accompanied her, slanty eyes, heavy coats, thick boots. The stink of rancid butter, the cutting edge of an impossible wind: and there, gleaming in the sudden sunlight, a pile of fire-bright yellow plaster with a thousand winking windows, a building, a lamasery strung along a mountain ridge. The nasal sound of distant horns and trumpets. The hoarse chanting of lotus-legged monks. What were they chanting? Om? Om? Om! *Om*, and flies buzzed around her nose, and she lay hunkered in a flimsy canoe, coursing silently down a midnight river in the heart of Africa; drowning in humidity. Brawny naked men with purple-black skins crouching close. Sweaty fronds dangling from flamboyantly excessive shrubbery; the snouts of crocodiles rising out of the dark water like toothy flowers; great nauseating orchids blossoming high in the smooth-shanked trees. And on shore, five white men in Elizabethan costume, wide-brimmed hats, drooping sweaty collars, lace, fancy buckles, curling red beards. Errol Flynn as Sir Francis Drake, blunderbuss dangling in crook of arm. The white men laughing, beckoning, shouting to the men in the canoe. Am I slave or slavemaster? No answer. Only a blurring and a new vision: autumn leaves blowing across the open doorways of straw-thatched huts, shivering oxen crouched in bare stubble-strewn fields, grim long-mustachioed men with close-cropped hair riding diagonal courses toward the horizon. Crusaders, are they? Or warriors of Hungary on their way to meet the dread Mongols? Defenders of the imperiled Anglo-Saxon realm against the Norman invaders? They could be any of these: But always that steady cool eye, always that unmoving consciousness at the center of every scene. *Him,* eternal, all-enduring. And then: the train rolling westward, belching white smoke, the plains unrolling infinityward, the big brown fierce-eyed bison standing in shaggy clumps along the right of way, the man with turbulent shoulder-length hair laughing, slapping a twenty-dollar gold piece on the table. Picking up his rifle—a .50-calibre breech-loading Springfield—he aims casually through the door of the moving train, he squeezes off a shot, another, another. Three shaggy brown corpses beside the tracks, and the train rolls onward, honking raucously.

Her arm and shoulder tingled with the impact of those shots. Then: a fetid waterfront, bales of cloves and peppers and cinnamon, small brown-skinned men in turbans and loincloths arguing under a terrible sun. Tiny irregular silver coins glittering in the palm of her hand. The jabber of some Malabar dialect counterpointed with fluid mocking Portuguese. Do we sail now with Vasco da Gama? Perhaps. And then a gray Teutonic street, windswept, medieval, bleak Lutheran faces scowling from leaded windows. And then the Gobi steppe, with horsemen and campfires and dark tents. And then New York City, unmistakably New York City, with square black automobiles scurrying between the stubby skyscrapers

like glossy beetles, a scene out of some silent movie. And then. And then. Everywhere, everything, all times, all places, a discontinuous flow of events but always that clarity of vision, that rock-steady perception, that solid mind at the center, that unshakeable identity, that unchanging self—with whom I am inextricably enmeshed—

There was no "I," there was no "he," there was only the one ever-perceiving point of view. But abruptly she felt a change of focus; a distancing effect, a separation of self and self, so that she was looking at him as he lived his many lives, seeing him from the outside, seeing him plainly changing identities as others might change clothing, growing beards and moustaches, shaving them, cropping his hair, letting his hair grow, adopting new fashions, learning languages, forging documents. She saw him in all his thousand years of guises and subterfuges, saw him real and unified and centered beneath his obligatory camouflages—and saw him seeing her.

Instantly contact broke. She staggered. Arms caught her. She pulled away from the smiling plump-faced blond man, muttering, "What have you done? You didn't tell me you'd show *me* to *him.*"

"How else can there be a linkage?" the telepath asked.

"You didn't tell me. You should have told me." Everything was lost. She couldn't bear to be in the same room as Nicholson now. Tom reached for her, but she stumbled past him, stepping on people. They winked up at her. Someone stroked her leg. She forced her way through improbable laocoons, three women and two servants, five men and a tablecloth. A glass door, a gleaming silvery handle: she pushed. Out onto the terrace. The purity of the gale might cleanse her. Behind her, faint gasps, a few shrill screams, annoyed expostulations: "Close that thing!" She slammed it. Alone in the night, eighty-eight stories above street level, she offered herself to the storm. Her filmy tunic shielded her not at all. Snowflakes burned against her breasts. Her nipples hardened and rose like fiery beacons, jutting against the soft fabric. The snow stung her throat, her shoulders, her arms. Far below, the wind churned newly fallen crystals into spiral galaxies. The street was invisible. Thermal confusions brought updrafts that seized the edge of her tunic and whipped it outward from her body. Fierce, cold particles of hail were driven into her bare pale thighs. She stood with her back to the party. Did anyone in there notice her? Would someone think she was contemplating suicide and come rushing gallantly out to save her? Capricorns didn't commit suicide. They might threaten it, yes, they might even tell themselves quite earnestly that they were really going to do it, but it was only a game, only a game. No one came to her. She didn't turn. Gripping the railing, she fought to calm herself.

No use. Not even the bitter air could help. Frost in her eyelashes, snow on her lips. The pendant Byrne had given her blazed between her breasts. The air was white with a throbbing green underglow. It seared her eyes. She was off-center and floundering. She felt herself still reverberating through the centuries, going back and forth across the orbit of Nicholson's interminable life. What year is this? Is it 1386, 1912, 1532, 1779, 1043, 1977, 1235, 1129, 1836? So many centuries. So many lives. And yet always the one true self, changeless, unchangeable.

Gradually the resonances died away. Nicholson's unending epochs no longer filled her mind with terrible noise. She began to shiver, not from fear but merely from cold, and tugged at her moist tunic, trying to shield her nakedness. Melting snow left hot clammy tracks across her breasts and belly. A halo of steam surrounded her. Her heart pounded.

She wondered if what she had experienced had been genuine contact with Nicholson's soul, or rather only some trick of Tom's, a simulation of contact. Was it possible, after all, even for Tom to create a linkage between two non-telepathic minds such as hers and Nicholson's? Maybe Tom had fabricated it all himself, using images borrowed from Nicholson's book.

In that case there might still be hope for her.

A delusion, she knew. A fantasy born of the desperate optimism of the hopeless. But nevertheless—

She found the handle, let herself back into the party. A gust accompanied her, sweeping snow inward. People stared. She was like death arriving at the feast. Doglike, she shook off the searing snowflakes. Her clothes were wet and stuck to her skin; she might as well have been naked. "You poor shivering thing," a woman said. She pulled Nikki into a tight embrace. It was the sharp-faced woman, the bulgy-eyed bottle-born one, bride of her own father.

Her hands traveled swiftly over Nikki's body, caressing her breasts, touching her cheek, her forearm, her haunch. "Come inside with me," she crooned. "I'll make you warm." Her lips grazed Nikki's. A playful tongue sought hers.

For a moment, needing the warmth, Nikki gave herself to the embrace. Then she pulled away. "No," she said. "Some other time. Please." Wriggling free, she started across the room. An endless journey. Like crossing the Sahara by pogo stick. Voices, faces, laughter. A dryness in her throat. Then she was in front of Nicholson.

Well. Now or never.

"I have to talk to you," she said.

"Of course." His eyes were merciless. No wrath in them, not even disdain, only an incredible patience more terrifying than anger or scorn. She would not let herself bend before that cool level gaze.

She said, "A few minutes ago, did you have an odd experience, a sense that someone was—well, looking into your mind? I know it sounds foolish, but—?"

"Yes. It happened." So calm. How did he stay that close to his center? That unwavering eye, that uniquely self-contained self, perceiving all: the lamasery, the slave depot, the railroad train, everything, all time gone by, all time to come—how did he manage to be so tranquil? She knew she never could learn such calmness. She knew he knew it. *He has my number, all right.* She found that she was looking at his cheekbones, at his forehead, at his lips. Not into his eyes.

"You have the wrong image of me," she told him.

"It isn't an image," he said. "What I have is you."

"No."

"Face yourself, Nikki. If you can figure out where to look." He laughed. Gently, but she was demolished.

An odd thing, then. She forced herself to stare into his eyes and felt a snapping of awareness from one mode into some other, and he turned into an old man. That mask of changeless early maturity dissolved and she saw the frightening yellowed eyes, the maze of furrows and gullies, the toothless gums, the drooling lips, the hollow throat, the self beneath the face. A thousand years, a thousand years! And every moment of those thousand years was visible. "You're old," she whispered. "You disgust me. I wouldn't want to be like you, not for

36

anything!" She backed away, shaking. "An old, old, old man. All a masquerade!"

He smiled. "Isn't that pathetic?"

"Me or you? *Me or you?*"

He didn't answer. She was bewildered. When she was five paces away from him there came another snapping of awareness, a second changing of phase, and suddenly he was himself again, taut-skinned, erect, appearing to be perhaps thirty-five years old. A globe of silence hung between them. The force of his rejection was withering. She summoned her last strength for a parting glare. *I didn't want you either, friend, not any single part of you.* He saluted cordially. Dismissal.

Martin Bliss, grinning vacantly, stood near the bar. "Let's go," she said savagely. "Take me home!"

"But—"

"It's just a few floors below." She thrust her arm through his. He blinked, shrugged, fell into step.

"I'll call you Tuesday, Nikki," Tom said as they swept past him.

Downstairs, on her home turf, she felt better. In the bedroom they quickly dropped their clothes. His body was pink, hairy, serviceable. She turned the bed on, and it began to murmur and throb. "How old do you think I am?" she asked.

"Twenty-six?" Bliss said vaguely.

"Bastard!" She pulled him down on top of her. Her hands raked his skin. Her thighs parted. Go on. Like an animal, she thought. Like an animal! She was getting older moment by moment, she was dying in his arms.

"You're much better than I expected," she said eventually.

He looked down, baffled, amazed. "You could have chosen anyone at that party. Anyone."

"Almost anyone," she said.

When he was asleep she slipped out of bed. Snow was still falling. She heard the *thunk* of bullets and the whine of wounded bison. She heard the clangor of swords on shields. She heard lamas chanting: Om, Om, Om. No sleep for her this night, none. The clock was ticking like a bomb. The century was flowing remorselessly toward its finish. She checked her face for wrinkles in the bathroom mirror. Smooth, smooth, all smooth under the blue fluorescent glow. Her eyes looked bloody. Her nipples

were still hard. She took a little alabaster jar from one of the bathroom cabinets and three slender red capsules fell out of it, into her palm. Happy birthday, dear Nikki, happy birthday to you. She swallowed all three. Went back to bed. Waited, listening to the slap of snow on glass, for the visions to come and carry her away.

Copyright © 1974 by Agberg, Inc.

Mike Resnick is, according to Locus, *the all-time leading award winner, living or dead, for short fiction, which includes five Hugo wins from a record thirty-seven nominations. This, the fifty-fourth Lucifer Jones story, marks his first appearance in* Galaxy's Edge.

PURE BEAUTY AND THE BEAST

A Lucifer Jones Story

by Mike Resnick

You'd think after all the books and poems that have been written about the mystical beauty of the sea, and the glory of sunset reflected on the water, that it would take you a lifetime—or maybe even two or three lifetimes—to get sick of the ocean.

Well, let me tell you, it just ain't so. After I took my leave of the headhunters on Borneo, I found myself adrift in a rowboat on a diet of raw fish (on them days when I had anything to eat besides my fingernails). I'm as forgiving as the next man, me being a preacher and all, but truth to tell I was getting mighty tired of being cast off to sea. Borneo was the seventh or eighth island I'd tooken my leave of, rarely leisurely or peaceably, and I was beginning to wonder if getting to Australia was worth all this hardship.

Then I remembered that Australia was the only major land mass I hadn't been permanently kicked off of, due to a series of innocent misunderstandings with forty-three different national governments on the finer points of the law, so I stopped feeling sorry for myself and just kept rowing.

I picked up a couple of fellow travelers along the way, a pair of sharks that I named Lum and Abner, though truth to tell I couldn't ever figger out which was which, and neither of 'em answered to their names anyway. But they was mighty good listeners and didn't hardly talk at all, and the only problem I had was that they must have both been mighty near-sighted, because whenever I reached over the side for some scraps left over from their dinner they kept mistaking my hand for a fish and would lunge for it.

Well, we went and we went and we went, and I had time to tell 'em all about my adventures and encounters and exploits, and the hazards I'd overcome (which I'm sure you've all read and memorized by now), and finally one day I looked ahead and lo and behold, there was land. I figgered it had to be Australia, since God surely wouldn't litter a pristine ocean like the Pacific with much more than half a dozen islands and I'd already fled for my life from more than that.

So I made my way toward land. When I got there I climbed out of the boat and dragged it ashore, and invited Lum and Abner to join me, but evidently sharks ain't no fonder of land that I am of the sea, so they didn't even say goodbye but just headed out to the middle of the ocean, wherever *that* was.

I looked a mile or two up the shore in each direction, saw nothing like a hotel or even a bungalow, and came to the conclusion that Australia wasn't nearly as civilized as I'd been led to believe. Still, less civilization meant fewer gendarmes, and probably more sinners to convert once I got around to building my tabernacle, and I decided I could have landed on worse islands.

Of course, that was before the tiger tried to have me for dinner.

I was kind of hungry, since all I'd had to eat were a few uncooked remains from my sharks' dinner, so I wandered off toward a jungle that had grown to within a couple of hundred yards of the ocean, and figured I'd get me some fruits and berries and maybe even some birds' eggs, though of course I didn't have no pan to fry 'em or even any match to start a fire.

I walked deeper and deeper into the jungle, singing psalms at the top of my lungs on the assumption that if Australians were godless heathens the psalms would frighten 'em off, while if they were God-fearing Christians they'd of course want to provide room and board to a man of the cloth.

Turns out that mostly what I attracted was a tiger. I came to a clearing from the right, he came to it from the left, we stopped and stared at each other for a mighty long minute, and finally I said, "I got right of way, so scram!" And he said something in tigerish that sounded mighty like a blood-curdling roar, and then I set an Olympic record for tree-climbing (if they have Olympic events in tree-climbing, and if they don't they should, because it surely is more a more valuable skill than curling).

I came to the first branch, maybe twenty feet up, and sat there as the tiger began climbing up after me, and when he was maybe two feet away I learned over and kicked him in the nose, and he fell back to the ground, making a noise that was halfway between a growl and an *oof!*

He climbed up three more times, I kicked his nose three more times, and finally he figgered there must be easier ways to get some dinner, so he headed off into the jungle…and about five minutes later he came racing back across the clearing, running hell for leather (not that tigers got any leather), and chasing him was an enraged antelope.

I decided that tiger wasn't long for a life in the jungle—and then it occurred to me that my life expectancy wasn't a lot longer than his unless I hooked up with civilization pretty soon.

Since the sun was just thinking of setting, I decided to stay in the tree all night, on the assumption that not all the local tigers were quite like this one. And in the morning, feeling totally refreshed and ready to seize the day, I slum down to the ground, took a deep breath of jungle air (which truth to tell wasn't no fresher at ground level), and followed a nice, wide path that headed inland.

I'd gone maybe a mile or so, and thought it was probably time to take a brief break of an hour or two to renew my phenomenal strength, when I heard a gunshot, and a bullet whizzed right by my nose.

"Hit the dirt, goddammit!" yelled a voice.

I turned and looked off into the distance to see who was yelling at me.

"Unless your canines have grown four or five feet since we last met," said a familiar voice, "get the hell out of the line of fire."

"Clyde?" I said, peering into the foliage as an elephant trumpeted behind me and raced off into the jungle. "Is that you?"

The owner of the voice stepped forward, and sure enough it was my old friend, Capturin' Clyde Calhoun.

"What the hell are you doing here, Lucifer?" he said, lowering his rifle and starting to walk toward me. "I ain't seen you since we captured King and Mrs. Kong back on that nameless little island." He paused for a moment, then added: "Matter of fact, as far as I can tell the only real difference is that this here island's got a name."

"It has?" I said.

He nodded his head. "Sumatra."

"Never heard of it," I said.

"Good," said Clyde. "I hate surprises. But if you never heard of it, what in tarnation are you doing here?"

"Mostly concentrating on being lost and hungry," I said.

"Ah!" he said, nodding his head. "Same as usual."

"How about you, Clyde?" I replied. "Last I heard you was going to take Kong to New York, put him on exhibition, and become a millionaire."

He nodded. "Seemed a good idea at the time."

"Then why didn't you?"

"Never got to New York," he answered.

"What happened?" I asked.

"Well, you know that they ain't never made a cage what could hold something as big as Kong," he said. "So we stuck him in the cargo hold, and every day I'd toss a few hundred bananas down to him. Now if you remember, Rosepetal Schultz was hanging out with me, so to speak, and one day she asked to see him, so I let her come along with me when we opened the slab at the top of the hold and I began tossing Kong his bananas. And that's when it happened."

"When *what* happened?" I said.

"Rosepetal ate a banana herself, and tossed the peel on the ground, and I slipped on it and fell into the hold."

"How did you survive?" I asked.

"She grabbed a gun and put a couple of shots right through his ear."

"And that was the end of him?"

He nodded sadly. "'Twas beauty killed the beast."

"So are you going back for Mrs. Kong?"

"Nah," he said. "I've had it with giant monkeys. I'm back to doing with I do best."

"Drinking and shooting things?" I asked.

He shook his head. "Bringing 'em back alive to put in Capturin' Clyde's 5-Star Circus."

"And you do that with a Lee-Enfield .303, do you?" I asked, since it was the same make of gun that Karamojo Bell and F. C. Selous each used to kill their hundred-plus elephants.

"Yep," said Clyde.

"And you shoot 'em with that and bring 'em back *alive*?" I said kind of dubiously.

"I bring back them few what *is* alive," he answered. "The rest pay for the safari, same as always."

"I didn't know there was any elephants or tigers on Sumatra," I said. "Hell, I didn't even know there was Sumatra."

"Got rhino, too," he said. "And honey bears. It's a real mixed-up island. Fortunately, it's also got natives to chop wood and set up tents and do natively things like that."

"I don't see none," I said.

"That's because a couple got betwixt me and my prey," answered Clyde. "Hospital says they'll probably live." He frowned and shook his head. "*Both* of 'em. I must have been having an off day." He stuck two fingers in his mouth and whistled, and three big burly guys wearing loincloths and kind of apprehensive expressions walked out into the clearing. "Getting hungry?"

"I been out of the habit of eating," I said, "but I reckon I could re-learn it right quick."

"Okay. We'd best start with a fire." He turned to the closest guy. "*Ooga mboga kiponi,*" he said in stern tones.

The feller turned to me with an apologetic look on his face. "I fear your acquaintance has an exceptionally awkward way of expressing himself," he said, and set to work building a fire.

Clyde led us over to a fallen tree that served as a bench, and we sat down while his team was cooking up whatever he'd slaughtered for lunch.

"Would I be very far off the mark if I surmised that Sumatra doesn't figger to be your permanent residence?" he said.

"I'm making my way to Australia, a country that knows how to greet and treat a man," I told him.

"So they threw you off Bora Bora and Tahiti and Fiji too?" he said, lighting up his pipe.

"No such a thing!" I replied heatedly.

"So you left of your own free will?" he asked.

"Damned right," I said.

"What if you'd stayed?"

"I'd have been speared or shot with an arrow, depending, and ultimately et," I said.

"But they didn't throw you off?" he said.

"Hell, no," I answered him. "Throwing me off was furthest from their minds."

"I do believe I got the picture," he said. "So what do you expect to find in Australia?"

"A warm, friendly welcome, and less guys with spears," I said.

"Well, you're welcome to travel with me until I hit the Philippines," he said.

"I appreciate that, Clyde," I replied. "Just out of idle curiosity, what's the Philippines got that's attracting you when there's still so many undead animals right here?"

"Kiyomi," he said.

"Gesundheit," I replied. "You were gonna tell me what's so special about the Philippines?"

"Kiyomi," he said.

"You got something caught in your throat, Clyde?" I asked.

"Kiyomi, dammit!" he growled.

"Would I be very far off the mark if I concluded that you're talking about someone named Kiyomi Dammit?"

"Well, you're half right," he muttered.

"Which half?" I asked.

"Kiyomi goddammit!" he snarled.

"Either you just raised him in rank, or—"

"He ain't a *he*," said Clyde. "He's a *she*." He paused for a moment. "I mean she's a she."

"And whatever she is, she's called Kiyomi?" I asked.

He stared at me long and hard for a minute. "You know," he said at last, "suddenly I feel a serious kinship with all them spear-throwers." He took a deep breath and let it out. Evidently he hadn't brushed his teeth in a few days, because every insect what had been crawling around his chin and shoulders suddenly headed south. "Kiyomi is the exquisite gem what I intend to marry," he said.

"I didn't know you could marry gemstones in the Philippines," I said. Then I shrugged. "What the hell. You live and you learn."

"Idiot!" growled Clyde.

"Hey," I said, "there ain't no reason to get mad, just because I ain't marrying a diamond or a ruby."

He leaned forward toward me. "Read my lips, Lucifer," he said, whereas what I mostly wanted to do was avoid his breath. "Kiyomi is the woman what has won my noble, masculine heart. In fact, in

Japanese her name means 'pure beauty,' and I tell you truly that she is the most gorgeous female on the face of the Earth."

All that meant to me was that he'd never seen Bubbles La Tour do her Dance of Sublime Surrender, but I congratulated him and asked what the hell he was doing *here* if his heart's desire was *there*.

"I figgered a hundred tusks ought to make a fitting bridal present for her," he replied. Then he frowned. "There's also the matter of her fiancé."

"He ain't into sharing, I take it," I said.

"No," admitted Clyde. "And neither am I."

"Well, if all else fails, you can blow him away and say that he looked like a gorilla from forty feet."

Suddenly he smiled. "I *like* that idea, Lucifer!" Then he frowned again. "Damn! They ain't *got* no gorillas at this end of the world." He shrugged. "I guess he'll have to look like an orangutan."

"Well, *that's* settled," I said. "How about some grub?"

"Sure," he replied. "Do you like your trunk with or without?"

"With or without elephant?" I asked.

"With or without condiments," he said.

I thunk about it for three or four seconds and allowed that condiments might help bring out the subtle nuances of the flavor.

"Okay," he said. "We got caterpillar, grubworm, and something kind of slimey that I ain't identified yet."

"Can't be no worse than raw fish," I said.

"You got it. *Bonga!*" he called, and one of the natives moseyed over.

"You called?" he said.

"*Boola mega spedumi,*" ordered Clyde.

Bonga turned to me. "I hope you'd had all your shots," he said, walking back to where the fire was and starting to slice off a pound or two of dinner.

"So tell me about this here perfect gem what's won your heart," I said.

"You'll meet her soon enough," replied Clyde. "I gotta tell you, Lucifer, she is truly the Red Grange or Babe Ruth of women."

Now me, I'd have preferred the Equipoise or Jack Dempsey of women, but like they say, there ain't no accounting for tastes, especially them what's worse than mine.

"So is she a hunter too?" I asked.

"No, I'll be doing the hunting for this family."

"Then maybe she's a acrobat or maybe a trapeze artist for Capturing Clyde's Circus and Thrill Show?"

He shook his head. "You don't understand the mysteries of the East, Lucifer."

Which had been proven time and again by Inspector Willie Wang and the mysterious Mr. Mako and a couple of dozen other representatives of the law, with whom I'd had my share of minor misunderstandings.

"Okay," I said. "Enlighten me."

"Her job is being beautiful."

"Okay, she gets up, does a quick hour of push-ups and running in place, takes a cold shower, and spends another hour making herself beautiful," I said. "What does she do with the rest of the day?"

"She gets admired."

"Okay," I said. "And then what?"

"Then she goes to bed, and does the whole thing again the next day."

"They got any job openings where she works?" I asked, thinking that maybe I wouldn't have to go to Australia after all.

"You still don't understand, Lucifer," said Clyde as Bonga brought us our elephant trunk. "It ain't that beautiful is all she *does*. All she *is* is beautiful."

"What happens if she wakes up one day with a wart on her chin?" I asked.

"That's can't happen," he said, and then frowned. "At least, it damned well better not."

"Uh, Clyde," I said, "I like talking about beautiful women as well as the next guy, and I don't want to change the subject—but I think my part of the trunk's still alive."

He guv it a quick look and shook his head. "Nah, that's just a bunch of bugs and mice and things trying to escape now that it's out of the fire." He paused for a moment, then added: "Them wooly spiders make mighty good appetizers."

I'd already et two or three by accident, and I couldn't vouch for where they ranked on the scale of appetizers, but they were clearly a lot better than the main course.

"You got any beer?" I asked him.

"Got a case of it chilling in yonder stream," he said, pointing to the stream in question.

"Good," I said, getting to my feet. "I'll fetch us each a bottle."

"I can have Bonga do it," said Clyde. I noticed that Bonga winced when he heard that. "He loves to do me favors." Bonga made sure Clyde was looking at me and not him, then shook his head vigorously.

"Nah," I said. "Ain't nothing difficult about getting us a couple of bottles."

I headed off toward the stream, and as I passed by him Bonga handed me his spear.

"It's not much," he whispered, "but it may help."

I chuckled. "I ain't gonna stab the beer," I told him. "I'm just gonna drink it."

He shrugged, and as I continued walking to the stream he began waving flies away, though if I didn't know no better I'd have sworn he was crossing himself.

I saw a big wooden box sitting halfway in and halfway out of the water, leaned down to pull it out, and suddenly got into a tug of war with a huge crocodile what was trying to pull it in. I figgered I could wade into the water and rassle him for it, but even though I am the possessor of a masculine physique that's the envy of every man (except for the parts what ain't), he had a lot more teeth than me, and they was a lot longer, so I decided I wasn't thirsty after all, and walked back to the fire empty-handed.

"I tried to tell you," said Clyde with a chuckle.

"Looks like you done lost a whole case of beer," I said, sitting down near him.

"Not really," he said.

"Surely you don't plan to fight him for it," I said.

"Of course not. He can have the first three or four bottles. Then pretty soon we'll hear him giggling, and finally he'll pass out and float all the way out to the ocean on his back with all four legs sticking straight up. Then Bonga will bring back the rest of the beer."

"I can see that even though I spent a few years in Africa, plus some time in the Brazilian jungles, there's a lot about safari life what has escaped me until today," I said.

"You ain't needed it up to now," Clyde replied. "You just keep what you need. Hell, the first thing I jettisoned out of my brain when I became a hunter was geometry."

"Makes sense," I said. "What about trigonometry?"

He shook his head. "I still let that one hang around in the back of my head until I can figger out if it's misspelled and is really *trigger*-nometry."

And then, since I'm much more interested in pure beauties, or even impure ones if push comes to shove, than I am in any kind of nometry, I asked him when I could set eyes on the exquisite Kiyomi.

"Just eyes," he said kind of sharply. "Nothin' else."

"Hey," I said. "I'm a gentleman."

"I see fiction ain't one of the things you jettisoned," replied Clyde.

He scratched his shaggy head, evicting no end of small lodgers. "What the hell, I don't like leaving Kiyomi alone in one place too long, what with her being engaged and all," he said at last. "I got about seventy-five or eighty tusks, and I don't think they teach math in beauty school, which so far as I know is the only school what she ever attended, so I'll just explain that eighty is another word for hundred."

Now, it's been my experience that even the few women I'd met in the course of my travels who couldn't read or write or spell sure knew how to count, and when the numbers were on cash what was being spent on 'em they could make Einstein look like a dummy. But I decided not to argue with him since if she got mad at anyone over being twenty tusks shy it was gonna be him, and if she was half as pretty as he said I'd be more than happy to comfort her in her hour of bitter disappointment. And if I played my cards right that hour might even extend to a few days or even a week.

"Sounds good to me, Clyde," I said. "I seen enough of Sumatra."

"We'll head out in the morning," he said. "Where'd you stash your stuff?"

"I'm wearing it," I said.

He chuckled. "Too bad we ain't got a mirror around here. You're wearing about half of it."

"So I'll pick up some duds in the Philippines," I said.

"You better," said Clyde. "I can't introduce you to the most beautiful critter alive looking like you do." Suddenly he frowned. "Of course, there's always a chance that she may be waiting for me at the dock, and there ain't no haberdasher between here and there." He scratched his head again, and still more stuff crawled out and ran for cover. "I got it!" he said at last. "Bonga, give my pal your loincloth."

Bonga just stared at him for a long moment, then at me, then at Clyde again, and finally he looked down and sighed.

And no matter what anyone tells you, that's the real story of how I came to be walking down the pier in Manila wearing a loincloth what had formerly been the personal property of Bonga, and before that of a bush pig what had been just a little too slow on his feet.

"Well, here we are," announced Clyde. "I'll send a boy back to pick up the ivory."

"Clyde, you got eighty tusks," I said, "and it looks like the smallest of 'em goes maybe forty or fifty pounds. I think you're gonna need more than one boy."

He shook his head. "Don't want to spoil 'em," he answered. "Let's go grab ourselves some rooms, and then we'll think real seriously about dinner."

"And maybe a bath," I added.

"What for?" he said. "I just bathed…lemme see, now…just three weeks ago."

When I thunk about that it suddenly made sense unless you had a cousin in the soap industry, so I just told him to lead on. And a few minutes later we were in the center of Manilla, which was never going to put New York or London out of business, but looked mighty luxurious compared to Sumatra.

"So where do we want to hole up?" I asked him.

"The Grand Hotel," he said.

"I don't see it," I said, looking around at downtown Manilla, which looked an awful lot like downtown Moline, Illinois, where I'd grown up, rather than one of the glittering capitols of the world.

"Me, neither," he replied. "But every two-bit town around the world's got a Grand Hotel, so Manilla figures to have one too."

And sure enough, in two more blocks we came to the Grand Hotel, entered the lobby, walked past a bunch of little guys in military uniforms, and stopped at the front desk.

"Welcome, Western scum," said the clerk with a happy smile. "How may I help you?"

"I just know it's gonna come as a shock to your system," said Clyde, "but we're gonna need three rooms."

"But there are only two of you," said the clerk.

"You must have been the best one in your math class," said Clyde. "Now, can we get down to business?"

"And you want three rooms?"

"I got a lot of luggage."

The clerk stared long and hard at him. "You want a whole room for your knapsack?"

"The rest of it'll be here by dark," said Clyde.

The clerk shrugged. "Who am I to argue with crazy Yankees?"

"You gonna take that kind of talk?" I whispered to Clyde.

"Why not?" he replied. "It ain't as if he accused us of being Red Sox."

So we signed in, and Clyde laid some money on the counter, and then we stood in the elevator for about ten minutes until we figgered out that it wasn't working and climbed all the way up to the second floor, then wandered down the hall.

"Well, this one's mine," said Clyde, checking the number and the little plaque that said it was the Presidential Suite. He stuck a key in the door and flang it open, and we found ourselves in a tiny room with a ceiling so low I had to duck my head just to walk into it without knocking myself out, and a single cot that almost touched three walls at once.

"They don't seem to think too much of presidents in Manila," I remarked as dust rose from the floor with each step I took.

"Nice view, though," he said, pointing to it.

"True," I agreed. "Might have been even nicer if they'd thunk to put some glass into the window."

"It may lack a tad here and there," he admitted, "but it beats the hell out of sleeping out in the rain in Sumatra."

"I think I'll go see what my room looks like," I said.

"You do that," he said. "We'll meet in the lobby and go out to dinner in five minutes."

I agreed, left the Presidential suite, and realized that we'd passed all but one room, and that the last one at the end of the corridor was obviously mine. I walked over and found I was mistaken, that it was clearly the permanent residence of some guy named Broom. I knocked a few times on the assumption that if he was there he could tell me what I'd done wrong and point me toward my room, but the door just swang open and I realized that they were in serious need of housekeepers, as no one had cleaned up all the rags that was littering Mr. Broom's floor.

Then I thunk that I might be looking at things all wrong, that maybe the room belonged to a Miss

Broom, or even a Mrs. Broom would be okay so long as she wasn't a fanatic about it, and I decided not to complain to the desk clerk after all.

I didn't have nothing to unload, so I wandered down to the lobby, avoiding all these little soldiers who kept giving me dirty looks even before I'd done anything with Miss Broom, and hung around the front desk waiting for Clyde.

"Is there anything more I can do for you, Yankee scum?" asked the clerk pleasantly.

"Yeah, if you can recommend a good restaurant," I said. And then, remembering the past few weeks, I added, "Preferably one that don't specialize in serving dead uncooked fish."

"Not a problem, American swine," he said with a smile. "The restaurant you want is the Garroted Hamiguitan."

"What the hell is a hamiguitan?" I asked him.

"A hairy-tailed rat, American swine."

Clyde showed up just then, and we made our way to the door.

"Do you get the feeling Americans ain't the most popular people in the Philippines?" I asked.

"Oh, they don't hate all Americans," Clyde answered. "Just folk like you and me, because we lead such noble, exemplary lives."

It made perfect sense to me, so I changed the subject and asked him about dinner. In fact, those were my very words: What about dinner?

"We eat it, of course," said Clyde.

"You got any favorite restaurant in Manilla?" I asked. "Especially one that don't specialize in the hammy guitar or whatever the hell it's called?"

"Not a problem," answered Clyde. "They tell me that the Tortured Tortoise serves a meal that Westerners can almost digest."

"Almost?" I repeated.

"Don't knock it," replied Clyde. "It was the most promising answer I could get."

We walked a couple of more blocks, being careful to avoid the occasional dead European on the sidewalk, and finally we came to it.

As we went in the door, a waiter walked up, bowed low, and then handed each of us a couple of pieces of cotton.

"What in tarnation are these for?" asked Clyde.

"They muffle the screams," explained the waiter.

"Of the dinner or the diners?" I asked.

"Yes," said the waiter with a happy smile. "Walk this way, please," he added, kind of mincing off toward the back of the restaurant.

"I ain't walked that way since I outgrew my first pair of shoes," said Clyde. "I'll just follow you."

"Whatever makes you happy, American pig," was the answer.

He sat us down at a table, handed us a couple of menus, and wandered off.

"So what looks good to you, Lucifer?" asked Clyde, staring at the menu.

"Nothing much," I said, mostly because I couldn't (and still can't) read a word of Manillan or Filipino or whatever the hell language they write in.

"Oh, come on," he said. "*Something* must look good."

"Well, the redhead two tables to the left looks about as good as anything in the restaurant," I said.

"I mean food, damn it!" growled Clyde. Then: "Though she *could* look mighty tasty covered in orange sauce and maybe pineapples."

The waiter came by and asked if we'd like to order something before Western society collapsed in ruins.

"I'll have a plate of the garroted gerbils," said Clyde, "and maybe a quart of Saki to wash it down."

"And you?" asked the waiter, turning to me.

I still couldn't read a word of the menu, so I finally just pointed at an item.

"Excellent choice," said the waiter. "Listen for the agonized scream, and you'll know that your crocodile is absolutely fresh."

"Or that he et the cook," offered Clyde.

The waiter shrugged. "Anyway, it'll be one or the other."

"So when do I get to meet this rare treasure that you're planning on absconding with?" I asked when the waiter had gone back to the kitchen.

"Tomorrow," said Clyde. "I've sent word to her that I've come to bring her a life of excitement and ecstasy and a bunch of other words beginning with 'e,' and told her to be ready tomorrow."

"Ready for *what*?" I asked. "You ain't planning on taking her back to Sumatra, are you?"

"Ready for *me*, damn it!" snapped Clyde.

I didn't want to disappoint him by explaining that if she was a normal healthy woman she wouldn't be able to resist throwing herself at me, so we just sat and pretended that all the screams and howls coming out of the kitchen were actually Glen Miller's band, or maybe one of them Doorstops or Dorseys or whatever they called themselves, and finally our waiter came out of the kitchen carrying a tray what looked at least as heavy as him and smelled a lot better, and then he put a plate in front of each of us, smiled, bowed, said "Enjoy and die, Yankee pigs," and wandered back to the kitchen.

There wasn't enough meat on my plate to choke one of Clyde's gerbils, and truth to tell I ain't never gonna become a serious fan of crocodile scales, but once you got used to the fact that all the salt had settled to cover the bottom inch of the water it helped wash away the taste of the scales. Even the water couldn't do much with the eyeteeth, of which crocs seemed to have about a hundred even though they only had two eyes.

Clyde didn't say much about his dinner, except to cuss it between mouthfuls. Finally the waiter came by and asked what we wanted for dessert, and then explained that bicarbonate wasn't on the menu any more.

"Any more?" asked Clyde.

The waiter shrugged. "We couldn't keep up with the demand."

We paid up, left him a generous tip of five Filipino pesos, which came to a little less than a penny in real money, and wandered out into the night. We walked maybe a block, looking for a friendly bar, when suddenly we heard a brass band coming from up the road. A minute later a couple of hundred soldiers in their dress uniforms came marching by, half of 'em blowing into their trumpets and trombones and whacking away at their drums, while the other half were pulling a wagon, and on it stood a little Oriental guy in a military uniform with a couple of hundred medals. He kept waving to the people, who waved right back and cheered at the tops of their lungs.

"Who the hell is that?" I asked a guy standing next to me.

"You really don't know?" he said, kind of half-shocked and half-outraged.

"Well, sure I do," I said quickly. "I was just testing you."

"He's the greatest general of all," answered the guy, walking forward so he could be even closer.

I figgered if he was all that important maybe I should introduce myself and see if he could get me a better room for the night. But by the time I'd thunk of it the parade had already passed by and turned left at the next street, and I decided maybe that was all for the best, since I didn't know if his band ever took a break and it'd be mighty hard to get a good night's sleep in his palace or wherever he hung his hat if the band kept playing all night, especially the trumpeter on the far right whose music was flat as a tire what had just lost a pitched battle with a couple of bullets and maybe an ax.

"This here looks like an inviting bar," announced Clyde as we walked a little farther and came to a bar what had a little stage in the back, and on it were maybe half a dozen young ladies who gave every indication of having dressed in a real hurry. But as we entered I realized that I'd done got it backward, and they were actually *un*dressing in even more of a hurry.

"What have you got?" asked Clyde as we sat down on a couple of stools at the bar and concentrated on admiring the almost graceful dancing of the almost dressed ladies while the bartender approached us.

"We've got Charina, Jaslene, Cheska, Glessie, Aijie, and Sadire," he answered.

"Never heard of any of 'em," I said. "What do they each taste like?"

He stared at me. "How the hell would I know?" he said at last.

"You're the bartender, ain't you?" I said.

"Yeah."

"Well?"

"Oh!" he said, snapping his fingers. "You're talking about our booze. I thought you were asking about the girls."

"It's a very adaptable question," interjected Clyde. "You can answer about the booze *or* the young ladies."

He stuck to the booze, and pretty soon I was very carefully sipping his notion of a martini, and the reason I was sipping it so carefully was that I found if I took even a medium sip the enamel on my teeth started bubbling. And when I swallowed it the parts of the croc I'd et for dinner kept biting at it and missing and chewing on my innards.

It just wasn't worth the agony, and I turned to Clyde after my seventh one and suggested that I was really getting ready to hit the hay (not that any bales of hay, or even a pitchfork full of it, could fit in Miss Broom's room).

"Might as well," he said. "Gotta get up fresh and fit to meet my pure beauty tomorrow morning."

"Does she know what time you're coming?"

"Nope," he said with a smile. "Think of how surprised she'll be!"

"Especially if she's entertaining the guy she's engaged to," I said.

"Hmm," he hmmed. "I ain't thought that far ahead yet."

"Far be it for me to tell you to use your brain, Clyde," I began, "but—"

"I got it!" he suddenly yelled.

"Knock it off wherever it is and stomp on it," I said, backing off a couple of steps.

"Don't understand me so fast!" he growled. "I mean I got the solution to this potential conundrum."

"What is it?" I asked.

"I'll send *you* in first," he said. "And then, if there ain't no gunshots and screams of hideous agony, I'll know he ain't there and the coast is clear."

"You're all heart, Clyde," I said.

"Well, *that's* settled," he said. "Let's go back to the hotel and get a good night's sleep before I surprise her."

"And her boyfriend is an officer?"

"Yeah, but he's probably in Japan with his troops, so you ain't got nothing to worry about," answered Clyde, and then added: "Probably."

We clambered off our barstools and went back out into the street.

"You know where she's staying, do you?" I asked.

"Of course."

"Maybe we could save time and go there now," I suggested.

He considered it for a minute, then shook his head. "No. This is the woman of my dreams. I got to freshen up for her."

"I didn't see no shower at the hotel," I said.

"I said I got to freshen up, not drown," answered Clyde. "I gotta run a comb through my hair and beard." And so saying, he pulled out a comb that was missing maybe half its teeth.

"Uh, Clyde," I said, "maybe we ought to stop off along the way and buy you a comb."

"Damn it, Lucifer," he said, "when you insult this comb, you're insulting *me*."

"I am?"

He nodded his head vigorously. "Damned thing's got more teeth than I do."

"Tell you what, Clyde," I said. "As long as you're paying for my room and my grub, it's only right that I do something in exchange for it, like give you a shave and a haircut and you can keep the six bits."

"Well, I call that right gentlemanly of you, Lucifer, to say nothing of being out of character. Clearly getting kicked off five continents and ten or twelve islands has made a better man of you." He paused, thunk about it for a minute, and then added: "Well, a better-traveled man, anyway."

We went back to the hotel, I checked to see if Miss or Mrs. Broom had returned while we were out, but the room remained pristine except for the rags and the mops and the smell of ammonia. I wandered across the hall to the Presidential Suite, found Clyde sitting on a rickety wooden chair with his shirt off—well, all except a few patches of shirt that still stuck to his body—and I went into the bathroom to get such shaving and cutting gear as he'd brung along.

There weren't no razors, but there was a handful of pretty sharp skinning knives, and I figured if they worked on some innocent dead animals what was sporting even less hair than Clyde that of course they'd work on him too, and probably even better.

I thunk of washing his hair first, but it was denser and gnarlier than some jungles I'd been in, and I didn't want to lose track and maybe possession of no fingers, so I just ran the comb through it once, which took care of the rest of its teeth, and since the bathroom didn't have no shaving cream I used a tube of toothpaste, and begun thinning it out while Clyde leaned his head back and began snoring.

I started humming to myself, and I was about halfway done with him when I decided to sing instead, and a couple of minutes later I realized that I'd done forgot some of the racier verses of "The Ring Dang Do," and I concentrated real hard on remembering 'em, and of course all that brainpower and concentration had to come from somewhere, and it turned out that it mostly came from Clyde's head, or to be more accurate what I was doing to Clyde's head, because when I finally remembered the words

I looked down and there was this bald pate shining up at me.

I thunk of gluing some of his hair back on, but I didn't have no glue nor even any paste. I did have some bandages, but of course if I used 'em to hold his hair on his head he wouldn't look no hairier, and even strangers would probably walk up to him and asked if he'd stuck his head in a blender or whatever had happened to him.

Then I figgered that he looked somehow out of balance. I walked around the chair a couple of times, staring at him, and finally it hit me that it just looked wrong to have four or five months of unkempt beard (though in truth I ain't never seen a kempt beard) while he was walking around with a shining bald noggin. So I went back to work and shaved his face too. When I'd done skinned the rest of it I realized that some women like a little hair on their men, so I decided to leave him with a really eye-catching handlebar mustache, but as I was putting on the final touches I sneezed and the left half of his mustache came away in my hand. I figgered half a mustache was better than none, so I waxed the half what was left and had it looking real elegant, with the tip pointing to the sky, and began to think if I didn't get around to building my tabernacle one of these days I could always make a handsome living as a barber.

I was too sleepy even to wander across the hall to see if Miss Broom was there, and if so was she a friendly, accommodating type of lady, so since Clyde was sitting on the chair snoring I lay down on his bed to catch forty winks.

About twenty-five winks into it I was awoke by a scream that would have woke such dead as weren't otherwise occupied, and then another one even louder.

"Damn it, Lucifer!" yelled Clyde from where he was staring at the cracked mirror in the bathroom. "You done scalped me!"

"Calm down, Clyde," I said, swinging my feet to the floor in case I had to make a quick getaway. "All I done was give you a little trim and a shave."

"Little?" he repeated, and then hollered "*Little?*" at the top of his lungs.

"Look at it this way," I said. "You won't need another haircut until your next safari is over."

"But she loved to run her hands through it!" he complained.

"Really?" I said, remembering just what it was like before I performed my beautification miracles.

"Well, until she busted two of her fingers trying to un-knot it," he admitted. He stared into the mirror again, then turned back to me and held up the only end of his handlebar mustache. "And what's the purpose of *this*?" he demanded. "Have you ever in your life seen a guy walk around with half a handlebar?"

"You're looking at it all wrong, Clyde," I said. "Just train it to point skyward and you'll always know which way the wind is blowing when you sneak up on an animal."

He frowned kind of thoughtfully, which made me realize I hadn't thinned out his eyebrows at all, and then looked up. "You know," he said, "I never thunk of that." He got to his feet. "Okay, Lucifer, let's grab some breakfast and go meet the purest beauty of them all."

"Sounds good to me," I said. I looked around for my boots, then realized I hadn't tooken 'em off the night before, and walked over to the bathroom. My comb didn't have any more teeth than Clyde's, but I'd been combing my hair with my fingers for months, so that didn't bother me none. I thought I'd grab a swallow of water, turned the tap on, saw a minnow swim out, and changed my mind.

"Ready?" he said when I came back out.

"Ready," I replied. "Where do we plan to eat?"

"There's a nice cheap joint in the alley behind this hotel," he said.

"Good," I said. "What's its name and what does it serve?"

"The Strangled Chicken," he said.

"Is that the name or the piece of resistance?" I asked.

"Both," he said, heading down the stairs.

"Have a nice day, Western Scum," said the desk clerk, giving us a smile.

"Do you get the feeling that Americans ain't the welcomest guests this here country's ever had?" I asked Clyde as we walked out into the street.

"It's all them Japanese soldiers," he said. "Though I don't know why the hell they're hanging around the Philippines or who they're planning to go to war with."

We walked for just about two minutes, and then Clyde announced we had arrived. We entered this little wood shack and sat down at one of its three tables, all of 'em empty.

The waiter walked up, took one look at Clyde, and giggled. "You lost an election bet, right?" he said.

Clyde offered his opinion of the waiter's pedigree piece by piece for the last seven or eight generations, then ordered some chicken and a cup of coffee.

"And you, American Pig?" asked the waiter, turning to me.

"Since we're on an island in the middle of the ocean," I said, "would it be possible to get me some lobster humidor?"

"You mean Thermidor," said the waiter.

"Whatever," I said. "You got any?"

"Yes," he replied, "as long as you don't mind if it takes like rare chicken."

"You mean like some real uncommon variety?" I asked.

"I mean like uncooked," he said.

So I ordered the lobster humidor, and that was when I learned that lobsters come with drumsticks.

We et pretty fast, figgering if we swallowed it real quick we wouldn't taste it, and we were almost right. Then we drunk our coffee, which truth to tell didn't look or taste much different from water except that it had a few soapsuds in it, and when a fly landed on my cup, took a sip, and expired, I decided it was time to go, which suited Clyde just fine, as he'd been ready two bites into his meal.

"So what hotel is she in?" I asked, once we got out of the alley and turned back onto the street.

"Kiyomi don't stay in no-star hotels like these here ones," he said. "She's too beautiful for that."

"The hotels around here kick anything that's beautiful out the door?" I said. "I should have figured that out yesterday."

"Don't understand me so fast, Lucifer," replied Clyde. "Her boyfriend puts her up in a luxury suite at the Dusit Thani, which is the fanciest hotel in town."

"Her boyfriend or her fiancé?" I asked.

"Same thing," he said. "Little Japanese guy. Some kind of officer in the army."

"So where is this Dusty Fanny?" I asked.

"Maybe four blocks," said Clyde. "And it's the Dusit Thani."

It took us about twenty minutes to get there, since we had to run a gauntlet of beggars and panhan-dlers, and more than a few tourists who wouldn't go away until Clyde and what was left of his handlebar posed for photos. But at least we reached the Dusit Thani, and a doorman, who was dressed sharper than most majors and colonels, opened the door for us and stood aside as we walked into the lobby.

"What do you think, Lucifer?" asked Clyde as I looked at my surroundings.

"Miss Broom can keep her damned room," I said. "This is the place for me."

"Skip your next six hundred meals and you can probably afford one night here," said Clyde, leading me over to a bank of elevators. We climbed into one, and a minute later emerged on the top floor.

"The penthouse," announced Clyde.

I looked around. All the walls went straight up and down, nothing was leaning in any direction, and I was at a loss to figger out what made the place a bent house, but I just kept my mouth shut and followed Clyde to a door at the end of the hall.

"Poor girl is probably dying to see me," he whispered, "so I'll go in first, and after she's spent ten or twenty minutes smothering me with kisses I'll open the door again and let you in."

Since I didn't have no overwhelming urge to see her kissing Clyde for even five minutes, let alone ten or twenty, I agreed and walked back down the corridor about halfway to the elevator, where I found a friendly wall and leaned up against it.

Clyde knocked on the door, it opened, he yelled "It's me, Honeybunch!", and he walked into the room.

A second later, or maybe it was only half a second, I heard a high-pitched scream, and then a crash, and then a *thud!*, and after another few seconds the prettiest Oriental-type lady I ever saw came rushing down the corridor right at me.

"Howdy, Miss Pure Beauty," I said. "What seems to be the trouble?"

"There's a hairless beast in my room!" she wailed. "Take me away from here!"

I figgered we'd best hurry, because if she'd seen what was left of Clyde's mustache she was maybe saying there were two beasts in her room, one hairless and the other mostly so.

As the elevator door closed behind us I looked her up and down and decided that whoever had named her had been guilty of an understatement, but that if it turned out that she was an Occasionally Impure Beauty that'd be okay too.

"We must escape!" she said.

"Doubtless my rugged masculine beauty has blinded you to the situation," I said, "but we just *did* escape."

"I mean from *here!*" she said. "It's not enough that this beast has probably killed and eaten Clyde, but my fiancé is incredibly jealous. If he finds this creature up there, he will assume the worst."

"I thunk your fiancé, whoever he is, would be at some barracks in Japan," I said.

She shook her head. "He is right here, in Manilla, and he has a terrible temper."

"Okay," I said. "We'll walk down to the dock, wait until I can find a ship what'll give us a free ride out of here, and the problem is solved."

"That will take too long!"

I allowed that I could always steal a rowboat and head inland.

"No!" she said firmly. "I have money. We will go to the airport and take the next plane out of here."

I couldn't believe my luck, that I had latched onto someone who was not only beautiful but rich.

"Lead the way," I told her.

She hailed a taxi. "Walking takes too long," she said.

So we hopped in the cab, and climbed out of it at the airport, and found that there was a flight leaving for New Zealand in half an hour.

"Well, that's that," I said.

"No," she replied. "I tell you Hideki is wildly jealous."

"Hideki?"

"My fiancé," she said. "He will see that you and I are flying to New Zealand and will follow us!" She paused for a few seconds, then smiled. "I have it! We will buy two tickets to Hawaii under our real names, then tear them up and buy the tickets to New Zealand under false names."

"Don't we gotta show our passports to get the tickets?" I asked.

She smiled. "I'll bribe someone to buy them for us, using his name."

Which is what she did, and half an hour later we'd tooken off and were on our way to New Zealand, which sounded a lot more modern than Old Zealand and was, according to Kiyomi, right next door to Australia, which had been my destination for the past three years.

And it was just as simple and innocent and blameless as that. We arrived at sunrise, checked into a hotel, and while I was grabbing a drink of water in the bathroom she picked up a newspaper what had just been brung to the room by a bellhop who had nothing else to do with his time, and hollered "Oh my God!" at the top of her exceptionally lovely lungs.

"What is it?" I asked.

"Hideki!" she said.

"He's here?" I said, looking around.

"No," she said. "But I must go back before he figures that we're in New Zealand."

"Why?" I asked.

"Our ruse worked." She held up a newspaper what was printed in English, which the New Zealanders spoke a kind of, and the headline said *"Japanese Bomb Pearl Harbor!!!"*

"What's that got to do with us?" I asked.

"Read it," she said, tossing the paper to me.

So I picked it up and began reading. It took me less than ten words to figger out what upset her so much: *"The Japanese, under the leadership of General Hideki Tojo…"* and there was also a photo of the little guy they'd been pulling on the wagon during the parade. I put the paper down. "This is *your* Hideki?" I asked.

She nodded. "It was nice knowing you, Lucifer, however briefly."

Then she was gone.

And no matter what General MacArthur and Admiral Halsey told the press, and what the history books claim, I'd saved a pure beauty from a fate worse than death—or if you add Clyde into the mix, from *two* fates worse than death.

There are days, and that was surely one of 'em, when I really wonder if it was worth my while to dabble in the hero trade.

Copyright © 2016 by Mike Resnick

Nancy Kress has won six Nebulas, two Hugos, a Campbell Memorial, and a Sturgeon Memorial, and co-authored Arc Manor's Stellar Guild novel, New Under the Sun. *Her most recent publication is* The Best of Nancy Kress *from Subterranean Press. This is her fifth appearance in* Galaxy's Edge.

PATENT INFRINGEMENT

by Nancy Kress

PRESS RELEGE

PRESS RELEASE

Kegelman-Ballston Corporation is proud to announce the first public release of its new drug, Halitex, which cures Ulbarton's Flu completely after one ten-pill course of treatment. Ulbarton's Flu, as the public knows all too well, now afflicts upwards of thirty million Americans, with the number growing daily as the highly contagious flu spreads. Halitex "flu-proofs" the body by inserting genes tailored to confer immunity to this persistent and debilitating scourge, whose symptoms include coughing, muscle aches, and fatigue. Because the virus remains in the body even after symptoms disappear, Ulbarton's Flu can recur in a given patient at any time. Halitex renders each recurrence ineffectual.

The General Accounting Office estimates the Ulbarton's Flu, the virus of which was first identified by Dr. Timothy Ulbarton, has already cost four billion dollars this calendar year in medical expenses and lost work time. Halitex, two years in development by Kegelman-Ballston, is expected to be in high demand throughout the nation.

✿

NEW YORK POST
K-B ZAPS ULBARTON'S FLU
NEW DRUG DOES U'S FLU 4 U

✿

Jonathan Meese
538 Pleasant Lane
Aspen Hill, MD 20906

Dear Mr. Kegelman and Mr. Ballston,

I read in the newspaper that your company, Kegelman-Ballston, has recently released a drug, Halitex, that provides immunity against Ulbarton's Flu by gene therapy. I believe that the genes used in developing this drug are mine. Two years ago, on May 5, I visited my GP to explain that I had been exposed to Ulbarton's Flu a lot (the entire accounting department of the Pet Supply Catalogue Store, where I work, developed the flu. Also my wife, three children, and mother-in-law. Plus, I believe my dog had it, although the vet disputes this.) However, despite all this exposure, I did not develop Ulbarton's.

My GP directed me to your research facility along I-270, saying he "thought he heard they were trying to develop a med." I went there, and samples of my blood and bodily tissues were taken. The researcher said I would hear from you if the samples were ever used for anything, but I never did. Will you please check your records to verify my participation in this new medicine, and tell me what share of the profits are due me.

Thank you for your consideration.

Sincerely,

Jon Meese
Jonathan J. Meese

✿

From the Desk of Robert Ballston
Kegelman-Ballston Corporation

To: Martin Blake, Legal
Re: Attached letter

Marty—

Is he a nut? Is this a problem?

Bob

✿

INTERNAL MEMO
KEGELMAN-BALLSTON

To: Robert Ballston
From: Martin Blake
Re: Gene-line claimant Jonathan J. Meese

Bob—

I checked with Records over in Research and, yes, unfortunately this guy donated the tissue samples from which the gene line was developed that led to Halitex. Even more unfortunately, Meese's visit occurred just before we instituted the comprehensive waiver for all donors. However, I don't think Meese has any legal grounds here. Court precedents have upheld the corporate right to patent genes used in drug development. Also, the guy doesn't sound very sophisticated (his *dog*?) He doesn't even know that Kegelman's been dead for ten years. Apparently Meese has not yet employed a lawyer. I can make a small nuisance settlement of you like, but I'd rather avoid setting a corporate precedent for these people. I'd rather send him a stiff letter that will scare the bejesus out of the greedy little twerp.

Please advise.

Marty

✿

From the Desk of Robert Ballston
Kegelman-Ballston Corporation

To: Martin Blake, Legal
Re: J. Meese

Do it.

Bob

✿

Martin Blake, Attorney-at-Law
Chief Legal Counsel, Kegelman-Ballston Corporation

Dear Mr. Meese,

Your letter regarding the patented Kegelman-Ballston drug Halitex has been referred to me.

Please be advised that you have no legal rights in Halitex; see attached list of case precedents. If you persist in any such claims, Kegelman-Ballston will consider it harassment and take appropriate steps, including possible prosecution.

Sincerely,

Martin Blake
Martin Blake

✿

Jonathan Meese
538 Pleasant Lane
Aspen Hill, MD 20906

Dear Mr. Blake,

But they're my genes!!! This can't be right. I'm consulting a lawyer, and you can expect to hear from her shortly.

Jon Meese
Jonathan J. Meese

✿

Catherine Owen, Attorney-at-Law

Dear Mr. Blake,

I now represent Jonathan J. Meese in his concern that Kegelman-Ballston has developed a pharmaceutical, Halitex, based on gene therapy which uses Mr. Meese's genes as its basis. We feel it only reasonable that this drug, which will earn Kegelman-Ballston millions if not billions of dollars, acknowledge financially Mr. Meese's considerable contribution. We are therefore willing to consider a settlement, and are available to discuss this with you at your earliest convenience.

Sincerely,

Catherine Owen
Catherine Owen, Attorney

From the Desk of Robert Ballston
Kegelman-Ballston Corporation

To: Martin Blake, Legal
Re: J. Meese

Marty—

Damn it, if there's one thing that really chews my balls it's this sort of undercover sabotage by the second-rate. I played golf with Sam Fortescue on Saturday and he opened my eyes (you remember Sam; he's at the agency we're using to benchmark our competition). Sam speculates that this Meese bastard is really being used by Irwin-Lacey to set us up. You know that bastard Carl Irwin has had his own Ulbarton's drug in development, and he's sore as hell because we beat him to market. Ten to one he's paying off this Meese patsy.

We can't allow it. Don't settle. Let him sue.

Bob

☼

INTERNAL MEMO
KEGELMAN-BALLSTON

To: Robert Ballston
From: Martin Blake
Re: Gene-line claimant Jonathan J. Meese

Bob—

I've got a better idea. *We* sue *him*, on the grounds he's walking around with our patented genetic immunity to Ulbarton's. No one except consumers of Halitex have this immunity, so Meese must have acquired it illegally, possibly on the black market. We gain several advantages with this suit: We eliminate Meese's complaint, we send a clear message to other rivals who may be attempting patent infringement, and we gain a publicity circus to both publicize Halitex (not that it needs it) and, more important, make the public aware of the dangers of black market substitutes for Halitex, such as Meese obtained.

Incidentally, I checked again with Records over at Research. They have no documentation of any visit from a Jonathan J. Meese on any date whatsoever.

Marty

☼

From the Desk of Robert Ballston
Kegelman-Ballston Corporation

To: Martin Blake, Legal
Re: J. Meese

Marty—

Brilliant! Do it. Can we get a sympathetic judge? One who understands business? Maybe O'Connor can help.

Bob

☼

NEW YORK TIMES

HALITEX BLACK MARKET CASE TO BEGIN TODAY

This morning the circuit court of Manhattan County is scheduled to begin hearing the case of *Kegelman-Ballston v. Meese*. This case, heavily publicized during recent months, is expected to set important precedents in the controversial areas of gene patents and patent infringement on biological properties. Protestors from the group FOR US: CANCEL KIDNAPPED ULBARTON PATENTS, which is often referred to by its initials, have been in place on the court steps since last night. The case is being heard by Judge Latham P. Farmingham III, a Republican who is widely perceived as sympathetic to the concerns of big business.

This case began when Jonathan J. Meese, an accountant with the Pet Supply Catalogue Store...

☼

Catherine Owen, Attorney-at-Law

Dear Mr. Blake,

Just a reminder that Jon Meese and I are still open to a settlement.

Sincerely,

Catherine Owen

Martin Blake, Attorney-at-Law
Chief Legal Counsel, Kegelman-Ballston Corporation

Cathy—

Don't they teach you at that law school you went to (I never can remember the name) that you don't settle when you're sure to win?

You're a nice girl; better luck next time.

Martin Blake

NEW YORK TIMES

MEESE CONVICTED

PLAINTIFF GUILTY OF "HARBORING" DISEASE-FIGHTING GENES WITHOUT COMPENSATING DEVELOPER KEGELMAN-BALLSTON

From the Desk of Robert Ballston
Kegelman-Ballston Corporation

To: Martin Blake, Legal
Re: Kegelman-Ballston v. Meese

Marty—

I always said you were a genius! My God, the free publicity we got out of this thing, not to mention the future edge—How about a victory celebration this weekend? Are you and Elaine free to fly to Aruba on the Lear, Friday night?

Bob

NEW YORK TIMES

BLUE GENES FOR DRUG THIEF
JONATHAN J. MEESE SENTENCED TO SIX MONTHS FOR PATENT INFRINGEMENT

From the Desk of Robert Ballston
Kegelman-Ballston Corporation

To: Martin Blake, Legal
Re: Halitex

Marty, I just had a brilliant idea I want to run by you. We got Meese, but now that he's at Ossining, the publicity has died down. Well, my daughter read this squib the other day in some science magazine, how the Ulbarton's virus has in it some of the genes that Research combined with Meese's to create Halitex. I didn't understand all the egghead science, but apparently Halitex uses some of the flu genes to build its immune properties. And we own the patent on Halitex. As I see it, that means that Dr. Ulbarton was working with **OUR** genes when he identified Ulbarton's flu and published his work. Now, if we could go after *Ulbarton* in court, the publicity would be tremendous, as well as strengthening our proprietorship position.

But the publicity, Marty! The publicity!

Copyright © 2016 by Nancy Kress

Dantzel Cherry has recently sold short stories to Fireside Magazine *and* Metro Fiction. *This is her fourth appearance in* Galaxy's Edge.

LESLIE'S LOVE POTION #4

by Dantzel Cherry

www.witchesbrew.com
Leslie's Love Potion #4
*** ½ stars, 19 reviews

W*arning: Please, for the safety of yourself as the brewer and the intended love interest, follow the recipe exactly. Do NOT make substitutions. Do NOT double the recipe.*

Ingredients:

1 tsp hemp seed oil
4 fresh jasmine flowers, harvested under a full moon, chopped
1 unholy dandelion, crushed
1 cinnamon stick
4 cups of fresh water
1 love letter, written in iambic pentameter
2 fig leaves, purloined
2 hairs—one from the giver of the drink, one from the intended recipient
1 small vial of virgin's tears
(*optional*) Chef Cheri's Crazy Creole seasoning, to taste

Instructions:

Start fire and set cauldron. While the flames are growing, warm oil and sauté jasmine and dandelion until fragrant. Combine the rest of the ingredients and, while loudly banging an extra ladle on the side of the cauldron with one hand, stir 13 times counterclockwise, then 13 times clockwise. Do not stop banging until you have finished stirring.

Cover and allow the concoction to simmer on low heat for 6 hours or until the love letter has completely dissolved, while occasionally stirring and whispering sweet nothings.

When the letter has dissolved, remove from heat and pour through strainer and into flask. Serve warm or chilled, to taste.

Yield: one serving

Reviews:

* WORST POTION EVER! I used dried jasmine, and a microwave in place of the cauldron, and my boyfriend couldn't stand the taste! I wish I could give this no stars. So disappointed. *~VictoriaVictorious*

*** He was into me, alright, but the smell of it took away any desire I had for love. This recipe must be calculated for someone else's pheromones. *~Val27*

***** Worked on me! My wife and I want to thank Leslie for five years of a piping hot marriage. *~Mike*

***** Best. Love. Potion. Ever. Most love potions only call for a hair from the intended recipient, but my own hair and the Creole seasoning really make this potion stand out! A huge hit at my party last night. Definitely recommend pairing this with Angelina's Forgetful Potion. *~fratboi22*

**** @fratboi22—Dude… no. Don't be that guy. Just no.
As for my actual review, well, this is exactly like the potion my granny used to brew. True love requires high quality ingredients, folks, so follow the directions. Also, for the reviewer talking about the smell, you must not have added your own hair like the recipe called for. Your bad. *~Dravik*

** Two stars for Leslie, because she left me for Cadrion Ambrosius. And that's not even his real name, it's Bryan. BRYAN. What kind of warlock name is that? *~DeclanTheMighty*

* Enforcement here. @fratboi22 won't be posting any reviews for a few years, folks. A strong reminder: International Witch Code #24532 states that it is ILLEGAL to sell the same customer a Love Potion and a Forgetful Potion, or to be in possession of both! ~*SomeCallMeTim*

**** Best love potion my girlfriend and I have tried yet. We've finally stopped arguing about the drapes in the front room! Hardest part was finding the unholy dandelion for a decent price. Thanks Leslie! ~*PotioneerPat*

** @*Dravik*—I don't need your advice, thanks. ~*Val27*

**** I was nervous about trying this, but I was feeling adventurous that day, so I gave it a shot! Worked great, but next time I'll hold the creole seasoning.

Also, I know that this tip will only work for the lucky (unlucky? IDK) potioneers, but if you're a virgin yourself, it's cheaper and less awkward to stock up on your own virgin tears before making your first love potion. They DO have a decent shelf-life of eight months, so you can give this "love" thing a solid chance. ~*Elphie*

***** I'm surprised this recipe doesn't have more rave reviews. Probably because of over-reactionary witches like @*Val27*. Adding another star to my review to counter her review. ~*Dravik*

* This is the first recipe I've made that I've had such a negative result from. I think I can give a fair rating. ~*Val27*

***** @*Val27*—I don't want to be rude, but this is a perfect recipe, and if it fails for you, that's your fault. A few tips about love potions, straight from my Granny Lelah:

- This recipe is only truly effective if your intended love is already somewhat attracted to you. This is a love potion, not a miracle potion.

- As stated, only stir 13 times clockwise and 13 times counterclockwise. Also, banging the ladle on the cauldron is critical.
- Write your love letter in pen—not pencil. Lead poisoning? No thanks.
- FOLLOW THE RECIPE and include your own hair next time. ~*Dravik*

* It was a love potion, alright, but I was looking for a One Night Stand Love Potion, and this was too sweet for my tastes. Perhaps my sweet nothings shouldn't have included a promise to call the next morning. ~*Antonio*

* @*Dravik*—You're all about banging on that ladle, aren't you? ~*Val27*

*** Is it just me, or is no good way to measure virgin's tears? I mean, do you fill the vial up to the top, or…? Anyway, I had fair to middling success with this potion. This is not for beginners. I'll make it again, but I need to practice my sweet nothings before giving this another attempt. ~*PhaedraLee*

***** @*Val27*—For good reason. Come over to my place sometime, and give it a try. I would totally cook a meal with you. ~*Dravik*

***** I made some pretty serious modifications to this recipes and it still turned out great. FWIW, I've found that virgin's tears are easier to collect and more potent at events like Comic Con. Five stars for sure! ~*Selina*

***** I'm sure everyone has their own favorite to-go love potion, but after a little practice, we've found that this really is the most effective LOVE potion recipe you can find when you're hoping for that true love's kiss. ~*Val27&DravikForever*

Copyright © 2016 by Dantzel Cherry

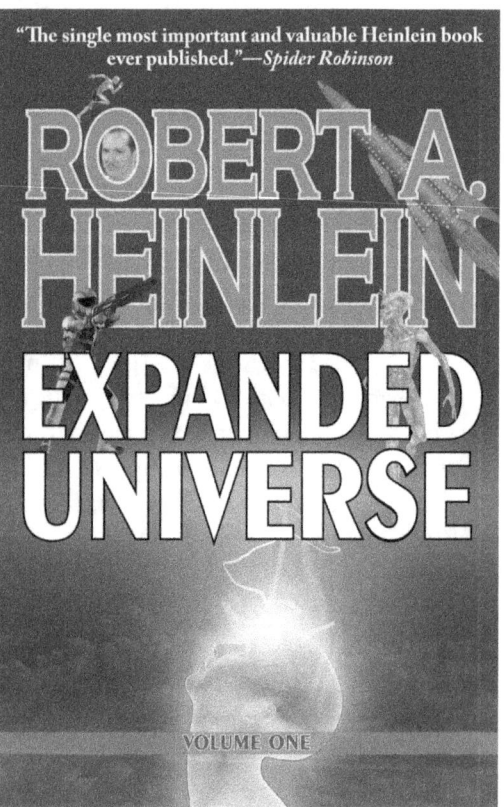

"Of all Heinlein's books, . . . Double Star is one of my three favorites."—*Connie Willis*

ROBERT A. HEINLEIN
DOUBLE STAR

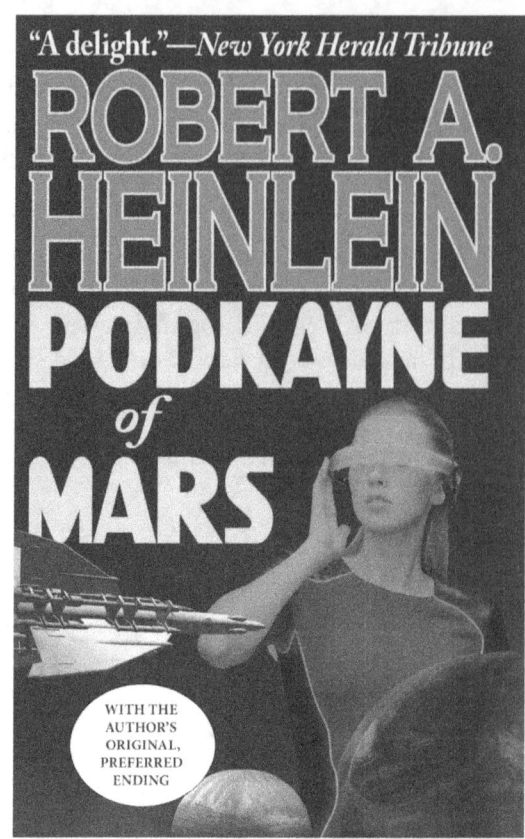

"A delight."—*New York Herald Tribune*

ROBERT A. HEINLEIN
PODKAYNE of MARS

WITH THE AUTHOR'S ORIGINAL, PREFERRED ENDING

"The single most important and valuable Heinlein book ever published."—*Spider Robinson*

ROBERT A. HEINLEIN
EXPANDED UNIVERSE

VOLUME ONE

"This is the book I've always wanted from Heinlein."—*John Bruni, GoodReads*

ROBERT A. HEINLEIN
EXPANDED UNIVERSE

VOLUME TWO

OVER THE WINE-DARK SEA

HARRY TURTLEDOVE

ORIGINALLY WRITING AS H. N. TURTELTAUB

THE GRYPHON'S SKULL

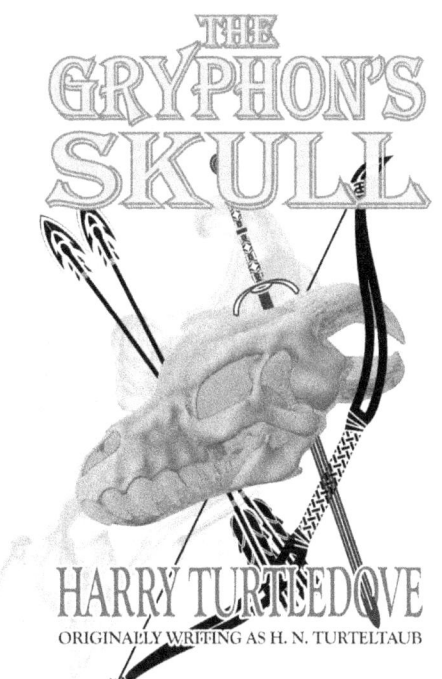

HARRY TURTLEDOVE

ORIGINALLY WRITING AS H. N. TURTELTAUB

THE SACRED LAND

HARRY TURTLEDOVE

ORIGINALLY WRITING AS H. N. TURTELTAUB

OWLS TO ATHENS

HARRY TURTLEDOVE

ORIGINALLY WRITING AS H. N. TURTELTAUB

Steve Pantazis is a Writers of the Future winner. His fiction has appeared in Writer's Digest *and the 2015* Writers of the Future *anthology. This is his second appearance in* Galaxy's Edge.

THE DEVIL WALKS INTO A BAR

by Steve Pantazis

If you're going to decide the fate of humanity, you might as well have a nice stiff drink to go along with it. At least that's my opinion.

I swilled the last of the whiskey in my double old-fashioned glass, held it up to linger in the cloud of cigar smoke from the blokes at the far table, and spoke a silent prayer before downing the delightful spirit.

Ah, I was going to miss this stuff. After today, I think a lot of people would.

This was the best twelve-year-old single malt they served here at the End of the World bar, and while there were other establishments that offered cask strength and twenty-five-year-old varieties, I decided this cozy little spot would do just fine. I chuckled, considering the name of the bar. It was apropos, all things considered.

The sleigh bells jingled over the front door, accompanied by a gust of cold, humid air with the unmistakable scent of the person I was sent here to meet: an acrid odor, like a match being put out in pig slop.

We made eye contact and he smiled, as if he were an old friend coming to visit; except he wasn't a friend. He was brutishly handsome by Hollywood standards, built like a professional tennis player, with a neatly-trimmed beard and well-defined jawline, a trait women of questionable morals lusted after, along with his British radio announcer's voice. Then there was his irreverent sense of humor, which I deplored.

I made no attempt to stand. I simply tipped my head and called him by the only name I could muster. His other names were unspeakable. "Hello, Luc."

He tipped his head in return and flashed his impeccably polished teeth. "Uziel. So good to see you." At least he was cordial, even if it was manufactured for the sake of civility.

Luc removed his overcoat and took the seat at the small table opposite mine. Before the rainwater from his wild locks of dark brown hair touched the table, Miller the barkeep was over with an empty glass and bottle of whiskey.

"Figured you could use a drink." He gave Luc a generous three-finger pour while I received a paltry finger-and-a-half.

I had trouble hiding my envy. The truth was Luc always got the better of me. Every time we met, anyone around us would fawn at his feet, laugh at his witty jokes, praise his comments, and fall prey to his guile. He was the CEO, in charge of a hell of an organization, and I was the lowly messenger boy. Part of me loathed his infernal swagger, the other part coveted it. It was a tortured existence.

"You shouldn't get down on yourself," he said, picking up on my jealousy. "Here. Let's toast to the end."

I clinked glasses, not wanting to look him in the eye. I did it anyway, knowing full well I'd better measure up if I was going to represent the Boss. His eyes were remarkably blue, unwelcomingly cold, like arctic frost. I drank half of what Miller gave me and set my glass aside. "Let's get on to business, shall we?"

"Always serious," he said in that playfully mocking tone he loved to torment me with. He took a thick, folded manila envelope from an overcoat pocket and placed it on the table. "Very well. Proceed."

I eyed the packet, satisfied I didn't have to pry it out of him. "There are certain rules we must adhere to in order to make our arrangement binding."

"Such as…?"

"Such as the need for a witness. Human, of course."

Luc called over to the bar. "Hey, Miller, you want to serve as our witness?"

The dimwitted barkeep looked up from drying a pint glass with a dishtowel. "Me?"

"Uzy here says we need a witness. No one in particular, just a mortal."

Miller scrunched his fat pickle of a nose. He was probably trying to figure out what Luc meant by "mortal." "Can I keep working while you talk?"

"Sure thing."

"Then I'm your fellow."

Luc turned to me. "Satisfied?"

"Fair enough," I said. "Onto the meat and potatoes. The Boss wants what we agreed to, starting with—"

"Chaos and bedlam, I know."

I hated when he finished my sentences. "Yes, that. Then there's fire and brimstone and all that jazz, too. Oh, and flies. Lots of flies. You can deliver on that, can't you?" I could hardly contain my excitement. Just the fact we were finally going through with this was a significant milestone after a millennium of careful planning.

"Spoken with gusto, Uzy! I'm impressed. Yes, I can deliver. Trust me; it would be much more dramatic than the whole locust thing the Big Guy came up with back in Egypt. That was second rate, you have to admit."

I continued, annoyed. "As for the souls, we'll need to divvy them up as they get weighed and judged. The Boss is worried about capacity. The Basement has been getting quite, ahem, crowded lately."

"Trust me, there's plenty of room. While the Upstairs is a pain-in-the-ass to get into, the Basement is always accommodating."

"It's not a hotel, Luc."

"More like the Hotel California, but do go on."

"Now, as you know, there is an entire list of activities outlined in the End-Times manual. I take it you've read it thoroughly."

"Front to back. Quite entertaining, I must say. I don't know why the Big Guy wants the whole theatrics with the breaking of the seven seals, or why there are bowls and trumpets signaling the end of times, or why we need four horsemen, but I get it: go big or go home, right?"

My tongue tied as I tried to respond to the inane question. "But you've prepared for your part, haven't you?"

He leaned back, a malevolent smile creeping up on his horribly beautiful face. "Hey, Miller, got a moment?"

The barkeep slung his dishtowel over his shoulder and walked over. "What can I do for you gents?"

"Uzy here wants me to sign off on the destruction of the civilized world. He says the Big Kahuna is ready to end everything, right now. Too much sinning and whatnot."

"Like the Rapture and stuff?"

"Exactly. We're talking about putting this corrupt world out of its misery; for fire and brimstone to rain down mercilessly on you transgressors; and for mankind to be judged for their mortal sins, all because you've run out of Hail Marys. What do you have to say about that?"

Miller picked at a barnacle-like bump on the bridge of his nose. "I'd say piss off. Sure, the world's gone to hell with cheaters, whores, politically-correct pansies, and us blokes who lie to the missus because we can't stand to hear them bitch, but it's our shithole, mate. I'm fine keeping it." He walked back to the bar and resumed drying glasses.

"There you have it," Luc said, knocking the last of his drink back and standing up. He took cash from a billfold and dropped it on the table. "That ought to cover it."

I jumped to my feet. "You're leaving?"

"Did you expect me to hang around? We're done here."

"But we haven't finalized our agreement!"

"The deal is off. I've changed my mind."

"But why? We've been planning this for centuries!"

He looked about the smoky bar. "This is working out pretty well for me, actually. If Miller's fine with the world going to hell, who am I to argue? More business for me." He flourished a roguish grin and donned his overcoat.

I wasn't about to let him get away so easily. I held up the manila envelope. "Are you forgetting you signed this?"

He regarded the envelope. "Oh, that? Keep it."

He tipped his head to me, then Miller, and left.

I tore open the envelope, expecting to see a signed contract, but pulled out a single sheet of cardstock with handwriting instead. "'Closed for the Apocalypse'?"

Miller chuckled. "Guess you won't be needing that anymore, mate."

I was at a loss for words, overcome with sudden helplessness. "But what do I tell the Boss?"

He shrugged and went back to work. "I'm sure you'll figure it out."

Copyright © 2016 by Steve Pantazis

Speaking of the professional, this is Nathan Dodge's first professional sale. It was written for—and won—a contest consisting of all the students of the 2015 Sail to Success cruise sponsored by Arc Manor.

THE PROFESSIONAL

by Nathan Dodge

As the express hydrolift rose swiftly and silently toward the luxury suite level of the hotel, Brea regarded the reflection that stared back from a full-length mirror on the rear wall of the lift.

Shoulder-length blonde hair, framing the face. Check. Wide-spaced blue eyes, a strong, upturned nose, lips with a naughty pout, a determined but diminutive chin. Check. Filmy metallic-gold dress, barely covering ample, upright breasts, small waist, hips with lots of curve. Check. Petite feet encased in gold spike heels. Check.

Always meet the client's expectations exactly.

The lift slowed, stopped, opened on the top floor. Across an expanse of dark blue carpet, a decorative young woman, though by no means in Brea's class, sat behind the concierge desk. To the rear of the desk and on either side, short halls led to each of the three executive suites. At her left, tall windows revealed a broad expanse of the spaceport, bustling with activity as ships either prepared for launch or disgorged passengers and cargo. Centered on the field, a blunt, bulbous jumpship lifted on a tail of flame, bound for the solar system rim, where the jump drive could freely operate. The windows shuddered as the thunder of the engines reached the hotel.

Behind the desk, the walls were a pale robin's egg hue. A calming color, designed to reduce the stress of the busy CEO or influential politician.

Approaching the desk, Brea noted the young woman's wide-eyed appraisal. The silence was about to become uncomfortable when she cleared her throat and said, "May I help you?"

Always be polite. It costs nothing and always engenders good will.

Brea smiled. "I have an appointment with Mr. Carson."

The young woman scanned a display screen. "Ms. Breuh?"

"It's pronounced b-r-a-y."

"Sorry." The concierge entered a code, pressed a button. "And your business?"

Brea increased the wattage of her smile. "I'm a therapist."

The woman frowned, then the light dawned. "Ah." Some hotel employees, and the occasional concierge, might act condescending or superior on learning Brea's profession. This one simply smiled, the look in her eyes showing that they shared a secret. In addition, there was the tiniest bit of desire behind the smile. She indicated the passage to her right. "Suite one."

"Thank you for your attention." Aware of the following eyes, Brea walked with an exaggerated hip roll to the suite door. Would the young woman catch the double meaning of her farewell?

Take time to cultivate potential clients.

Carson opened his door instantly. Somewhat taller than Brea, his face a bit florid, his body still stood erect, stocky but not paunchy. Into middle age, but still not bad looking. Seeing Brea's face, his breath caught.

After a frozen moment, he retreated into the room. Brea entered, closed the door. He was still speechless, lost in Brea's smile.

As usual, research had been extensive. Brea knew the client, although they had never met. Knew his habits, his desires, his longings. His first name was Charles.

Brea approached him until they were face to face. His glance took in the barely-concealed form, the angel face. Putting a hand out, he touched long blond tresses, caressing the soft skin of Brea's shoulder.

For a moment, he simply stared at her. Finally, Brea leaned in, brushed lips against his cheek. "It's okay to touch me. I am yours for the evening." The client brought their lips together, drawing them closer, his breath quickening.

After a moment, Brea began to loosen his belt. "Why don't you remove all those clothes and let's sit on the bed?"

✧

Exiting the room near dawn, Brea left the client exhausted and asleep. A quick check via personal mobile showed the payment already credited, plus a tip more than twice the fee.

The size of the tip shows the level of satisfaction.

At the concierge station, the same young woman still occupied the desk, looking weary. She glanced up and inhaled sharply.

"Your... therapy session is complete?"

Brea smiled. "Yes, Mr. Carson is fast asleep. The therapy was a success."

The concierge smiled timidly. "I'm sure you are always successful." She hesitated, sucked in a breath, as though afraid to say something. She looked up, her face an agony of indecision.

"Go ahead," Brea encouraged.

"It's just," the woman blurted, "I've never seen anyone as beautiful as you in my life."

Which hasn't been so long, thought Brea. Aloud, "What a nice compliment."

"The thing is," the young woman rushed on, "I'll probably never see you again."

"Oh, I'm here from time to time."

"Yes, but even if I do see you, I'll always think about this first time. Would you, that is, could I have... a kiss?"

Free samples are often a good investment.

Without a word, Brea leaned forward. The concierge lifted her head, and their open lips touched, joined.

After a long moment, Brea turned and moved toward the elevator. The young woman's face held a worshipful expression. Sliding onto the lift, Brea turned, smiled, and blew her a kiss.

✧

In the hotel room, Brea slipped off the dress, stood examining his naked form, smiling. Moving to the computing unit on the desk, he activated it, pulled up the current schedule.

The next client was a jumpship tycoon, Rezzed, who would be checking in this evening. A prestigious client, and scheduled half a hydra cycle ago. Quite a coup, even for him. Summoning his comm list, Brea selected Mazl and pressed the call button.

After maybe a dozen rings, a click was followed by a raspy voice. "First chance I get in weeks for a good night's sleep and... Brea?" The display lightened and a cockroach-like head appeared. After a moment,

its mandibles began to vibrate, then opened wide, a sign of pleasure.

"Hey, Mazl," Brea grinned at the image. "How's it hangin'?"

"Good, good. Just got done with the client; trying to catch a couple hours downtime."

Brea smiled. "Sorry to interrupt your rest. How'd that go? I didn't think the Ba'rx'hnn went in for our services."

"Not usually. I was a stand-in for the prime patriarch. You know how they got those extended families."

"Yeah."

"He died last year. They have some rite every few cycles and she wanted to have him there, like he was still alive. She's very sentimental. Sent me tri-vids, bought a full week of service. I had time to perfect his look. She was real pleased; got a hell of a bonus."

"Good for you. You still got tonight reserved, right?"

"For you? Absolutely! Who's the customer?"

"Big-time client, worth a zillion."

"What is it, some sort of three-way?"

"Naw, he's Zaeran. They're trisexual, remember? He's an alpha male. I got the female covered, I need you as the beta male."

"Gotcha. No problemo. You got his forms?"

"Sent them to you last evening. Check your mail."

The cockroach-head swiveled toward the upper corner of the screen, then returned to Brea. "Got it. I'll catch a little more rest, then start the conversion."

Brea gave him a thumbs up. "Pay attention to his preferences list. He likes a little one-on-one with his beta."

"Fine with me. That's an extra, right?"

"Twenty percent. He didn't even argue."

"Hey, how come I never get to be the female?"

"Cause I'm better at it."

"True, true. Hey, want to catch dinner tonight?"

Brea scowled. "No, I hate the restaurant in this place. Besides, the client promised refreshments, and he ought to be able to afford gold-plated appetizers."

"Fair enough. I'll come by your room."

"Meet me here at second ten. We're under contract till noon tomorrow."

"Geez, another night without sleep."

"You can catch up next week, Mazl. This is a big payoff, and a nice tip if he's pleased."

The roach-head eyed him. "Tell me something, Brea. I've known you two thirds of your life, maybe twenty hydra-cycles. You've been top of the heap for at least ten, raking in twice as much as anybody else in the business. You're fixed for life—hey, you've helped *me* get fixed for life. Ever think about just chucking it all and retiring?"

Brea stared at the screen, surprised. He shrugged. "Not really. You know, our family's been in the business since my grandparents started it. Mom was one of the best, the first to be popular in several systems. She loved what she did. 'Making people feel good,' she told me, 'is a good way to make a living.' The thought just hasn't come up."

"I seem to remember your mom retiring."

"Yeah, but not that long ago. She got me started, helped me get established. Encouraged me. She always had these 'words for the wise.' Things to do to make sure the client got the best experience possible, to be a success in your job. She had a great attitude. For instance, her mantra was, 'Always do what you like and you'll never have to go to work.' She always had a saying like that handy."

"Sounds like a smart old broad."

"Yeah, yeah, she is." Brea smiled.

Mazl's mandibles spread again, showing humor, then vibrated up and down, a farewell sign. "See you later." The screen darkened.

Brea stood, approached the mirror again. The female human form had always been one of his favorites, with its soft, symmetrical breasts, flat stomach, and gently curving hips. Today's creation had surely been his best work. The Change was already starting, however, breasts deflating, six vestigial arms becoming visible, the mating hooks starting to grow at his shoulders and hips. He had studied the background information and knew exactly what was required. The client would certainly hate to see him leave tomorrow.

Always leave 'em wanting more.

Copyright © 2016 by Nathan B. Dodge

George R.R. Martin is a four-time Hugo winner, former Worldcon Guest of Honor and one of the best-selling author's in the world. Last year the television series "A Game of Thrones," based on his work, was up for twenty-four Emmy Awards, winning twelve of them. It shows no signs of slowing down.

STARLADY

by George R. R. Martin

This story has no hero in it. It's got Hairy Hal in it, and Golden Boy, and Janey Small and Mayliss, and some other people who lived on Thisrock. Plus Crawney and Stumblecat and the Marquis, who'll do well enough as villains. But it hasn't got a hero… well, unless you count Hairy Hal.

On the day it all began, he was out late, wandering far from the Plaza in the dock section near the Upend of the Concourse. It was night-cycle, the big overhead light-panels had faded to black, and here the wall-lights were few and dim. Elsewhere, just down the Concourse, the Silver Plaza was alive with music; multi-colored strobes were flashing, and joy-smoke was belching from the air ducts. But Hal walked in darkness, through silent halls full of deserted loading trucks, past shadowed stacks of freight. Here, near the docks, Thisrock was much as the Imperials had known it. The corridors near the Plaza were all shops and disfigured plastic; the walls of the Concourse were covered with boasts and slogans and obscenities. But here, here, the only markings on the shining duralloy were the corridor numbers that the men of the Federal Empire had left. Hairy Hal knew the business was elsewhere. But he'd given up on business that night, and he was here.

Which was why he heard the whimper.

Why he followed it is something else again. The starslums were full of whimpers, plus screams and shouts and pleading. Hairy Hal was a child of the starslums, and he knew the rules. But that night he broke them.

In the black of a cross-corridor, up against some crates, he found Crawney and his men, with their victims. One victim was a youth. He stood in shadow, but Hal could make out a slender, graceful body, and his eyes. His eyes were immense. With him was a young woman, or maybe just a girl. She was backed up against the wall, under a yellow wall-light. Her face was pale, scared. And dark hair fell past her shoulders, so clearly she was off-world.

Crawney confronted them, a short slim man with black and red skull stripes and a mouth full of teeth that stuck out too far. He dressed in soft plastic, and he worked for the Marquis. Hal knew him, of course.

Crawney was unarmed. But the pair with him, the silent giants with the heads painted black, each of them carried a dark baton, and they waved them gracefully in front of them. Stingsticks. They kept the victims cornered.

So Hairy Hal, unnoticed, knelt in darkness and watched it all. It was a bleak episode, but one he'd seen before. There were soft threats from Crawney, delivered in a mild slurring voice. There were pleadings from the woman. There was a lightning pass from a stingstick, and a scream from the boy. Then whimpers, as he lay crumpled on the floor. Then another stingstick pass, a touch to the head, and the whimpering stopped.

Finally there were two rapes; Crawney, amused, just watched. Afterwards they took everything, and left her there crying beside the boy.

Hairy Hal waited until they were long gone, until even the echoes of their passage had faded from the corridor. Then he rose and went to the woman. She was naked and vulnerable. When she saw him, she gave a small cry and struggled to get up.

So he smiled at her. That was another of Hal's trademarks; his smile. "Hey now, starlady," he said. "Easy. Hal won't hurt you. Your friend might need help."

Then, while she watched through wide eyes, he knelt down near the boy and rolled him under the wall-light with one hand. The youth was blacked out from pain, but otherwise unhurt. But Hal didn't notice that much. He was staring.

The youth was golden.

He was like no boy Hal had ever seen. His skin was soft cream gold; his hair was a shimmery silver-white. The ears were an elf's, pointed and delicate, the nose small and chiseled, the eyes huge. Human? Hal didn't know. But he knew it didn't matter.

Beauty was all that mattered, beauty and glowing innocence. Hairy Hal had found his Golden Boy.

The woman had dressed, in what Crawney had left of her clothing. Now she stood. "What can you do?" she said. "I'm Janey Small, from Rhiannon. Our ship...."

Hal looked up at her. "No, starlady," he said. "No ship no more. Crawney got the name tabs, the Marquis'll sell. Some insider will be Janey Small, from Rhiannon. See? Happens, well, every day. Starlady should have stayed on the Concourse."

"But," the woman started. "We have to go to someone. I mean the man with the striped head, he said he'd show us the good stuff. He hired the other two for us, as bodyguards. Can you take us to the police?" Her voice was even, quiet, and the teartracks on her face were dry now. She recovered fast. Hal admired her.

"Starlady landed on Thisrock," he said. "No police here. Nothing. Should've hired a real bodyguard. Crew would give you a steer as usual. Crawney hit, instead. Starlady wasn't Promethean, wasn't insider, wasn't protected, probly four-class passage, right?" He paused, she nodded. "So, right. Crawney wanted tabs, starlady was stupid, easy hit." Hal glanced down at Golden Boy, then up at the woman again. "With you?" he asked.

"Yes. No." She shook her head. "Not precisely. He was on the ship. No one could understand him, and no one seemed to know him, or where he was from. He started following me around. I don't know much about him, but he's good, kind. What's going to happen to us now?"

Hal shrugged. "Help get Golden Boy over Hal's shoulder. Come with, to home.

☼

Hairy Hal's home; a four-room compartment on a cross-corridor near the Concourse, just off the Silver Plaza. It was good for trade. The door was heavy duralloy. Inside was a large square chamber, with a low couch along one wall and opposite a built-in kitchen. Above the couch were racks of books and tapes; for a starslummmer, Hal was an intellectual. A big plastic table filled most of the room and closed doors led off to the bedrooms and the waste cube. A glowing globe sat in the center of the table, sending pink reflections scuttling across the walls as it pulsed.

Hairy Hal dumped Golden Boy, still out, on the couch, then sat down at the table. He pointed to a second chair, and Janey sat too. And then, before either of them could say anything, a bedroom door opened and Mayliss entered.

Mayliss was very tall, very regal; sleek legs and big breasts and a hard, hard face with small green eyes. She painted her head bright red to let people know what she was. What she was was one of Hal's girls. At the moment, she was his only girl.

She stopped in the door to her bedroom, studied Janey and Golden Boy, then looked at Hal. "Spin," she said.

So Hairy Hal spun it. "Starlady got hit," he told her. "Crawney did a bodyguard grabtab, threw in rip an' rape." He shrugged.

Her face grew harder. "Hairy Hal scoped it all, right? Did nothing?" She sighed. "So?"

"Seal it, Mayliss," Hal told her. He turned back to Janey Small, smiled his smile. "Starlady know what comes now?" he asked.

Janey wet her lip, hesitated. Finally she spoke. "If there really are no police, I guess we're stuck here for a while."

Hal shook his head. "For good. Better face that, or you'll get hurt. Easy to get hurt on Thisrock, starlady, not like Rhiannon. Look." With that, his left hand reached across his body, grabbed a corner of his heavy green cape, and flipped it back over his shoulder. Then he took his right arm by the wrist, and lifted it onto the table.

Janey Small did not gasp; she was a tough woman, Janey Small. She just looked. Hairy Hal's right arm wasn't really much of an arm. It bent and twisted in a half-dozen places where an arm ought not to bend, and it was matchstick-thin. The skin was a reddish black, the hand a shriveled claw. Hal clenched his fist as it lay there, and the arm trembled violently.

Finally, when she'd looked enough, he reached over again with his left hand, and took it off the table.

Then he smiled at her. "Easy to get hurt," he repeated.

She chewed her lip. "Can't you get it replaced?"

He laughed. "Probly, starlady, on Rhiannon. Probly Prometheans could, too. But Hal's here, and Thisrock forgot a lot during the Collapse. No. Not even if Hal was an insider, an' Hal is no insider. Hairy Hal is a starslum pimp."

Janey's eyes widened. "I don't care," she said. "You're better than those others. You helped us."

Behind him Mayliss laughed. Hal ignored her. "Hey now, starlady," he said smiling, "Listen and learn, an' learn quick. Starslummers don't help anyone, less they get a slice. Hal is no hero, he didn't even try to stop that rip an' rape, right? But Hal is offering you good, and straight, so listen to him spin. Starlady and Golden Boy can stay here till day-cycle. When the lights come on, they got to pick. One, go out and take their chances, and good luck. Two—" he cocked his head questioningly— "they stay and work for Hal."

He lifted his right arm then, struggling and trembling, without using his left. It hit the table with a thump. Mayliss was laughing again. "Hairy Hal was good with a no-knife," he said, patting his arm with his good hand. "Still, this. Pick."

Well, I told you he wasn't a hero.

Janey's face went baffled at first, as she listened to Hal's words. Then, despite herself, she began to cry. Mayliss kept on laughing, but Hal's smile faded then. He shrugged, and shook his head, and went to bed.

The tears stopped in time and Janey sat alone, watching pink shadows race across the room. After a long time, her gaze wandered to Golden Boy asleep on the couch, and she went to him and curled up on the floor so her face was close to his. She stroked his silvery hair, and smiled at him, and thought.

But, of course, she had no choice. When day-cycle came Janey told Hal what she must.

He gave her a smile. He did not get one back.

"You'll work the Silver Plaza," he told her, as he stood across the table and buckled a plastic belt. "Starlady's fresh, an' young, an' she smells of stars, an' that's all good for trade. Mayliss'll take the Concourse. Hal will take you round today, an' spin out all the rules. Listen."

She looked at the couch. "What about the boy?"

"*Mayliss!*" Hal bellowed. When she came, glaring, he gestured. "Stay an' feed the Golden Boy, spin him soft when he blinks, an' don't let him fly. Hal's got plans for Golden Boy." He went back into his bedroom.

Mayliss watched his door shut with a sullen expression, then turned on Janey. "Why don't you run, ship girl?" she said. "Run back to your ship. You don't click here, and Hairy Hal don't click so good himself. Scope him smart before you root, he isn't all that much. You and Golden Boy will get shoved up an air duct if you believe his wobbly spin."

Hal emerged from the bedroom, dressed in a black swoopshirt and his cape. "Seal it, redhead," he told Mayliss. Then, to Janey: "First lesson, listen flow." He reached across his body, beneath his cape, and his hand came out holding a finger-sized rod of black metal.

"No-knife," he said. He did something with his thumb, and suddenly there was a humming, and a foot-long blue haze that stuck out from his fist. "They make them, well, not here. They come on ships. The force-blade'll cut anything, cept durloy, an' it's clean an' quick. Hal was good once, now not so good, but still he's better than most. This is your protection, starlady. This is why you don't get hit no more. Today Hal's parading you round the Plaza, an' the word gets out. Tomorrow no one touches you."

"Cept Marquis," Mayliss said. Her tone was cutting. "Cept Marquis and Crawney and Stumblecat, and any other blackskull who wants you. They get you free, starlady, and they do anything they want with you, and Hal don't do a thing. Right, Hairy Hal? Spin that at her."

Hairy Hal made a palming motion, the ghost blade blinked out and the black rod vanished beneath his cape. "Dress, starlady," he told Janey. "Take something from Mayliss, anything you like, an' cut it to size."

"Hey now," Mayliss started, but Hal raised his voice and bulled right over her.

"You pick, you get, starlady," he said. "Keep your hair, so they know you work for Hal. But tie something red round your head, so they know you work."

Afterwards, they left Mayliss and Golden Boy alone, and went out into the corridor down to the Concourse, out towards the Plaza. Janey Small wore a red headband and a gossamer yellow dinger and a cool, pale face. She did not talk. Hal did all the talking, Hal in black and green, who smiled and kept his arm around her.

The Concourse, already, was jammed. Hal pulled Janey to a food stall, nodded to the man behind the counter, and they both ate crusty brown breadsticks and cubes of cheese. Janey put her elbows up on the counter. Hal put his arm around her, rubbed her shoulder, and pointed at people with his eyes.

That one's a thief, he told her, and that one pushes dreams, and the other with the wide eyes and the drools, well, he's that buys them. And there's another pimp, but his girls are old and baggy, and there's Bad Tanks who owns a stall out near the plaza. Don't ever eat there, though, cause he laces his sticks with dust to bring in more new dreamers. French is a joy-smoke merchant, he's quick but you can trust him, but Gallis don't sell nothing but a spin.

They started down the Concourse together, past the grimy plastic walls and the countless shops, past fat, half-naked women with shaved red skulls who glared at them resentfully, past swaggering youths with stingsticks who gave Hal a wide berth. All the time Janey Small walked in silence while Hal kept on his lessons.

The place with the blue curtains is Augusty's, he told her, he rents you bodyguards that you can trust. But never, never get a guard from Lorreg, worse than Crawney, only half the brains. That fat man with the green stars on his head? He's a pimp, a straight one if someone gets to me, you go to him. Dark Edward pimps too, yes, but don't go near him, he used to be much bigger than he is. Over there you've got yourself religion, if you're the kind who likes to mumble in the dark. The guy in the silver swoopsuit, he don't have long to live, he talks too loud and he's going to get a stingstick up his ass.

They reached the Silver Plaza: a huge open place at the end of the Concourse, a ceiling far above that spilled down silver lights, tiers of balconies and shops, welling music all around them, a troupe of dancers whirling in the street. Hal pushed his way toward them; Janey followed. He watched, smiling. One of the women, a blur in scarlet veils, spun up against him, stopped, and grinned. He reached under his cape and pressed something into her palm. She grinned again, and danced away.

"What did you give her?" Janey asked, curious despite herself, after they'd elbowed free.

"A coin," Hal said, shrugging. "The dancing clicks for Hal, starlady. Probly that's another lesson for you. You won't get hit cause you're with Hal, right? But you don't hit no one, see? Hal spins straight, the ship men give steers to pimps who serve up girls without the stingsticks."

Suddenly his arm tightened on her shoulder. "An' there," he said, pointing with his chin "There's two more lessons for starlady, walking right together."

She looked in the direction he'd indicated. A man and a woman were making their way across the Plaza slowly. The man was broad-shouldered and blond, dressed in a dark floor-length cloak with heavy gold embroidering. The woman was brown-skinned, with kinky black hair and a pale green uniform.

Janey was still looking when she heard the voice from behind her. "The man is one of the leading citizens of Thisrock," the voice said, in a mellow, purring tone. "We call his kind insiders. The woman is an officer from a Promethean starship, of course; I expect that you knew that, dear. And your lesson, I'd guess, was to be that both insiders and Prometheans are to be treated with deference. They are powerful people."

They turned. The speaker was wearing a Promethean uniform, too; but unlike the woman's his was thin and patched. He had nothing else in common with the starship officer, or with anyone else in the crowd. Instead of being hairless, his face and hands were both completely covered by a soft gray fur. His ears were pointed, his nose was black, his eyes feline. He was, in fact, a man-cat.

"Hello, Hal," he said, in the oddly gentle voice that mocked the stingstick swinging from his belt. Then he smiled at Janey. "Right now you're full of questions," he said. "I know them all. First, I don't talk like the others because I'm not from Thisrock, and I have an education. I don't look like the others because I was genetically altered. A game they play with the lowborn on Prometheus, you know. My alterations were not satisfactory, though, so I wound up here. Some of them work, however. I heard Hal's last comment from quite a distance. Now, yes, that should cover it." He smiled. His teeth were very sharp.

Hal did not smile back. "Janey Small," he said, pointing. "Stumblecat."

Stumblecat nodded. Janey stood frozen.

"You're clearly a star-born," Stumblecat said in his cultured tones. "How ever did you wind up with Hal?"

"Starlady was passing through," Hairy Hal said sharply. "She hired the wrong bodyguard. Listened to Crawney spin, an' wound up raped and ripped. Now she's with Hal."

"You always were one to take advantage of a ripe situation, Hal," Stumblecat said. He laughed. "Well, I'll keep the starlady in mind the next time I'm looking. She might be an interesting change."

Hairy Hal was not amused, but he kept from showing it. He shrugged. "Yours anytime, Stumblecat," he said slowly.

"For a spin and a smile, Hal?"

Hal's face was dark. "For a spin and a smile, Stumblecat," he said slowly.

Stumblecat laughed, stroked Janey with a soft furred hand, then turned and left.

And Janey, hot eyes glaring, turned on Hairy Hal. "I agreed to work for you because you gave me no choice. I don't like it, but I recognize the situation I'm in. There was nothing said about you giving me to your friends."

Hal frowned hard. "An' nothing done, either. Listen to the biggest rule, starlady. Insiders, Prometheans, you scope them good, an' give them room, an' let them be customers. Nobody gets you free, cept black skulls. *Yes*, starlady. Like the ones who raped you up, don't look so white. For them, you do anything, be nice, charge nothing less they offer to pay. An' also for the black skull bosses. Like the Marquis, who Hal will tell about. Like Crawney, who hit you. An' Stumblecat.

"Hey now, starlady, you look shocked. Why? Mayliss spun you straight, you knew it. Probly you thought Stumblecat was a good guy, right? Cause he talks like you, only better. Well, starlady just did another stupid. First she hums to Crawney, now to Stumblecat. Next thing you'll be cuddling the Marquis himself; you already got both his leetenants."

His good hand was pinching her shoulder painfully as he spoke, and people in the crowd were throwing quick looks their way. Janey, furious, spun free.

"What about all that *protection*?" she shouted. "If I don't even get *that* much, why should I wear *this*?" She tore off her headband, thrust it at him.

Hairy Hal stood there, looking down at it. When he spoke, his voice was low. "Maybe you shouldn't," he said, shrugging. "Up to you, starlady. Hal doesn't force no one." He smiled. "But he's better than them."

Janey stared at him, saying nothing, holding the red rag out in her hand. Hal looked at the ground and scratched his head. And, in the awkward silence, a third man approached.

He was short, heavy, off-world; his clothes were rich. And his eyes moved constantly in a nervous scramble to see if anyone he knew was around. "Excuse me," he said. Quickly, quickly. "I—that is—the man on my ship told me to look for a man with a green cape and, well, ah, hair." He waited expectantly.

Hairy Hal looked at him, then at Janey. He said nothing.

Her hand fell. She stared at Hal's face, then at the ground, then—finally—at the off-worlder.

"Come on," she said at last.

Somewhere along the line, her name got lost. Janey Small of Rhiannon was gone, flown away on a ship hardly remembered. She was Starlady, and she did a thriving trade.

It wasn't the off-worlders so much; after the first, they came to her no more than any other. It was the starslummers who gave her business, the kids with the hand-me-down stingsticks and the whooping swoopsuits who caught the scent of the stars. They'd grown up with shaved-skull hard-eyed redheads, and they wanted hair and dreams and maybe innocence. They hummed to Starlady. They came to Starlady.

And she learned, yes yes, she learned.

There was a night-cycle near the docks, when a corridor club got a hold of her. The queen of the club was a blue-skulled dreamer, and the man she hummed to had gone to Starlady. So she stared and smiled and drooled while her three underboys stripped their catch and started to play with their stingsticks. Ah, but then Hairy Hal was there! Starlady had friends all along the Concourse, and the friends had seen the grab, and they got to Hal, and he knew the dock section where the club called home. Such a short fight. An underboy swung his stingstick, Hal lifted his humming blue ghost blade, the baton sheared neatly in two, and the club ran.

And she learned, yes yes, she learned.

There was an afternoon at Hal's in the third bedroom, the special one with the canceller that wiped out Thisrock's gravity grid. But the customer wanted more than free-fall fun; he had a nervelash, which is like a stingstick, only worse. She screamed, and Hal was there, kicking off and floating fast and graceful, bringing his no-knife up and around. Afterwards they had to turn off the canceller, to ground all the droplets of blood.

And she learned, yes yes, she learned.

There was a conference at Hal's one night, and she met Dark Edward with his hot red eyes and his double stingstick and his plans for being emperor again, plus Fat Mollie who ran a stable of boys. They wanted Hairy Hal to join them. "It's a straight spin, Hal," Dark Edward said in a ponderous voice. "We can hit him good, and I'll make you my leetenant." He talked and talked and talked, but Hal just shook his head and threw them out. Afterwards he and Mayliss fought for hours.

But there came a silver morning two weeks later, when Crawney and Stumblecat dragged Dark Edward screaming to the center of the Plaza. At first Janey just watched Stumblecat, in all his soft-furred clumsiness, and noted the lack of feline grace that Hal had told her of, the curious lack that made him a reject from Prometheus and gave him his curious name. Then she saw the Marquis, and she knew what was going to happen.

The Marquis had all of Stumblecat's stolen grace. He wore black boots, and the robes of an insider, but he was very silent. His skull was silver; it shone in the Plaza light. Around it, covering his eyes, was a solid ring of tinted blueblack plastic.

While Janey watched, while hundreds watched, he took Dark Edward's double stingstick and turned it on. Crawney and Stumblecat held the victim. The Marquis played for hours.

And she never saw Fat Mollie after that day, either.

Oh yes, she learned, and soon she knew the rules. She was Starlady, and Hairy Hal was her protection and she was safer than most around her. The blackskulls never bothered her. She was beneath them.

"The Marquis is a stupid," Hal told her after Dark Edward's death, when she came home early from the Plaza. "Dark Edward, well, he was worse, but still.

Listen, the dreamboss clicks, right? The dust comes in on ships an' his men get it quiet an' sell it quiet an' no one knows the dreamboss an' no one knows how to touch him. Lametta tried, got hit. *Hard!* Probly the dreamboss will buy himself inside someday, the way he clicks. See?

"But Marquis, he doesn't click. Too *loud.* Everybody knows the Marquis, everybody chills to him, only he won't *never* buy his way down inside. The insiders don't want him marching round the Ivory Halls, less he's got an exotic for them and a quick exit-pass.

"He started with exotics, Starlady. Alters like Stumblecat, an' a couple Hrangans, green gushies, Fyndii mindmutes, that kind. Got all the exotics on Thisrock, right? The insiders, well, some of them hum sick, but they want to hum bad, an' they want to hum quiet, an' they pay a lot. Prometheans come too. The Marquis hums sick himself, but different, he hums to pain, an' power probly, but mostly pain. Good with a stingstick, though, an' he got the exotics. After that he got a lot of other things, joy-smoke and grabtabs and ripping, all his now. Exotics are still a big slice, the Marquis has them all.

"Only, well, he's so loud, an' it'll kill him. Someday he'll try to hit the dreamboss, or squeeze an insider for quiet-money, or *something.* Maybe Stumblecat will take him. Stumblecat spins quieter, Starlady, an' Hal knows he don't like seconds. Hitting Dark Edward in the Plaza was just a *stupid.* The Marquis wants to chill everybody, cept it won't click."

He was sitting at his table eating as he spoke, his cape thrown back, his claw-like right hand clutching the plate as his left cut and speared with a kitchen knife. Janey sat across from him. In the corner of the room, regarding them both with immense blue eyes, Golden Boy sat on the couch.

Golden Boy had an easier time of it than Janey. Hairy Hal had run boys before, he said, but he wasn't running Golden Boy, not yet. He just kept saying that he had plans. The youth sat around the compartment all day, eating and staring at people, never saying a word. Somehow he seemed to know what was required of him, whenever something was. Mayliss, after mothering him for a week, had finally gotten tired of the way he shrank away in fear whenever she came near him. She clawed him badly with

sharpened nails, then ignored him after Hairy Hal promised her a taste of no-knife if she did it again. "Golden Boy's got to stay *pretty,*" he told her, with his ghost-blade in his good hand. She'd been backed up against her bedroom door, looking terrified but oddly ecstatic. That night she and Hal had slept together, the only time since Janey Small and Golden Boy had arrived.

Most times Hal slept alone. That first night, he'd tried to sleep with Janey, but she'd pulled away and glared at him. "I did it for you all day, and you've got the money," she said. "I'm not going to do it *with* you too."

And he'd let her go and shrugged. "Starlady, you're a strange one," he said. Then he went to his room by himself. Janey sat by Golden Boy on the couch, looking at his eyes and brushing back his silver hair. Finally they'd gone to sleep together in the free-fall chamber, arms wrapped around each other as they nestled in the sleep-web. Golden Boy simply held her and slept. He knew what was required of him.

It was that way every night. Hairy Hal tried once more, after he'd saved her from the corridor club. Back in the compartment, he'd sat by her on the couch and kept his arm around her until she stopped her trembling. Then he got up and went to his bedroom. He paused at the door, favoring her with a smile and one of his cock-the-head questioning looks. "Janey?"

"No," she said. He shrugged, and gave up trying.

After all, he wanted Janey, and Janey was long gone. She was Starlady and she had her Golden Boy.

Then one day, when Janey came back from the Silver Plaza, Golden Boy was gone. She looked around the compartment frantically; he'd never left before. But there was no one home but Mayliss and a paunchy off-worlder, afloat in the free-fall room. Mayliss glared at her as she stood in the doorframe, but the man just chuckled and said, "Well, well, c'mon in."

When he'd left finally, Mayliss put on a sheath and came storming and spewing out at her. "I'll chill you down good, Starlady, and if Hal don't like it I'll cut off his crottled arm. What's the big spin?"

"Golden Boy is gone."

"So? Hal's out selling him, little girl. Grow up."

Janey blinked. "*What?*"

Mayliss snorted in disgust, and put her hands on her hips. "I spun you straight. Why'd you think Hairy Hal let Golden Boy sit round here all day and powder his ass with dreamdust like he was an insider or something? Cause Hal clicks right, is that what you figured? So, wrong. Hal was waiting for a big sell. He spun it all out to me. With all those fun boys coming through here every day, sooner or later word's probly going to get down inside, that's where Hal wanted it, see? Lots of insiders like little boys, and he knew they'd pay big for a little *golden* boy with pointy ears and big eyes and silver hair. Only Hal couldn't zactly parade round the Ivory Halls giving out handbills, right?"

"He won't do it," Janey said stubbornly. "Golden Boy won't do it!"

Mayliss laughed. "You warm me, Starlady, you're such a *stupid*. Listen good, cause I'm going to spin you right. Golden Boy will do zactly what Hal says. You think you learned a lot, but you don't know *nothing*. Stead of a clear skull, you got a head full of hair and stars. I think you hum to Golden Boy, you know, and that's so warm it's *boiling*."

"I love him," Janey said, with storms flashing across her face. "He's kind and gentle and he's never done anyone any harm, and he's a hell of a lot better than anyone else on Thisrock."

But Mayliss only laughed again "You'll learn, Starlady. Hal don't click, but at least he clicks better'n Golden Boy. Listen, I used to hum to Hal once. I had to learn."

"What? That he uses people? Well, I learned *that* fast enough," Janey said. She turned and went to the couch and sat down.

Mayliss followed her. "No, Starlady, you got it spun up all wobbly and tangled. I thought Hairy Hal was a big hero. He was faster with his no-knife than *anybody*, and he looked good, and he spun big about how he was going to click. Yes, and little Mayliss believed it all. Cept one night, after Hal'd been doing too good, there was this knock on the door, right? Crawney. Back then, Hal had me and two other girls and a couple boys and some exotics plus he had some 'sticks working for him, and he was spinning about a slice of joy-smoke. Well, Crawney came to chill him

down. The Marquis wanted joy-smoke, you see, and the Marquis didn't like Hal having exotics.

"Well, Hairy Hal just laughed at Crawney, and I hummed to that. It was a long time ago, right, and the Marquis wasn't so big and Hal wasn't so small, and Lametta was even still round. Hal had plans.

"Cept Crawney didn't like being laughed at. A couple cycles later, the blackskulls grabbed Hal and me and took us down by the docks. Crawney was there, and Stumblecat, and the Marquis. They made me watch, while the blackskulls broke his arm all up, again and again until he was screaming. Right? Then the Marquis just smiled and said, 'Hey, Hal's arm is broken, he needs a splint,' and they splinted it with a *stingstick*, and just stood there and watched him on the floor.

"Afterward, all the nerves were crottled or something, and Hal wasn't nothing with his no-knife. Everybody left him; his 'sticks, his girls, everybody. The Marquis took his exotics. Hairy Hal had nothing cept *me*. Little stupid Mayliss, she still hummed to him, and I stayed. I helped him use his other hand, and I thought once he was good again, he'd take his no-knife and go *after* the Marquis, right?

"Well, wrong. That's where my spin went wobbly on me, and I learned. Hairy Hal was scared and he still is. He's never dared to get big again cause the Marquis gives him big chills. Every once in a while one of the blackskulls'll come by to have me, and they never pay, and Hal never does anything. They'll do it to you, too, watch. You'll learn, Starlady. You're a *stupid* if you hum to *anyone*, or buy anybody's spin, or do anything for anyone but *you*!"

Janey waited until the outburst had passed. Then, very quietly, she said, "If you gave up on Hal, then why are you still here?"

Before Mayliss could answer the door opened, and Hairy Hal and Golden Boy were back. Hal was smiling broadly. He reached under his cape, pulled out a packet, and tossed it on the table. Mayliss looked at it, grinned, and whistled.

"Golden Boy clicked *good* down in the Ivory Halls," Hal said. Then, startled, he stopped and looked at Janey. She'd gone to Golden Boy and wrapped her arms around him and now she was fighting not to cry.

So things began to click.

Down inside, in the Ivory Halls and the Velvet Corridors, in the great cool compartments around the Central Square, the word was loose. And the customers came; sleek blond men in woven robes, matrons in dragon dresses, adventurous girls in soft plastic. Others sent for Golden Boy, and Hairy Hal took him to them, walking the streets inside as if he were born to them. He handled things quiet and smooth, and he sold Golden Boy only for big money. No starslum funboys got their hands on him; Hal had his wide-eyed gold mine reserved for men of taste.

And Golden Boy went, and did what was required of him. He never spoke, but he seemed to understand, sometimes even without Hal telling him. It was almost like he knew what he was doing.

Sometimes the insiders would buy him for a night, and Janey would float in her sleep-web alone.

On one of those nights, Hal returned from inside by himself, carrying a heavy book under his good arm. He was sitting at the table, poring over the pages, when Janey and a customer returned from the Silver Plaza. He ignored them and kept poring.

When the man had gone, Janey came out and looked at him sullenly. "What's that?" she asked.

Hal glanced up, smiled. "Hey, Starlady. Come an' look. Hal got it for Golden Boy tonight from an insider. It's old, you know, pre-Collapse. Straight spin!"

Janey walked around behind him to peer over his shoulder. The pages were big, glossy, full of closely packed text and bright holostrations of strange creatures in colorful costumes.

"There's something here, look here, about a race that might be Golden Boy's. Look at that picture, Starlady, the same, only the hair is the wrong color. Still. They were a Hrangan slave-race before the war or the Collapse. So, probly Golden Boy is a little Bashii. Unless…." He riffled some more pages. "Here, this part about genetic alteration experiments an' cloning an' that stuff. The Earth Imperials were trying to clone their best pilots an' such, duplicate them. An' you had alters, like Stumblecat cept he's a defect. See starlady, it has this bit about *esthetic* alters on Old Earth, pretty boys, being worked up. So. Maybe he's one of those. From Old Earth, what a spin! Thisrock hasn't heard from that far in, well, long time. It chills you, right Janey?"

His enthusiasm was a flood; Janey felt herself smiling at him. "I don't think he's from Old Earth," she said. "If he were, he could talk to us. He's probably a Bashii. But I really don't care what he is. He's just Golden Boy."

"*Just!* Janey, you're positively warm. Listen, he's clicking for us, Starlady. They hum to him down there, they hum high an' hot, an' probly they're going to want him down there more, right? But he won't do it right less Hal wants it, *an'* Janey, of course. In a while, Starlady, we can buy down inside, all of us, cause Golden Boy is Golden Boy. An' cause Hairy Hal is quiet, right?"

"Not quiet enough, Hal," the voice said from the doorway. Stumblecat stood there, smiling, his hand on his stingstick. "Not quite quiet enough."

He sauntered in with the clumsy ease that was uniquely his. Crawney followed, pushing Mayliss ahead of him. She stumbled up against the table, reeled, then pulled away towards the bedrooms.

"They want to see you," she said, looking apprehensively at Crawney and Stumblecat. "They found me on the Concourse and took my keyplate."

Hairy Hal closed his book and stood. "Spin it," he said. His face was a guarded blank.

"You know it all already, Hal," Stumblecat said. Such a soft voice he had, such a civilized purr. "You've known it all along. We told you long ago that we bear you no grudge. You can pimp all you like, girls, boys, anything. But exotics, well, you know. The Marquis has a sentimental attachment to exotics. He collects them, you might say."

"You been spinning us wobbly," Crawney put in, grinning at Hal and showing off all his teeth. "But you can straighten out. Just give us your exotic."

"Golden Boy, I believe he's called," said Stumblecat.

"Yes," Hal said. "Only Golden Boy isn't an exotic. Would Hal spin you wobbly, eh? He's just human, an alter, look at the book." He tapped it, offering.

"I'm not interested in any books, Hal," Stumblecat said. "An alter is exotic enough for the Marquis. And even if you were right, well, the sad fact is we'd still want him. That much inside business is too tempting."

"You want to get your other arm crottled?" Crawney said. "Wrong? Then you'd better hum to us, Hal."

Hal did not move. But Mayliss did. She came around the table, grabbed him, shoved him towards them. "*Hal!*" she shrieked. "Hey, this is your *chance!* Only two of them, and Crawney never carries nothing, and Stumblecat is a clumsy stupid with his stick. *Take* them!" She pushed him again from behind.

And he hesitated, then whirled and slapped her hard. "You want to spin me cold, redhead," he said. "There might be more outside."

Mayliss pulled back, said nothing. Stumblecat and Crawney just watched and smiled. Janey frowned. "Hal," she said. "You can't give Golden Boy to the Marquis. You can't do that, Hal, she's right."

But Hal ignored her. "Golden Boy's gone now," he said, turning back to the two men. "He'll be back, straight spin! You can have him."

"We'll wait," Crawney said.

"Yes," said Stumblecat "And Hal, you haven't treated us very hospitably, you know."

Hal's lip trembled. "I—no, Hal will set you right. Drinks?"

"Later," said Stumblecat. "That wasn't what I had in mind." He walked over to Janey, reached out and stroked her hair. She shivered.

Hal looked at her. "Janey?" he said. "My Starlady? Will you…." But she was already gone, with Stumblecat, to the bedroom.

Crawney, not to be left out, took Mayliss.

☼

They watched pink shadows run as the globe pulsed.

Two of them.

Alone together.

The insider had brought Golden Boy back at last, and the blackskulls who'd been outside had taken him. Mayliss had left too, packing all her things in silence. Now there was Hairy Hal and Starlady.

She sat there, calm, cold, and watched him and the shadows. This time Hal was crying.

"I can't, Janey," he said, over and over, in a broken voice. "I *can't*. He chills me, Starlady, and I've seen him with his stick. The no-knife, yes, it's a better weapon, quicker, cleaner. But *him*, the Marquis, he's too *good*. Probly Hairy Hal could've taken him, he thought he could've, one on one, no-knife against stingstick. No chance, though.

An' now, Hal's all crottled. Marquis'll never face him alone anyhow."

"You're Hairy Hal," Janey said evenly. "If he could take Marquis once, you can take him now. You can't leave Golden Boy with him. You *can't*. I love Golden Boy."

Hal looked up, wincing. "Hey, Starlady," he said. "I'm spinning you straight. You want Hal cold?"

"If you won't do anything," she said. "Yes."

He shrugged. "I hum to you, Janey," he said suddenly, staring at her with something that was almost fear.

"Wonderful. But you'll never see me again." She stood up. "Give me your no-knife, Hal. If you won't try, I will."

"They'll kill you, Starlady, or worse. Root down an' listen. You won't even find the Marquis."

"Yes I will. And he'll face me one on one, too. You told me how, Hal. The Marquis is loud, remember? Well, me too. I'll stand in the middle of the Silver Plaza and shout for him until he comes. He can hardly have his blackskulls gang up on me then. If he did, who'd ever get chilled again? Will you give me the no-knife?"

"No," he said, stubborn. "You're wobbly."

"All right," she replied, leaving.

☼

Night-cycle in the Plaza, and the silver-shining overheads were out. The wall-lights provided a different illumination, winking through their color-phases, alternately dyeing the faces of the revellers blue or red or green or violet. The dancers were out in force, music was everywhere, and the air was thick with the sweet gaiety of joy-smoke.

On the polished stairway that curved up towards the second tier of shops, Starlady took her stand and began to spin.

"Hey," she called to the throngs below her, to the people pushing by, "Hey, stop and listen to me spin. You won't soon have the chance. The Marquis is going to kill me."

Below, the off-worlders paused, curious, admiring. Whispers were exchanged. Prometheans shook their heads and grinned. And the swaggers in their swoop-suits, the redheads out to sell, the drooling dreamers and the men who doled out dreams, the pimps, the bodyguards, the dancers and the thieves—well, they knew what was going on. A show was coming. They stopped to watch.

And Starlady spun, Starlady with the shiny, dark hair, in a suit of milky nightwhite that took the colors of the lights, Starlady with a black rod in her hand.

"Marquis took my lover," she shouted to the gathering crowd. "He chilled down Hal and stole the Golden Boy, but he hasn't chilled down me." And now the no-knife in her hand was alive, its ghost blade flickering strangely in the violet light. And Starlady was sheathed in purple, her face stained grim and somber.

"I'll kill him if he comes," she said, as they drew away around her, leaving her alone on the stairs. "Me, Starlady, and I've never used a no-knife in my life." The Plaza was growing quiet, tension spread outward like ripples in a pool. Here the talking stopped, there the dancers ceased to whirl, over in the corner a joyman killed his smoke machine. "But he won't come, not Marquis, and I'll tell you why. He's chilled."

And now the light clicked over, and Starlady was a vision in green, the ghost blade a writhing bluish shadow. "You've seen him kill, starslummers," she said, with a shake of emerald-dark hair. "And you've heard the wobbly spins, right? Marquis, who hums to pain. Marquis, Thisrock's top 'stick." She threw back her head and laughed. Over on the far side of the Plaza, they were muting their music and drifting her way. "Well, think now, have you ever seen him *fight*? Without his blackskulls? Without Crawney—" she pointed, and a man with a shiny striped skull straightened and glared and rushed towards the nearest corridor— "and Stumblecat—" she whirled the other way and picked him out lounging against a food stall, and Stumblecat smiled and lifted his stingstick and waved— "to hold the arms of his victim?"

The light clicked again, and she was bright blue and glowing, and the no-knife was suddenly invisible. Now the Plaza was dead, still, captive to the Starlady. "No," she shouted, "you haven't, no one has. Straight spin! Remember what you see tonight, watch when the blackskulls come and take me, watch how they hold my arms when Marquis kills me, and remember how he was too chilled to come alone!"

A murmur went through the throng, and eyes lifted. And Starlady turned and smiled. Two

blackskulls were coming down the stairs behind her, their faces hard chalk-blue. "See?" she told the crowd. "I spun you straight!"

Only then someone bounded out of the audience below, a yellow-faced youth with sparkling circles on his head and a glittery gold-flake swoopsuit. He took the stairs three at a time, past her, and a stingstick was in his fist. He waved it at the blackskulls. "No, no," he shouted, grinning. "No grabs, soursticks. I'm humming to a show."

The blackskulls drew their own sticks and prepared to take him. But then another swagger joined him, all aglow in dazzlesilk. And then a third, and a fourth with a wicked white nervelash. And others came running down behind them, sticks drawn.

Out in the plains of the Plaza, a dozen other blackskulls found themselves surrounded. The mob wanted Marquis.

And Starlady, shining crimson, stood and waited, and when she moved the red reflections flashed in her hair like liquid fire. Till another voice challenged hers.

"You spin a wobbly spin, Starlady," Hairy Hal said from the foot of the stairs. They'd gone for him, of course. By now the news had rippled far beyond the Silver Plaza. "Probly little Janey Small of Rhiannon hasn't seen the Marquis kill, but Hairy Hal has. He's *good*, redhead, an' Hal is going to watch while he teaches you how to scream."

Heads turned, people murmured. Hairy Hal, well, wasn't he her lover? No, the answers came, she never hummed to him, so maybe his hum's gone sour.

"There's Hairy Hal," Starlady called from her perch. "Hairy Hal the quiet pimp, but you ought to call him Chilly Hal. Ask Mayliss, and she'll tell you. Ask me, too, about Golden Boy and Hal."

Stumblecat, his stingstick sheathed, pushed his way forward and stood next to Hal. "Hal's just smart, Janey," he said smiling. "You, sadly, are not. Though you *are* pretty. Maybe the Marquis will let you live, and rent you out to nerve lash freaks."

Hal laughed, coarsely. "Yes. Hal could hum to that."

Her eyes flashed at him, as the red light flicked to gold. Then Marquis came.

He walked easily, gracefully, swinging his stingstick and smiling. His eyes were lost behind their dark ring. Crawney scrambled beside him, trying to keep up.

As if on signal, Stumblecat drew his stick and gestured. People pulled back, leaving a clear circle at the base of the stairway. A wall formed to keep onlookers out; blackskulls and Starlady's swaggers, working together.

Starlady descended, golden.

The ring closed around her. Inside was only Crawney, Stumblecat, the Marquis, and Hairy Hal. Plus her, plus Starlady. Or was it Janey Small, from Rhiannon?

The light went violet again. The Marquis smiled darkly, and Janey Small suddenly looked small indeed. She shifted her no-knife nervously from one hand to another, then back again.

As they advanced, Stumblecat sidled up to Hairy Hal. He grinned, and lifted his stingstick, and jabbed Hal very lightly in the chest. Pain sparkwheeled out, and Hal winced.

"Your no-knife, Hal," Stumblecat said. "On the ground."

"Hey, sure, Hal's on your side," he said. His good hand reached under the cape, came out again, and dropped a dead knife to the floor. "Straight spin, Stumblecat! Starlady needs a stinging, she never learned the rules, right?"

Stumblecat just smiled. "Maybe," he said. "Maybe that's what you think." He eyed Hal speculatively. His stingstick wandered under the corner of the cape, began to lift it. Then, suddenly, he glanced over at the Marquis, laughed, and changed his mind. Stumblecat put the stick away.

"They all saw me disarm you, Hal," he said, nodding.

Meanwhile Janey circled, holding her no-knife out clumsily, trying to keep the Marquis at bay. He hadn't moved yet. He just grinned at her and waved his stick, like a snake preparing for the strike.

When the light clicked from purple to green, she jumped, bringing the ghost blade down at his baton. One touch, cut it in half, and he was hers. She'd seen Hal do it oh, so often.

But the Marquis just flicked his stick back, blinking-quick, and her no-knife severed air. Then it whirled forward again, to brush her wrist. Janey screamed and pulled back. The no-knife rang upon the floor.

She backed away. The Marquis followed. "Not over, silly ship girl," he said to her softly, as she clutched her wrist. "I'm going to chill you good, and hurt you, and teach you how things work. Come to me, Starlady."

And he darted at her, his stick brushing one cheek. She screamed again, as an angry flush appeared. The Marquis had his stick set on maximum.

He was cornering her, advancing towards her, herding her toward the ring of stingsticks that kept the crowd away. As he drifted in, oh so slowly, the watchers pushed and shoved for better position, while inside the ring, Crawney and Stumblecat and Hairy Hal followed behind him.

Janey took one step too far backwards, came up against a stick, yelped, jumped forward again. The Marquis stroked her lovingly, down her side, and heard another scream.

She rushed at him then, tried to grab the stick, screamed again as she finally caught it and had to let it go. He gave her another swat as she rushed past, past him and Hal and Stumblecat, towards the fallen no-knife.

Marquis swiveled and started to follow. But Hal stepped beside him, then, and the Marquis shoved up against his cape.

And cried a gurgling cry.

And fell.

It was quite an ordinary kitchen knife sticking through Hal's cape. Beneath, clutching it and trembling, a crottled blackened hand.

By then, Janey had recovered her no-knife. She finished the Marquis as he lay there bleeding.

There were loud noises from the crowd. Stumblecat snarled and gestured, and suddenly the ring broke, the blackskulls began swinging their sticks and people shouted and shrieked and scattered. A few swaggers fought briefly before running. And Crawney was still standing open-mouthed while Stumblecat picked up Hal's no-knife, moved in behind him, and neatly slit his throat. There was only room for one emperor at a time.

In the center of chaos, Hal stood smiling. Janey knelt by the Marquis. "Hey, Starlady," Hal said. "We did it. I did it. Now we can get back an' buy our way down, an'…"

"I still don't have Golden Boy," she said coldly.

Stumblecat walked over and smiled down at her. "Ah, but you do. He doesn't seem to understand us. I think he had some sort of empathic link with you, or Hal, or both. Join us, Starlady, and you'll have him every night."

"*Hey!*" Hal said, angrily.

"All right," said Janey.

He looked at her shocked. "*Janey*," he said. "You're spinning wobbly. I killed him for you, Starlady, my Starlady. Like you wanted."

"That's what Mayliss wanted, Hal," she said, standing. "I just wanted Golden Boy. And I'm going to have him. He's not like the rest of you. He's still clean, and kind, and I love him." She smiled.

"But," said Hal. "But, Starlady, Hal hums—I *love* you. What about me?"

"What about you?" Starlady said.

And she went off with Stumblecat, to find her Golden Boy.

✧

In the end, some of them were dead. The rest survived.

Copyright © 1976 by George R. R. Martin

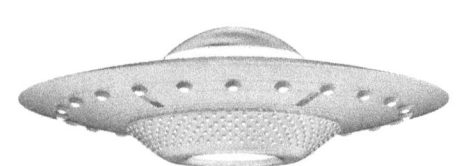

Jody Lynn Nye is the author of forty novels and more than one hundred stories, and has at various times collaborated with Anne McCaffrey and Robert Asprin. Her husband, Bill Fawcett, is a prolific author, editor, and packager, and is also active in the gaming field.

RECOMMENDED BOOKS

by Bill Fawcett and Jody Lynn Nye

Meet Me in Atlantis
by Mark Adams
Penguin Random House/Dutton
April, 2016, reprint edition
ISBN-13: 978-1101983935

Many who read this magazine probably don't think Atlantis is real. Others are devoted believers. But most of us, deep inside, have to admit we wish Plato's story of the city was true. This is not yet another book defending some theory of where Atlantis was located. Nor is it speculation on mystical powers or anything you might expect, or dread, with Atlantis in the title. *Meet Me in Atlantis* is really a journey through Atlantology, the speculation and researching of the Atlantis myth, and the people who continue to search for the lost continent.

Beyond excellent writing and storytelling, one of the great appeals of this book is that Mark Adams is not a "true believer," but rather an explorer. The book begins with an easy-to-follow look at the basis of the Atlantis myth. Then you join Adams as he travels across the world to meet a wide range of men and women, each of whom are trying to solve the riddles involved with Atlantis as described by Plato. These are the self-proclaimed Atlantologists who often fervently believe contradictory things. While you journey along you will absorb in an entertaining and comfortable way an impressive amount about the myth, the theories it has spawned, and the history of the time when the Greek philosopher Plato wrote his tale of a great empire lost and island submerged. Among the many twists Adams finds is that Plato may not have really described Atlantis as an island. The Greek word he used could also mean a peninsula or possibly even coastal plain. Another is that there were two lengths of time, "years" in the Egyptian calendar, meaning the solar year, but also a lunar "year" that we would call a month. This dichotomy means that Plato may have been describing events not from 9,000 BC, but only 9,000 months or only seven hundred and fifty years before he was writing.

To be honest, I began reading with a bias against the book just because of the title. Books about Atlantis, Bigfoot, and King Arthur tend to be tedious at best. There simply isn't enough time to sit and view all the TV specials, each of which proves a different location for the lost city, much less read the mountain of speculation Plato's *Discourse* has engendered. But within a few chapters I was a believer, not in Atlantis, but that Mark Adams is an amazing storyteller. He will carry you enjoyably along on his exploration of Plato's story and the people who believe it is true. At the end when he summarizes the theories and speculations, he comfortably leaves you to draw any final conclusions.

If you have any interest in Atlantis, especially even a cautious and cynical one, this is the one Atlantis book you will truly enjoy. If you are among those of us who rather doubt the tale is true, but would be thrilled if it was, this book will be a treat. If you are interested in how people who live and think a bit differently are part of their own subculture, *Meet Me in Atlantis* will fascinate you. There are a lot reasons to read this book, but perhaps the best one is that you will enjoy it.

The Lost Stars, Shattered Spear
by Jack Campbell
Ace Science Fiction
May, 2016
ISBN-13: 978-0425272275

The *Lost Stars* books are more a parallel series than a sequel to the deservedly successful *Lost Fleet* novels. In the *Lost Fleet*, an officer who was thought to have died heroically a century earlier is discovered floating in space cryogenically preserved. The war, lasting more than a hundred years, had degenerated on both sides to the point where the recovered officer's knowledge on tactics and strategy allow him to lead a fleet trapped behind enemy stars to a war-ending victory. The enemy was the ultimate nightmare of bureaucracy and corporate abuse run wild. After losing, the "Syndicate" shatters, with many worlds trying to become independent. The central core that remains of the corporate state is using what is left of its resources to retain control. All this is complicated by the presence of an implacably hostile alien empire. The *Lost Stars* novels combine space opera and politics in the story of one planet, Midway, that is on the edge of the alien menace, trying to remain free and create a more humane and democratic way of life. The leaders, beset from all sides, are handicapped because of Syndicate managers and are distrusted by their people. They try to ensure the survival and independence of their changing world.

As they begin, Shattered Spear, a nearby solar system valued only for its jump gate, is ruthlessly invaded by the aliens. Possessing the gate means that the aliens would be within easy striking distance of Midway. Unwilling to leave their home world helpless, the leaders decide to split the already weak Midway fleet. At virtually the same time, those defending the planet face off with a more powerful Syndicate fleet while the rest of their ships and no fewer than three other powerful space fleets battle for control of the planet and jump gate.

The combat elements are excellently shown and powerful. The convolutions of leadership and the challenges facing those who are trying to defend Midway are equally compelling. This is space opera at its best. Without losing sight of the excitement of combat, you are also drawn into the reasons why humans fight and sacrifice for home and freedom. The entire series is a truly good read, but the *Lost Stars* novels are also full of compelling characterizations and unexpected twists. Warning: start these books early in the day, so you don't stay up half the night reading. You will find yourself cheering for the good guys, when you can figure out which ones they are. Each book is more sophisticated and a better read than the one before it. Since they started strong, this bodes wonderfully for the future. You can comfortably start reading with *Shattered Spear* or any book in the *Lost Stars* and enjoy it as a stand-alone. That there are fifteen in the series is just a bonus.

Anyone who likes space battles, planetary politics, and stories with an interstellar scale will enjoy all of the *Lost Stars* and *Lost Fleet* novels. Look for tales well told with heroes, villains, and explosions enough to satisfy anyone. They are combined with some real morals and character depth. If you have enjoyed other military SF series, this is a must-read.

✿

Familiar Spirits, anthology
edited by Donald J. Bingle
54-40 Orphyte
September, 2015
ISBN-13: 978-0692532959

Gathered in this book are a number of really excellent ghost stories. This is not a book full of friendly or gentle ghosts. The "bump in the night" for most stories is really a solid smash. The collection begins with Sarah Hans's tale of revenge by an abused and murdered woman and ends with Jean Rabe's highly original story giving a ghost dog's eye view of a murder set in one of the most fascinating locales ever, the Coon Dog graveyard in Tuscumbia, Alabama. Not a collection for the younger reader, *Familiar Spirits* will appeal to you with its darkness.

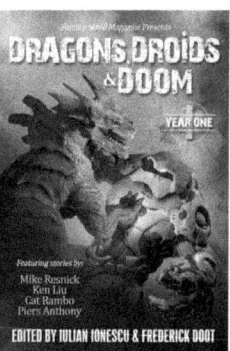

Dragons Droids and Doom, anthology
edited by Iulian Ionescue and Frederick Doot
Fantasy Scroll Press
November, 2015
ISBN-13: 978-0991661992

By all rights we should not be reviewing this anthology. It is a collection of the best stories published by a competing magazine. But the goal of this column is to present to you with books that are worth reading, and this definitely is one of them. The range of the stories is matched only by their number. All the stories, being the best of what they already had selected by *Fantasy Scroll's* editors, run from good to strong. With fifty stories in one volume, this book is a bargain for your reading dollars. The tales are only loosely themed and include stories ranging from very dark to a wonderfully written and gentle told romance by Piers Anthony. There are stories by new talents, as well as from some very respected names such as Mike Resnick, Cat Rambo, Ken Liu, and others. This is a great collection to read a story from when you only have a few minutes.

✿

The House of Daniel
by Harry Turtledove
TOR Books
April, 2016
ISBN-13: 978-0765380005

This is an extraordinary book about a rather ordinary man living in an alternate 1930s America. In this world magic had long been used and is commonly known, if not commonly practiced. The 1929 Crash was caused not by manipulations in the stock market, but by a sudden collapse of the magic that was used on an industrial scale. Harry Turtledove writes some books with a grand, sweeping scope. This is a more personal story. The main character, beautifully drawn but not really a hero, is a part time baseball player who gets in trouble with the local crime boss in Enid, Oklahoma. Later, the boss's wrath comes back and adds an element of suspense and danger. To escape possibly fatal punishment, the ball player goes on the road and lucks into a replacement slot with a traveling, semi-pro team calling themselves the House of Daniel. Like many teams of the era they barnstorm around the Southwest in an old bus, playing the local

teams for a split of the gate. The integration of magic is seamless even down to the resentment the many unemployed feel for the zombies who will work slowly, but sleeplessly and for no pay.

The world is fun, with the added delight of the baseball games themselves. The voodoo priests chanting to help the opposition, for example, don't exist in the real world's ball games, curses on the Chicago Cubs being the only probable exception. Seeing a world from the perspective of a center-fielder trying to just get by in the Depression in a world where magic is mundane is so well handled that it feels real. But it is not the skill of the writing you will see, but rather the enthralling story about ordinary baseball players moving through a different and yet familiar landscape.

The insider's view of baseball in a world of every day magic is by itself entrancing. It is easy to get into and keeps you entertained. If you have enjoyed any of Harry Turtledove's many other alternate history or alternate universe novels, enjoy another. If you have played any baseball or even just like movies such as *Major League* and *Bull Durham*, this will be a treat. Definitely a home run.

✿

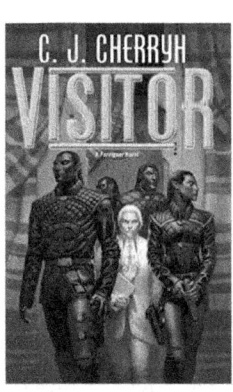

Visitor, book seventeen in the Foreigner series
by C.J. Cherryh
DAW Books
April, 2016
ISBN-13: 978-0756409104

The *Foreigner* series, called by its author First Contact and divided into an ever-increasing cluster of trilogies, began with the story of a starship bringing human beings out from the Sol system to a habitable world around which they intended to build an enormous space station known as Alpha. The failure of their vessel, the *Phoenix*, in hostile space, leaves them orbiting the world of the atevi, another humanoid race. The atevi, tall people with ebony-black skin and golden eyes, are technologically behind humanity, but far ahead in their knowledge and understanding of mathematics. Math forms their language, in which disharmonious sentences and expressions are as offensive as insults. Their cultural structure is designed around their natural impulse for loyalty to others, known as *man'chi*, as opposed to humanity's tendency to seek power for its own use. As a result, neither people really understand the other. A single human, known as the *paidhi*, is permitted to live among the atevi and learn from them, to become the interpreter between them and humankind. Eventually, the atevi cede an island, Mospheira, to human control in exchange for technological advances. The balance between the two is often uneasy, but they come to cooperate, usually due to the careful diplomacy of the *paidhi*.

Two hundred plus years after the initial contact, that *paidhi* is Bren Cameron. He has gained trust from the atevi, to the point of becoming a semipermanent escort of Ilsidi, the *aiji*-dowager, grandmother of the current ruler, Tabini, and her great-grandson Cajeiri.

Visitor begins in the aftermath of a change of power on the human-owned space station circling the atevi world. Another alien race, the touchy and dangerous Kyo, whom Bren and Ilsidi have encountered before, is on their way toward the atevi world and Alpha. The kyo destroyed portions of humankind's second space station, Reunion, rendering its population refugees now crammed into nooks and crannies aboard Alpha. Bren has one contact among the Kyo that trusts him. With the atevi only recently recovered from a failed coup, and facing an influx of humans desperate to escape from the return of their enemy, Bren has to negotiate his greatest feat of diplomacy on a very narrow tightrope indeed.

Fans of C.J. Cherryh's other works will enjoy this series and its exploration of other-thinking aliens. Her writing is a joy to read. Even if this is the first volume you pick up, you'll be drawn into the culture and situation without getting lost. Good for those who love space adventures as well as political dramas.

Altered America: Steampunk Stories, collection
by Cat Rambo
Plunkett Press
June, 2016
ISBN-13: 978-1-945477-03-4

I truly enjoyed *Altered America: Steampunk Stories*. This short book by accomplished author Cat Rambo explores an alternate world in which steampunk technology exists side by side with magic. All of the tales are linked, but diverse in their approach to the milieu and their protagonists or narrators. Rambo has a gift for immersing her reader into a vivid universe full of adventure, sensuality, wit, and poignant observation. She gives us a brilliant story filled with wry humor told by a man very much of his time in "Clockwork Fairies"; a touching and sad tale as seen from the lower classes in "Rare Pears and Greengages"; and hints of a much larger narrative to come in "Laurel Finch, Laurel Finch, Where Do You Wander?"; and her stories of the psychic Pinkerton agent, Elspeth Sorehs and her phlogiston-powered mechanical partner, Artemus West. Highly recommended for anyone who enjoyed "The Wild, Wild West" and other steampunk stories.

erences, so fans of Monty Python and other television shows will have a leg up on other new readers, but the Discworld is a marvelous place to be, and *The Colour of Magic* is your gazetteer to the series.

Copyright © 2016 by Bill Fawcett and Jody Lynn Nye

The Colour of Magic, The Color of Magic
by Terry Pratchett
Smythe Publishing (UK) HarperCollins (US)
January, 2013, reprint
ISBN-13: 978-0062225672

This month's classic is *The Colour of Magic,* the first in Terry Pratchett's immensely popular Discworld series that eventually ran to forty novels and associated works. From the prologue describing the structure of the world itself to the last page, it's filled with humor ranging from wry to outright slapstick. Twoflower is a seemingly gormless tourist visiting Ankh-Morpork, the city divided by the polluted and frighteningly magical river Ankh. With him is his Luggage, a chest made from enchanted pearwood that follows him everywhere on a myriad of "dear little legs." He falls into the company of Rincewind, a wizard, or if you read his hat, 'wizzzard.' Naturally, the local falls out of his depth immediately, but the tourist comes to show hidden talents.

Pratchett's stories are told with wit and insight, as well as increasingly complicated and hilarious footnotes, some of which poke fun at more weighty and pretentious fantasy epics. He introduces us to other denizens of the Discworld, such as witches, wizards, merchants, talking dogs, bureaucrats, the city guard, and Death himself, a seven-foot-tall skeleton in a black cloak who speaks entirely in capital letters… all of whom a reader will come to feel are real people, and some of whom are downright lovable. The title refers to the eighth color in the spectrum, octarine, which comes somewhere in between violet and red. The humor is decidedly British in character and ref-

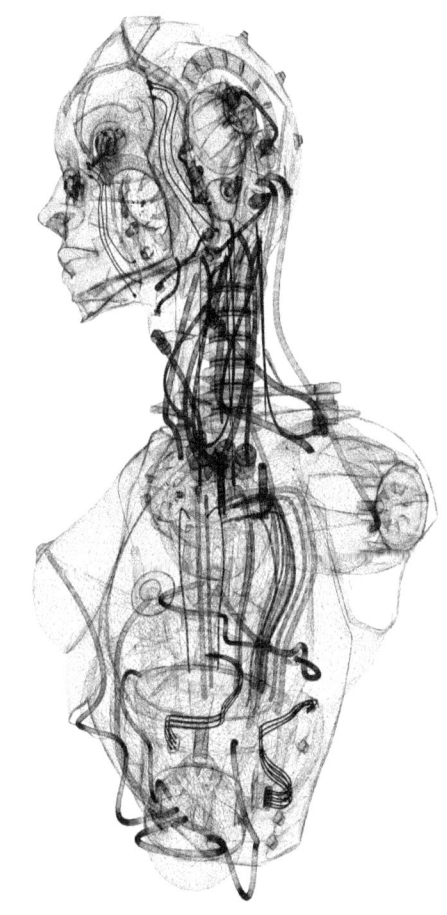

Gregory Benford is a Nebula winner and a former Worldcon Guest of Honor. He is the author of more than thirty novels, six books of non-fiction, and has edited ten anthologies.

A SCIENTIST'S NOTEBOOK

by Gregory Benford

IMAGINING THE REAL

Lately I've asked a wide number of my scientist friends two questions:

(a) did you ever read science fiction;
(b) what did you like?

These questions assume that working scientists don't read much fiction any more, which turns out to be true for the majority. Their answers were remarkably similar, whether I asked physicists, chemists, biologists or even engineers. Well over half did read sf, most haven't the time now, but they preferred "hard" science fiction when they did indulge.

None of this surprised me, but it does raise further questions about how this particular brand of SF relates to scientists themselves. We all know that a small but rather determined band of SF authors actually are scientists, and they tend to write the "hard" stuff. Is it obvious that they should?

As one who does, it's a personal point, and I'm going to worry it a bit here, without unmasking all the mysteries.

By hard science fiction I mean that which highly prizes fidelity to the physical facts of the universe, while building upon them to realize new fictional worlds. It sticks to the *facts*—unless some crucial new experiment or discovery changes those—but can play fast and loose with *theory* as it likes. It's important that any new scientific theory must explain the facts we already know, though it can twist your head around to do the job. Einstein's explanation of gravity as warped space-time doesn't sound like Newton's forces acting at a distance--but they explain the same elliptical orbits and falling apples, with Einstein winning in the fifth decimal place.

Our century has been a playground for physics, which with electronics, the atom, and the rocket has remade the world. Because physics makes the most precise predictions, hard SF often uses it to anchor speculations. Astronomy provides the largest possible landscape for adventures, often action-filled, but also for cosmic perspectives, a hallmark. Maybe some of all this authority will rub off.

Science fiction arose in a time affected by science's unsettling revelations about ourselves, about our position in the natural order—and by relentless technology, science's burly handmaiden. SF has tried to grapple with ideas which disturb our sense of being at home in the world. While botany, or human anatomy, or zoology do not really separate us from our common world, physics, chemistry, and especially astronomy certainly do. This alienation may be why these latter sciences turn up so much in hard SF, as it struggles with the emotions they kindle. Advances in genetics shall soon lead to bioengineering, effectively alienating us from our bodies, making us see ourselves and nature even more as machines—so hard SF has lately drawn this area into its province. Many stories expend a lot of effort trying to offset or reconcile with these poisoned gifts.

Robert Frost remarked that free verse was like playing tennis with the net down. At first maybe a netless game seems fresh, exciting—but soon nobody wants to watch you play. Hard SF plays with the net of scientific fact up and strung as tight as the story allows.

H.G. Wells admonished writers to make one assumption, as fantastic as we like, and then explore it remorselessly. A world of infinite possibilities is boring because there can be no suspense. If you write a sonnet with, say, seventeen lines, you haven't written a good or bad one—you haven't written a sonnet at all. The same way the iron rules of the sonnet can force excellence within a narrow frame, paying attention to scientific accuracy can force coherence on fiction. This aesthetic is central to hard SF, and why scientists like it.

Scientists like the joy of discovery, which means uncovering an unsuspected aspect of the world, usually implicit in what you knew before. Detective stories hold similar pleasures in a smaller compass. There is a particularly hard-SF flavor to this delight, though, suggested by a passage from Clement's *Mission of Gravity*:

> Dondragmer spent much of the time on the downstream trip examining the [differential] hoist. He already knew its principles of construction well enough to have made one without help; but he could not quite figure out just *why* it worked. Several Earthmen watched him with amusement, but none was discourteous enough to show the fact—and none dreamed of spoiling the Mesklinite's chance of solving the problem himself.

Problems as a source of pleasure do not have to be explained to the reader.

Mission of Gravity's detailed descriptions of a high-gravity planet and its insectlike natives was meticulous and well-argued. This novel may mark the true beginning of hard SF as a recognized subgenre, though the term itself doesn't seem to have come into use until the middle 1960s, perhaps in reaction to the New Wave literary movement. (Though the New Wave was important in opening the field to wider influences, its greatest effect may have been to make hard SF into a recognized opposite.) Clement's bizarre but scientifically plausible world is a raw setting in which the protagonists struggle upward against great weight, a reflection of the sometimes grim but usually hopeful tone of hard SF.

Much of the charm of Frank Herbert's hugely successful *Dune*, written several years after *Mission of Gravity*, lies in its working out of the implications of life on a desert planet. Herbert used massive research to buttress his imagination, and the book compels us because the consequences of the rigorous environment, as the plot unveils them, seem logical and *right*. Fred Pohl's *Gateway*—a New Wave-influenced novel with futuristic psychotherapy and *angst* as a frame—uses stellar astronomy, scrupulously rendered. Except for some superstrong materials to wire it all together, Larry Niven's *Ringworld* conforms to physics as we know it now. It follows a band of explorers who trek across an immense ring which circles a star, spinning to create centrifugal "gravity." The ring is so immense it can harbor life across a surface many times larger than the area of the Earth. Making this all work is great fun, with ideas unveiled by plot turns at a smooth pace. The sheer size of everything overwhelms the reader, but the game is played straight and true, no cards up the sleeve.

Well, almost. I noticed, along with many others, that the ring had a distressing property—shove it sideways and it coasts into its star. This instability can be righted by installing attitude jets on the outer rim. Niven didn't know this, but he added the jets to his sequel—a good example of holding true to the ideas of contemporary physics.

The crucial opening assumption can be pretty fanciful, though. Suppose Earth has been immersed in a medium which dumbed down all species, as in Poul Anderson's *Brain Wave*. What would happen when we got suddenly smarter—and so did the animals, including Rover and Puss? In *Shield* Anderson asks: What happens if somebody invents a perfect defensive screen against all weapons, making Jeffersonian individualism a hard fact? Or suppose there is a gene which confers immortality against disease and aging—though not against, say, being crushed by a landslide? Near immortals would be very different people. Anderson's *The Boat of a Million Years* follows a handful of these developing oddities through ancient history up to the present, then beyond. Most specialists on aging believe it arises as a side effect of relentless natural selection for reproductive efficiency in younger years, a menu of traits which make for more and better children but take their toll in the end. Given that one gene, though, Anderson's logic proceeds smoothly to a grand finale.

Robert Heinlein's "By His Bootstraps" examines time travel—a far more fanciful notion than a moon colony—in all its overlapping paradoxes, turning the plot on its head in strictly logical fashion. Time travel brings into play immense possibilities, but it lies at the margin of hard SF. Are paradoxes inevitable—or can you really shoot your grandfather and still survive? There is a considerable body of sophisticated theoretical research devoted to probing whether physics can in principle exclude time travel, and the jury—after many physics papers about faster-than-light particles (tachyons) and wormholes in space-time—is still out. Nearly all physicists are very doubtful. But no *fact* makes these ideas mistaken. I consider a properly couched time travel yarn marginally within the hard SF boundary—and so do the scientists I know. I spent a lot of time justifying this to myself in a novel, *Timescape*, which wound up having to use quantum mechanics to escape paradox. Hard SF writers will do a lot of work to make their creations as solid-seeming as possible.

SF can reach even further afield than time travel and keep its credentials. Asimov used his broad knowledge of science to make an apparent impossibility—element plutonium 186—become real, by inventing a scientifically plausible method of connecting parallel universes. *The Gods Themselves* is his most scientifically oriented novel, producing the "feel" of hard SF through meticulous logic. His *Foundation* series, on the other hand, envisions social science as hard as physics, capable of making exact predictions—but somehow, the "hard" affect is less telling than in *The Gods Themselves.*

The drone of meticulous explanation appears often, almost like a bizarre fetish—because the authors want to retain the authority of nonfiction, its touchstones of an external (though provisional) truth. Thus the writer may stretch a quantitative point for dramatic effect, but not commit the unpardonable sin of lying—giving scientific misinformation to the reader. This sets tensions afoot in the plot, from the peculiar difficulty and excitement of building narrative suspense.

Rigor can have other drawbacks. Stories can turn on whether a match will stay lit in an orbiting spacecraft (convection of hot smoke away from the flame depends on hot air being lighter; Hal Clement, "Fireproof"). This sets up a tension between narrative drama and fidelity to facts. Most writers feel that scientific errors or finessed facts should be at least invisible to the lay reader—remembering, though, that the best reader is sophisticated and not easily fooled. They love to catch each other in oversights. Heinlein once skewered me about the freezing point of methane, and I was mortified.) They even show off a bit by pioneering, rationalizing territory previously regarded as the province of fantasy. In "Magic, Inc." Heinlein treated magic as a technology with rules as strict as a chess game. Larry Niven followed with stories in which magic (mana) was simply a natural resource, used up in ancient times (*The Time of the Warlock*), leaving us with merely the scientific laws we know now.

To really get the science right, you have to know the scientists. This is an aspect of *verisimilitude*—imbuing fantastic events with convincing detail. Piling on well-worked-out nuances derived from the science and technology. C.S. Lewis termed this "realism of presentation," as in his *Out of the Silent Planet*; in its simplest form it uses names, geography, maps, titles of nobility, etc. Fantasy shares this trait, as in Tolkien, but the distinctive hard SF method is to fix upon a few surprising but logical consequences of the scientific facts. The most unexpected, the better. The moon colonists in Heinlein's "The Menace from Earth" notice that their low gravity allows people to fly in pressurized domes—creating a tourist industry. In *The Rolling Stones*, Heinlein's savvy traders deduce that Martian gravity and sandy soil will make bicycles a thrifty, overlooked method of transport. They make a killing, like many self-sufficient hard SF heroes.

Getting the voice right is essential. Fred Pohl's "Day Million" is a frustrated rant, expressing the author's despair at ever conveying to his reader how wondrously different the far future will be—yet it tries anyway, with compact expository lumps like grumpy professorial lectures. This is one of the voices of hard SF itself, trying to punch through humanist complacency about the supposed centrality of human perspectives and comforts. Tom Godwin's "The Cold Equations" also hammers relentlessly (and melodramatically), invoking the constraints of gravity, orbital mechanics, and fuel levels. These two stories talk across the rapid social evolution between Godwin's (1954) and Pohl's (1966). Godwin used the indifference of the universe to frame a morality tale in which a woman suffers because she tries to use her innocence to avoid responsibility. Pohl doesn't personify human insularity in a woman, but in the reader himself—and ends by directly addressing that reader, assumed to be a callow young man, indeed, perhaps even the techno-weenie some see as the hard core hard SF audience.

The most important voice to get right is the style of scientists themselves. This takes considerable craft; scientists at work are less interesting than watching paint dry. James Gunn's *The Listeners* opens each portion with lengthy quotations from the scientific literature, with radio astronomers debating the philosophy of listening for extraterrestrial intelligence. Fred Hoyle's *The Black Cloud* uses crisp, though long, arguments between astronomers, complete with equations. They try to cope with an immense, super-intelligent plasma cloud which swoops out of interstellar space and envelops the entire inner solar system. The astronomers are sharply rendered, shrinking the huge perspectives down to clashes of style and personality. Outside their observatories and conference rooms, the rest of humanity panics, resorting to religious frenzy and misled by dull-witted politicians who pay little attention to the scientists (a favorite Hoyle theme). Much SF struggles to reduce the vast canvas of astronomy to human scale by rendering the scientists in detail—jargon, warts and all.

Science can make the world seem surreal, a symptom of culture lagging behind technological reality; Blake's tilting at his satanic windmills plays differently now, because while they may still seem ugly to us, they are no longer bizarre. This is the problem with using current emblematic objects, as J. G. Ballard does with abandoned Cape Canaveral launch pads and traffic islands. Declaring this way that "modernity" ends in unreal landscapes fixes the author in the moment, tied to aesthetic attitudes which date quickly. Hard SF has a more flinty view of external artifacts, often taking them matter-of-factly.

2001: A Space Odyssey, Stanley Kubrick's fruitful collaboration with Arthur C. Clarke, uses both major realms of hard SF—the near-future grittiness, and far-flung symbolism. In its symbolism and philosophical import science has the most impact, I feel.

Since the eighteenth century, science has been widely seen as a better way to understand our world than either myth or religion—two elements which, used at face value in fantastic fiction, typically yield fantasy. Hard SF favors a universe which cares nothing for us, yet furnishes wondrous perspectives, like an immense cathedral of an unfathomable alien faith.

In Poul Anderson's *Tau Zero*, a runaway starship cannot brake itself and so must accelerate forever, leaving our galaxy, boosting ever closer to the unreachable speed of light. As relativity theory dictates, time slows on board while the universe outside expands, galaxies age, and finally the expansion halts and an inevitable contraction begins. Against this exterior majesty Anderson contrasts the petty wrangles and sexual misadventures of the crew trapped in a cramped human vessel, responding only fitfully to the massive perspectives they witness. They pass through the inward collapse of the universe, through to the rebirth, scrapping and struggling all the way.

Anderson achieved this effect by using a technique of Olaf Stapledon. His first chapter covers a few hours, the second a few days, the third several weeks—a logarithmic progression in time. Each chapter has about the same wordage, which allows the reader enough time to get used to this new time span, then whisks her up another order of magnitude. New perspectives demand new literary techniques.

The hard SF symbolism of H.G. Wells' crab scuttling across a worn beach at the end of time announced that the young genre could talk about the biggest of questions. Immensity comes naturally to astronomers, who daily deal with events and distances which we literally cannot comprehend except through mathematical notation.

Even missions to our outer planets take for their planning, launch, and rendezvous a working scientist's lifetime. Everywhere, as science pushes on, time and space transcend our ready perceptions. With a taste for the huge, novels such as Stanislaw Lem's *Solaris* portray alien intelligences which are literally enormous (in this case, a planet-covering ocean which doesn't fit Darwinian ideas, to say the least). Lem's career has often dealt with science's limitations as hopelessly, human-centered, with no true credentials to talk about the world as it truly is—a posture owing much to the rather dated views of the philosopher David Hume.

A favorite device casting human mortality against the inexorable laws of the universe appears in Arthur Clarke's "Transit of Earth." Here the doomed astronaut witnesses the uncaring clockwork precision of planetary orbits, communicating his awe and dread back to people comfortably safe. This motif contrasts human social insulation with the distance assumed in the physical and biological sciences. This method appears in James Gunn's "Cave of Night," and Clarke has used it many times, notably in a story with an astronaut who seems doomed to crash back onto the moon in a spent rocket, and radios goodbye to his wife on Earth—but manages a solution at the last minute, a more typically pulp ending. Both "Transit of Earth" and Tom Godwin's "The Cold Equations" profit from not attempting a pleasant finish, remorselessly sticking with the assumptions of the story. The impersonality of the universe ultimately stands for its authority.

Immensity has a beauty all its own, one of the cliches of the field. The beautiful often demands the cultivated exclusion of natural forces, so artifacts emerge cool and serene, as in *2001*. The horrific is then the repressed return of those forces, the breakdown, as in so many disaster novels.

In contrast, we meet the very small in Paul Preuss's *Broken Symmetries* (particle physics and its mileau) and James Blish's "Surface Tension." Whatever the symbol—giant quasisexual spacecraft, divine aliens, Edenlike planets—many writers seem searching for the sense of strangeness. Robert Forward's *Dragon's Egg* explores life on a neutron star, with gravity so strong the atmosphere is an inch high. Conventional literature occasionally embraces the strange, as in William Golding's *The Inheritors* about Neanderthal and Cro-Magnon, and Richard Adams' *The Plague Dogs* with its passages told from a canine point of view.

Yet all this rational hardness gives over frequently to mysticism. Edgar Allen Poe's "A Descent into the Maelstrom" uses a natural, though exotic, phenomenon to reveal the arabesques of reality. His hero escapes by solving his problem rationally, and the experience unsettles his worldview. The concrete whipsaws us against the ineffable.

Awe can arise naturally from as simple a childhood question as: If the sun was an orange and the Earth a pea, how big would the solar system be? (About a mile.) While Darwin won the battle with religion in the nineteenth century, spirituality, after all, isn't as easy a target as organized religion; in fact, often they conflict. Transcendental beauty and awe are always with us in literature, from Lucretius' observation that exquisitely interconnected nature yields inexpressible joy. Sometimes this corkscrews into SF heroes who become the Messiah (*Dune, Stranger in a Strange Land*). At its best it gives vis-

tas beyond conventional literature, as in the images of ascending into new states in Clarke's *Childhood's End* and Greg Bear's *Blood Music*.

These novels echo the man I consider the first grand master of hard SF transcendentalism, Olaf Stapledon. From his first work, *Last and First Men*, through *Star Maker* and *Sirius*, he gave us cool condensates of pure imagination, uncluttered by the apparatus of novels—characters and incidents, talk and action—yet quite fictional. His imagination moved with a grave solemnity, seldom granting a nod toward the everyday. Stapledon had digested Darwin-Wallace evolution, together with the just-emerging view of stars, too, as evolutionary.

With graceful cadence, he paired the progression of intelligence as another element in the natural scheme, with the lives of stars from early compression to fiery death-throes, the slow massive workings of red giants and white dwarves—anthropomorphic names for vast, imponderable energies. Cosmic evolution from brute matter, up through stellar element-building, through simple primordial chemistry and into blossoming life, is a far more beautiful image than the popular view of evolution. Stapledon anticipated this in the 1930s, blending the nineteenth century flavor of Schopenhauer's philosophy of being with Spengler's clockworky cyclic history into a vision of man as "a fledgling caught in a brush fire."—certainly not the expansive, humanistic "measure of all things."

At times Stapledon seemed one of those "intellects vast and cool and unsympathetic" in H.G. Wells' unforgettable description of the Martians, itself the grandest nineteenth century hard SF novel. Stapledon directly inherited much in method and manner from Wells. Other British thinkers such as J.D. Bernal and Fred Hoyle follow this tradition. (Jules Verne became the forefather of the other face of hard SF, twentieth century optimistic technophilia.) Brian Aldiss termed Stapledon's work "great classical ontological epic prose poems." Yet *Last and First Men* against this sober canvas, the largest ever constructed in fiction, concludes that "Man himself, at the very least, is music, a brave theme that makes music also of its vast accompaniment, its matrix of storms and stars." This mirrors the tension in hard SF between its inhuman landscapes which dwarf us, and the fictional demand that makes people, especially their emotions, central. Stapledon's solution, fiction without people in the foreground, was extreme—and has outlasted innumerable works of humanistic merit.

How does hard SF sit in the recent cataloging of literature by critics—structuralist, post-modern, deconstructionist, etc.? To many SF writers, me included, "post-modern" is simply a signature of exhaustion. Its typical apparatus—self-reference, dollops of irony, self-conscious use of older genre devices, pastiche and parody—betrays a lack of invention. Some deconstructionists have attacked science itself as mere rhetoric, not an ordering of nature. I suspect they seek to reduce it to the status of the ultimately arbitrary humanities.

At the core of hard SF lies the experience of science, which conventional literature mostly ignores—though as J.G. Ballard remarked, the trouble with SF is often that it is not a literature won from experience. This means that hard SF is finally hostile to the current fashion in criticism, for it values its empirical ground. Deconstructionism's stress on a contradictory or self-contained internal differences in texts, rather than their link to reality, often merely leads to literature seen as empty word games.

Post-modernism seems to most hard SF writers as fiction about media-saturated cultures, with the attention span of MTV, and not about the deeper facets which make that culture—particularly, not about the implications of science seen up close. Postmodernist literary theorists have embraced some SF authors who display a conspicuous stylistic gloss—Ballard, William Gibson—because they write primarily about the surfaces of the technosphere which now envelopes us. This places these writers at the edge for hard SF, for the "info-universe" immersing us stems directly from advanced technology—though they often don't fathom the underlying ideas which produces the shiny technical surfaces.

"Cyberspace" is a realm inside computer spaces, which characters can inhabit. In Vernor Vinge's pioneering *True Names* and Charles Platt's *The Silicon Man* atmospheric weirdness dominates the mood. More often cyberspace is a magical realm with a high-tech gloss, as in Gibson's *Neuromancer*. Depicting computer-saturated futures is difficult if you actually don't have a clue how computers work—but it can make compelling reading, as in Gibson's "Johnny Mnemonic." Still relevant are earlier stories, such as Asimov's "The Last Word" and Gordon Dickson's "Computers Don't Argue."

Directly opposite this concern with the present, science fantasy uses the trappings of hard SF—spaceships, jargon, high tech ornaments—awash in the devices and thought-patterns of fantasy. Galactic cultures coexist with feudal planets, complete with their swords, queens, and quests. A near neighbor is hard SF, though—techno-empire SF, such as Larry Niven and Jerry Pournelle's *The Mote in God's Eye*. The science is right and the action supports conflict and military virtues as eternal features—plausible assumptions, alas.

Like other subgenres of fantastic literature, hard SF works in part because it is an ongoing discussion. Its authors speak of "playing the game"—getting striking but physically plausible scenes into their work, and being able to defend their extravagances with "hard" scientific arguments, even calculations. This resembles the pleasures of police procedural novels and classic puzzle mystery stories, with their meticulous accuracy of method and logic.

Genre readers immerse themselves in a system of thought, so that each fresh book or story is a further exploration of that system, mental play illuminated by all the reader has discovered before. Genres layer.

Science and technology are more complex systems than crime or international intrigue or westerns or romances, affording both wider and odder pleasures. The flipside of this is a daunting genre vernacular, making works somewhat unintelligible to the newcomer until he learns the ropes. With learned genre competency come the pleasures of cross-talk—the books speak to each other in an ongoing debate over big issues, such as our place in creation, the nature of consensual reality, etc. Both readers and writers form a kind of "virtual club" which inspires real feelings of companionship and loyalty.

So George Zebrowski's *Macrolife* speaks to Stapledon and Clarke and Aldiss; Joe Haldeman's *The Forever War* and Harry Harrison's *Bill, the Galactic Hero* answer Heinlein's *Starship Troopers*; Clarke and Charles Sheffield publish novels in the same year about building towers from Earth to high orbit; David Brin's *Earth* reflects the early ecological themes of George Stewart's *Earth Abides* and John Brunner's *Stand on Zanzibar*. The mathematical lattices of computer intelligences inform Rudy Rucker's *White Light*, the concepts evolving through Greg Bear's *Queen of Angels* and Charles Platt's *The Silicon Man*. John Varley's *Steel Beach* and Allen Steele's *Lunar Descent* take up from Heinlein's sense of the future as a frontier, rewarding hard-nosed ambition with head-spinning possibilities. Michael Kube-McDowell's *The Quiet Pools*, Roger McBride Allen's *Ring of Charon* and Thomas McDonough's *The Architects of Hyperspace* glance over their shoulders at galaxy-spanning epics of A.E. Van Vogt, E.E. Smith, and Jack Williamson. The long perspectives in time of Anderson's *The Boat of a Million Years* achieve a lofty yet warmly human view, as Brian Aldiss did in his Helliconia trilogy.

This contrasts strongly with "serious" fiction, which proceeds from canonical classics that supposedly stand outside of time, deserving of awe, great and intact by themselves. Genres are more like immense discussions, with ideas developed, traded, varied; players ring changes on each other—a jazz band, not a solo concert in a plush auditorium.

But hard SF and other genres are no less "serious," merely less solemn. I suspect readers of "serious" fiction are probably more likely to blame themselves if they find a book from the approved canon boring; a genre reader blames the writer.

Genre pleasures are many, but this quality of an on-going discussion may be the most powerful, enlisting lifelong devotion in its fans. In contrast to the Grand Canon view, genre reading satisfactions are a striking facet of modern democratic ("pop") culture. Hard SF writers have an unusual camaraderie, even within the genre. They produce more collaborations than other types of science fiction authors, and in the free trading of ideas often behave like scientists. Modern science itself shares many genre features of steadily developed ideas, communal feeling, and open discourse, especially in a time when papers in learned journals can have fifty authors.

I think hard SF ultimately is the voice of a class, the scientifically literate, which listens to a music they can hear best. Their needs are not met by conventional fiction, and won't be, for it caters to other classes, other cultures.

Hardness in fiction, whether SF or a police procedural novel, is a cultivated taste. In a nation of declining science-related skills, written hard SF may reach a shrinking audience, though its taste for high-tech imagery may continue to be widely influential.

Still, I hope its aesthetic goals may still occupy the center of the field—even though much recent SF has returned to the old styles, in which fidelity to scientific facts and world view are subordinated to conventional literary virtues of character or style or setting. In this sense, alas, hard SF may be a paradigm more often honored in the breech than not.

Barry N. Malzberg is the winner of the very first Campbell Memorial Award, a multiple Hugo and Nebula nominee, twice the winner of the Locus Award for Best Nonfiction Book, and the author of more than ninety books.

FROM THE HEART'S BASEMENT

by Barry N. Malzberg

DECADENCE

"Define it," said James Morrow after I had flung the word ("science fiction now is an exercise and a recursion in decadence"). And in one of those rare moments when the Prophet whispers in your ear, I said: "That state of the art at which form overtakes function." (Or as in the case of post-twelve tone composition, lack of form overtakes function.) Science fiction had become in the late 90s when I said this a self-referential and self-investigating exercise; the tropes, cues and formulations had become so involved and hermetic that the good old time religion, ad astra, deadpan extrapolation, integrated technology, could serve only as reference points. Alfred Bester was perhaps our first modern, post-Campbellian decadent giving light and life to Horace Gold and all the acolytes of *Galaxy*, but Bester really knew the territory, had periscoped it pretty well in between radio and comic book adventures in the 40s. Bester also had a real love for the junk, the downside, the grit of extrapolation, and he funneled that love through raunch and outrage. A comic book guy. No disrespect whatsoever. Shakespeare with his appropriated plots and bloody juxtapositions would have been a great story man for *Weird Science* even if his grasp of technology would have been necessarily shaky.

Decadence—and Bester had wild fun in the 50s, torturing junk plots and contrivances into poetic furioso, sending the Men Who Murdered Muhammed up and down their discrete time tube—is the key to any true understanding of Horace Gold's decade. But epiphany is on a very short fuse, and that decade looked very much like innovation at the time. Seemed to be purely innovative as the 40s had

been consolidated into the Conklin anthologies and almost beneath notice had become historical. But the illusion of ad astra, of course, persisted...what Campbell's central crew had thought they were doing in the 40s was now in the hands of Gold and his legions, who were working at inverting every astounding protocol and making clear that the downside of technology was not the fatuity of Kuttner's Proud Robot but something more ominous. Gully Foyle abandoned. A Bad Day For Sales. Richard Wilson's idiots from earth.

Thirty years after his collapse, marginalization, and sad death I remain as obsessed with Alfred Bester as I was in the 50s. And piece by piece the two novels and a dozen great short stories of that decade were landing on me as a series of astonishments which I could barely apprehend and knew I could never duplicate. Clearly he was aware of the secret life of this country as no literary writer of his time...his time machine, mad spacemen, crazed Ben Reich (no coincidence in that last name), his clanking, murderous robot. There was nothing comparable outside of his work, just as Sturgeon's Mr. Costello or Saucer of Loneliness had nothing comparable. "...And Now The News" preceded Oswald by seven years and Hinkley by a quarter of a century. No one in or out of science fiction had the clarity of that story, and it was twenty years past its publication that Scorcese's "Taxi Driver" brought that simple and terrible news to the world.

So to read the contents page of *Best American Short Stories* or the O. Henry Awards volumes of the 1950s is to see perhaps most significantly the awful missed opportunity in our literature. Kerouac might have grasped this truth, but Kerouac was as much an outsider as Bester (and ultimately he ended as badly). And by the time the vision of *On the Road* had reached the wider culture it was already severely dated, historic, a letter from Garcia. After Oswald, *On the Road* was sentiment.

This was not true of Bester, but he was essentially buried before he was buried, a ghostly, self-mocking Convention presence. But even after his decade, the science fiction he had influenced, at least in its better examples, was pushing forward even as it seemed to glance backward. Not only stylistically but thematically there seemed to be a crossing of borders.

Generalities are dangerous (this one too) but *Dune* and *The Moon is a Harsh Mistress* were the refractions of a world different from that of *Dragon in the Sea* or *Stranger in a Strange Land*. Thomas M. Disch's 1965 novel *The Genocides* infuriated Budrys, who saw it as a self-conscious exploitation of entropy as a metaphor. Disch never forgave him for this *Galaxy* review and celebrated Budrys' death in June 2008, preceding by less than three weeks Disch's more direct suicide. But Disch in that novel was still dealing with the traditional tropes of science fiction.

Michael Moorcock's *New Worlds* crew of the mid-to-late-1960s was not, and that was when the situation shifted. Technology was only the cause and effect of alienation; more intricate technology rendered alienation more intricate. That was Ballard's central issue, first in the novels and short stories of disaster ("The Drowned Giant," *The Crystal World*) before he moved on to the "condensed novels" of the late 60s, whose fragmented outrage and outraged fragmentation was labeled clearly as the product of television and the ravaging architecture which would turn the world into slow glass. Ballard was the most important writer ever to have emerged from the field: there was a roster of those who were equally important to science fiction (Bester, Pohl, Kornbluth, Sheckley, Klass). But from start to finish their science fiction was contained within the field, never reached even the slivers of general readership which, say, were reached by *Limbo*, a novel by the one-time *Galaxy* author Bernard Wolfe. Ballard got all the way out with *Crash, High-Rise,* and of course *Empire of the Sun*, and in that sense it could be argued that he abandoned the dialogue, was no longer addressing (as had "Terminal Beach") the essential material of science fiction.

Inside or out, however, the mission of Moorcock's *New Worlds* was to explain and explore the rancid consequence of the collision of science fiction with contemporary events. And within the field, in this country, the effects were immediate: spilling into the category were writers and anthology markets encouraging the anatomy of entropy in all of its phases, and the original anthologies *Orbit, New Dimensions, Nova,* and of course both *Dangerous Visions* anthologies represented a kind of outsourcing of this thematic material. Gardner Dozois publishing in *New Dimensions* and *Orbit* was then in his early career. He was not the best of the entropy peddlers at his young age (b.1947) but he might have been the most prototypical. Damon Knight, an acerbic and bitter guy who was plotting his own revenge against science fiction which he felt had trapped him, was perhaps the strongest advocate of this approach and, not surprisingly, *Orbit* was for the 40s and 50s readers and writers the most destructive influence.

Science fiction—here is its secret, pounding heart—always wanted to die as much as it wanted to live. Post-apocalyptic science fiction was substantively a metaphor for science fiction itself. Perhaps I will get to this next time.

And perhaps I will not.

Copyright © 2016 by Barry N. Malzberg

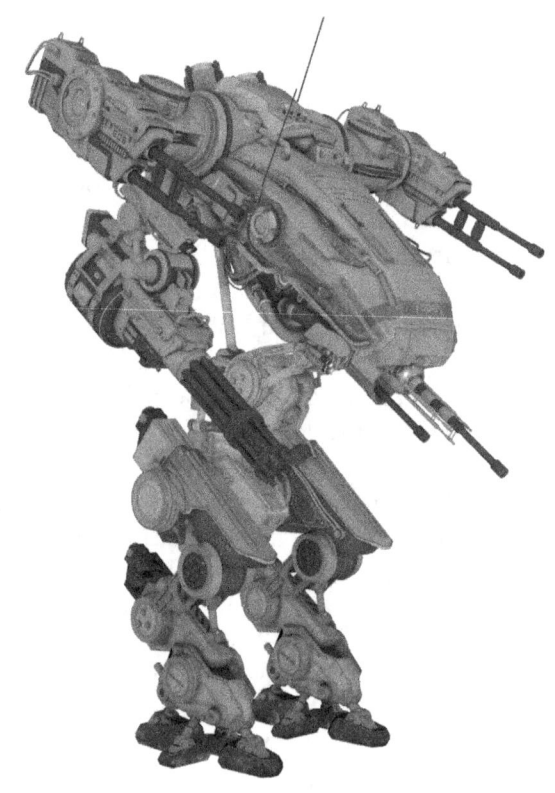

Joy Ward is the author of one novel. She has several stories in print, in magazines and in anthologies, and has also done interviews, both written and video, for other publications.

Robert J. Sawyer is the winner of the Hugo, the Nebula, Canada's Aurora, Spain's UPC, and Japan's Seuin-sho Awards. Canada's leading science fiction writer, he was recently given an honorary Doctor of Laws degree by the University of Winnipeg.

THE *GALAXY'S EDGE* INTERVIEW

Joy Ward interviews
Robert J. Sawyer

Robert J. Sawyer has won almost every award given in science fiction. He was kind enough to give us a few minutes for an interview at the 2015 Worldcon.

Joy Ward: How did you start writing?

Robert J. Sawyer: I was a science fiction fan from being a little kid. I was born in 1960. I grew up watching *Star Trek* and also watching the Apollo Space Program going to the moon. In 1968, my father took me to *2001: A Space Odyssey*, which was in its first run in theaters. I got fascinated by the fact that there was this literature about the future. Very shortly thereafter, I realized people wrote these stories professionally. From about ten years old, it was something I wanted to do—write science fiction stories. I have been very, very grateful that it has been doable as a career.

I was living in Toronto, Canada, and that was an interesting fact that it didn't matter where I lived to do this. There are all kinds of professions where you have to go somewhere. If you want to be a film or TV star you have to go to Hollywood. Subsequent to my youth, if you wanted to be in computer science you probably went to Silicon Valley. But you could be an author anywhere. I loved the notion of the portability of the profession. I never wanted to have a nine-to-five job. I never wanted to have anything anybody would call a career with a retirement date built into it. This seemed to be the ideal itinerant thing to do with one's life.

JW: What's the first thing you got published?

RJS: My very first published work was in my university's literary magazine. It was a literary annual called "The White Wall Review," from Ryerson University in Toronto. Ed Greenwood, who went on to be a very major fantasy and Dungeons & Dragons author (he's a Tor author), was two years ahead of me at that university and was the editor of the magazine. He was sympathetic to "genre" contributions, even though it was the literary review. My first story, a fantasy actually, not a science fiction story, was selected for inclusion. That was the start.

JW: So that was the first time you saw your work in print…

RJS: Yes and there's a typo in the last line of the story, and they left my middle initial out. I've always written as "Robert J. Sawyer" in homage to Arthur C. Clarke and Robert A. Heinlein and James T. Kirk—and there's my middle initial missing. They left a word out of the last line of the story. So my first experience was, oh, there are frustrations. This is not a dream that is easily realized. But nonetheless it was intoxicating to be in print. It had been a goal. I was only twenty when it first appeared…sorry, I was nineteen and it was something I wanted to have it happen over and over again.

It is funny for me to use that adjective, because I don't drink. I guess whatever highs I've had in my life have come from either reading or writing transformative fiction. It has always been my greatest pleasure, reading a good book. People sometimes say I've read a lot about life prolongation and they ask why I want to live forever and I say, "Simply, there are just so many books that I haven't read and they keep writing more! There's no way I'll ever catch up!"

JW: What was your first professional publication?

RJS: My first professional publication, my first professional sale—that is one SFWA recognized, was not a print sale. The Strassenburgh Planetarium in Rochester, New York had a contest in the summer of 1980, judged by Isaac Asimov, to choose a story to be adapted into a planetarium star show. Mine did not win. The winner turned out to be a lovely little vignette that was not at all suitable for making a planetarium star show out of. It was charming, and the producers realized that they needed something else other than what Asimov had selected. They did adapt the vignette. They had decided to buy two other stories and do a trilogy—a star show that had three science fiction visions of the future in it. The producers had liked my entry even if the good doctor had not. So they reached out to me and asked if they could buy the rights to do it, and they did. It was performed one hundred and eighty-six times in the summer of 1980 in Rochester, New York. I went to see it several times. I dragged indulgent friends to see it repeatedly.

It was very interesting because I was studying Radio and Television Arts at Ryerson University at the same time, with a goal to becoming a screenwriter. That was my aspiration: to write film and television science fiction, not to write novels. So this was my first taste of something actually being produced. I think I would have gone down that route, had it not been for the fact that the year I graduated, 1982, from the top broadcasting program in Canada, was the first year that the CBC, the Canadian Broadcasting Corporation, had had massive layoffs for the first time in its history. There were no jobs, not even beginners' jobs, to be found in the broadcasting industry. So I had to do something else with my science fictional visions. I turned back to print. That took on a life of its own and it was many decades before I came back to scriptwriting.

I guess I really started to be noticed when I was doing short stories for *Amazing Stories* in the 1980s, and particular in the summer of 1988. I had a cover story novelette in *Amazing Stories* with a beautiful Bob Eggleton cover, which I loved so much that I actually bought the original art from him. It was a marriage made in heaven. It still hangs in my bedroom—the original painting. That story, "Golden Fleece," I expanded from a novelette into a short novel, 60,000 words. You can't sell those these days. But I used the novella, the novelette, and the fact that it had been the cover story to attract an agent to represent the expansion.

It's a long time ago now, but it was absolutely lovely, partly because this time there were no typos. All the words were there. My "J" was there, and the Bob Eggleton cover painting was spectacular. It was a wonderful experience! Some of my other friends were publishing in *Asimov's* and *Fantasy & Science Fiction* at the time and even one person in *Analog*, which had bigger circulations than *Amazing* at the time. But none of them had had a cover story. I may not have hit the top market, but I got the cover and that let me hold my head up high in what was the burgeoning Toronto SF community of that day.

It was a damn good story. It was as simple as that. I was very ambitious. It actually probably was a compressed novel. There were so many ideas and bits of business in it. I worked very, very hard on it. It was very wondrous for me that the editor at the time, a fellow named Patrick Lucian Price, had taken a liking to my work. I owe an awful lot of what my career turned out to be to that magazine editor who championed me early on.

It made me feel wonderful! It made me feel that I was on my way!

I definitely knew that the next step had to be a novel. As much as they had actually paid me well for that novella—$1,250 for that novelette! It was a lot of money for a short work. But you had to have a book, if you were going to be a serious writer in this field. I knew that I had to proceed to write books. I didn't have any idea that I was going to be able to write more than one but I was embarking on a career that I had to test and at least see if I could write and sell a book to a major U.S. publisher.

JW: How did you decide what was going to be your first novel?

RJS: It was because this cover story novelette had been received so well; it just seemed natural to expand it. Also, two of my friends in Toronto, Terence M. Green and Andrew Weiner, both had taken stories of theirs, one from *Fantasy & Science Fiction* in Terry's case, and one from *Asimov's* in Andrew's case, and expanded them to their first novels. So it had seemed like this was the way to do it! The novel isn't coming cold to an editor. You can say, here, it is, an expansion of a work that has already proven to have a certain degree of marketability.

JW: Please tell me about one of the high points in your life involving writing?

RJS: I was very gratified about ten years ago when I got a letter from a young woman who'd just finished her PhD in geology. She had started out by studying paleontology, a science she'd gotten interested in by reading my novel, *Calculating God*. That came out fifteen years ago now. She'd read it in high school and hadn't had any interest in being a paleontologist until she read my book. Ultimately, after an undergrad in paleontology she'd gravitated toward pure geology. That was an enormously satisfying moment to realize that somebody's whole career and a decade of study, had come out of the inspiration that they had taken from something I'd written.

It made me feel quite like I was contributing something to the world other than entertainment, and that was nice.

I think science fiction serves an important social purpose, a societal purpose.

JW: Another high point of your career?

RJS: Oh, it was winning the Hugo Award for Best Novel of the Year. There's no question about that. We're here on the eve of this year's Hugo Award ceremony and twelve years ago, I was the lucky guy to take home what George R. R. Martin, who presented my Hugo to me, called "the big one." There's no question that nothing before or since has equaled that. I can't imagine anything that could.

It meant that my readers had decided that I had done the job I'd set out to do better than anybody else had done it in the previous year. There's nothing more gratifying than actually having satisfied customers.

It made me feel terrific!

It made me feel that this very financially risky, career path, eschewing a 9 to 5 job, a pension, benefits package—had been the right choice to make.

JW: Where do you see science fiction going?

RJS: You ask where science fiction is going. Will there be science fiction as a separate category of publishing in ten years? When I started publishing with Ace Books, that was the early 90s, and Ace did six titles a month then. They do six titles a month now. Back then, it was five science fiction books and one fantasy book. Now it is five fantasy books and one science fiction book. So, if we extrapolate forward another decade or two, will there be any science fiction at all on their list? Two months ago, there were five fantasy novels and one alternate history novel. We can argue academically that alternate history is a subset of science fiction, but to most of the world it is not perceived as such. In other words, Ace Science Fiction had a month where they did no science fiction. That's sort of like the summer where the snow doesn't melt, where you've started the Ice Age. We may be falling into a science fictional ice age. There will be science fictional properties published as mainstream. Andrew Weir's *The Martian* is a pure quill science fiction novel that says science fiction nowhere on the cover.

I dislike the trend toward endless series. I think it is bad creatively for writers. I think it is bad economically for writers. So many of my friends have been dumped by their publishers because Volume four, five, six in a series did not perform well. When they say, "I'll write something different," the publisher will say basically, "But you didn't have fans; that series did. Those fans dried up." So, so many publishers push to create a series brand. It is very easy to sell the next book in an ongoing series. So you end up with writers who were extraordinarily cutting edge early on, like Orson Scott Card who is still mining the Enderverse thirty years later, instead of giving something new. I don't think that's good for the field.

JW: What else is not good for the field?

RJS: The consolidation of publishers. The fewer markets for us to sell our work. Ace and Roc used to be two separate imprints, two separate companies. Now they are all consolidated under Penguin. Penguin and Random House used to be two separate companies. Del Rey and Bantam, which were consolidated, were two separate companies. Now Ace and Roc and Del Rey and Bantam are all the same company. So what used to be four possible buyers for a science fiction novel, which let you have some competition amongst tastes, and competition for getting a better price for your work, have consolidated to essentially one buyer. That is very unfortunate for authors. I think also, very unfortunate for having a plurality of works and a variety of voices in the field. It is no coincidence that the huge debates about diversity in the science fiction and fantasy genres have risen up precisely in the era of consolidation of publishing companies. When you have a single buyer, it is not surprising that you have a limited taste.

There should be more diversity than there is. There is a lack of diversity. You would think there would be more diversity than there is. When Warner was not part of Hachette, Warner used to do the Warner Aspect first novel competition. Betsy Mitchell bought Nalo Hopkinson's first novel—she's a woman of color. She was the first winner. The second winner was Karin Lowachee, also a person of color. There used to be an opportunity to do that sort of thing. We don't see that happening on an ongoing basis anymore.

JW: You are known for excellent background research.

RJS: It isn't possible to have too much science in science fiction, like it isn't possible to have too much sex in pornography. It is what it is about. I am a research junkie. To be perfectly honest, the only reason I write my novels is to support my research habit. I love being able to follow in whatever vagary of depth any topic that interests me for as long as I want and then completely change what it is that I am pursuing. There are not many jobs that will let you do that. I like to say that being a hard science fiction writer is like being a graduate student who gets to change his or her thesis topic at a whim, as often as he or she wishes. For science fiction to be taken seriously, it has to be realistic. It has to be plausible. I think it is important that it be taken seriously. Any social commentary it can bring to the table can be easily dismissed if the underlying science behind the future that is being portrayed can be easily dismissed. The scaffolding is the science that lets you say, "No, here is something realistic and important that you should be paying attention to."

I am learning things all the time! There's a line from classic *Star Trek* where a woman named Rayna says she's interested in the totality of the universe, and anything else is a betrayal of the intellect. That's what I'm interested in. This genre lets me explore just about everything that exists, did exist, or ever could exist! I can't ask for a bigger platform than that.

JW: Well if you weren't doing this, what would you be doing? Where do you go next? What's the difference for you between doing film or video and doing a book?

RJS: The biggest difference is that at this stage of my career, everything that I write gets published. At this stage of anyone's career in film or television, most of what they write never gets produced. You get paid very well for development work, you get paid very well for drafts that are discarded, you get paid very well to write pilots that nobody ever sees. So you do one for economic reasons, and you do the other because you actually want your vision to be realized. I wish the twain met more often, but they are very different paths.

JW: How do you want to be remembered? You'll be writing for a while yet.

RJS: I don't know that. I don't know that. And I think actually far too many authors continue writing after they've had anything interesting to say, or have the patience to take the time to say it well. So I don't know that. If this twenty-third novel, *Quantum Night*, turns out to be my last, either due to the vicissitudes of the market place or because my own interests shift to somewhere else, I'll be content. I've won fifty-four awards for my fiction. I've won the Hugo, the Nebula, the John W. Campbell Memorial Award, thirteen Aurora awards, Lifetime Achievement Award from the Canadian Science Fiction and Fantasy Association, the top science fiction awards in Japan, China, France, and Spain How do I want to be remembered? As an accomplished and prolific hard science fiction writer who always gave his readers value for their money.

JW: What do the awards mean to you?

RJS: The first one that was really major was winning the Nebula Award. What it meant was, as my editor at the time, John Douglas, put it, "You've gone overnight from being a promising newcomer to an established, bankable name." Since I won the Nebula in 1996, I have not had any economic worries and I don't antici-

pate any for the rest of my life. It meant that I was a commercially viable author in a very competitive industry. The Hugo, which was subsequent to that, simply added luster to that, but the reality was that it was the major award wins that made it possible for me to be the sole income earner for my family, for decades now, and who have enjoyed a pleasant and prosperous existence on this ball of dust.

JW: What advice would you give young writers?

RJS: Write things that you are passionate about. Never ask what's selling, what's hot, what's the trend, what should I be doing? Write the things you most passionately care about. Write them as surpassingly well as you can. Put everything you can into your work. Try to become a distinctive voice in the landscape. Don't emulate others. Don't do it for commercial reasons. If you are good at what you do, in all likelihood you will find both artistic and economic fulfillment. If you decide that all you want to do is to churn out carbon copies of things that already exist, you will probably find it a rather empty life.www

I have had things that I thought were worth sharing with the world. I think having people talk about one's work after you've gone is at least as important as having them talking about you after you've gone. It is a contribution to human culture that transcends your circle of acquaintances. I am proud to have made my little tiny piece of that.

You know, to be perfectly blunt, my younger brother died two years ago. He died of lung cancer. He didn't expect to be checking out when he checked out. But when he did, he said, "In the end, I can't complain. It wasn't as long a life as I wanted it to be, but it was a good life." Just before he died, he won an Emmy award from the International Academy of Television Arts and Sciences. He'd achieved the top distinction in his career. There'll always be an entry on him in the databases and encyclopedias of his profession. They say you're not dead when the people remember you, but the reality is that the people who remember you will soon be dead too. However, work can live on for centuries. That's the only immortality outside of science fiction that any of us have hitherto obtained.

Copyright © 2016 by Joy Ward

SERIALIZATION
THE LONG TOMORROW

by Leigh Brackett
Phoenix Pick, 2012
Trade Paperback: 202 pages.
ISBN: 978-1-61242-013-4

Leigh Brackett was one of the greats. She began writing in the pulps, where her Martian tales rivaled those of Edgar Rice Burroughs. Hollywood called, and she wrote major screenplays for Humphrey Bogart (The Big Sleep) *and John Wayne* (Rio Bravo). *Hollywood paid better, but science fiction was her first love and she kept coming back to it, resurrecting her hero, Eric John Stark, for three novels in the 1970s. She also wrote the initial screenplay for* The Empire Strikes Back. *Leigh and her husband, science fiction writer Edmond Hamilton, were co-Guests of Honor at the 1964 Worldcon. We are thrilled to bring you the serialization of Leigh's* The Long Tomorrow.

THE LONG TOMORROW

Part Four

by Leigh Brackett

ELEVEN

The main square of Refuge was wide and grassy, with trees to make shade there in the summer. The church, austere and gaunt and authoritative, dominated the square from its northern side. On the east and west were lesser buildings, stores, houses, a school, but on the southern side the town hall stood, not as tall as the church but broader, spreading out into wings that housed the courtrooms, the archives, the various offices necessary to the orderly running of a township. The shops and the public buildings were now closed and dark, and Len noticed that some of the shopkeepers had put up their storm shutters.

The square was full. It seemed as though all the men and half the women of Refuge were there, standing around on the wet grass or moving back and forth to talk, and there were others there, farmers in from the country, a handful of New Mennonites. A sort of pulpit stood in the middle of the square. It was a permanent structure, and it was used chiefly by visiting preachers at open-air prayer meetings, but political speakers used it too at the time of a local or national election. Mike Dulinsky was going to use it tonight. Len remembered what Gran had told him about the old days, when a speaker could talk to everybody in the country at once through the teevee boxes, and he wondered with a quivering thrill of excitement if tonight was the start of the long road back to that kind of a world—Mike Dulinsky talking to a handful of people in a village named Refuge on the dark Ohio. He had read enough of Judge Taylor's history books to know that that was the way things happened sometimes. His heart began to beat faster, and he walked nervously back and forth, vaguely determined that Dulinsky should talk, no matter who tried to stop him.

The preacher, Brother Meyerhoff, came out of the side door of the church. Four of the deacons were with him, and a fifth man Len did not recognize until they came into the light of one of the bonfires that burned there. It was Judge Taylor. They passed on and Len lost them in the crowd, but he was sure they were heading for the speaker's stand. He followed them, slowly. He was about halfway across the grassy open when Mike Dulinsky came from the other side and there was a general motion toward the center, and the crowd suddenly clotted up so he couldn't get through it without pushing. There were half a dozen men with Dulinsky, carrying lanterns on long poles. They put these in brackets around the speaker's pulpit, so that it stood up like a bright column in the darkness. Dulinsky climbed up and began to speak.

"Tonight," he said, "we stand at a crossroads."

Somebody pulled at Len's sleeve, and he turned around. It was Esau, nodding to him to come away from the crowd.

"There's boats on the river," Esau said, when they were out of earshot. "Coming this way. You warn him, Len, I got to get back to the docks." He looked furtively around. "Is Amity here?"

"I don't know. The judge is."

"Oh Lord," said Esau. "Listen, I got to go. If you see Amity, tell her I won't be around for a while. She'll understand."

"Will she? Anyway, I thought you were bragging how nobody could—"

"Oh, shut up. You tell Dulinsky they're coming. Watch yourself, Len. Don't get in any more trouble than you can help."

"It looks to me," said Len, "as though you're the one in trouble. If I don't see Amity, I'll give the message to her father."

Esau swore and disappeared into the dark. Len began to edge his way through the crowd. They were standing quiet, listening, very grave and intent. Dulinsky was talking to them with a passionate sincerity. This was his one time, and he was giving everything he had to it.

"—that was eighty years ago. No danger menaces us now. Why should we continue to live in the shadow of a fear for which there is no longer any cause?"

A ripple of sound, half choked, half eager, ran across the crowd. Dulinsky gave it no time to die.

"I'll tell you why!" he shouted. "It's because the New Mennonites climbed into the saddle and have hung onto the government ever since. They don't like growth, they don't like change. Their creed rejects them both, and so does their greed. Yes, I said greed! They're farmers. They don't want to see the trading centers like Refuge get rich and fat. They don't want a competitive market, and above all they don't want people like us pushing them out of their nice seats in Congress where they can make all the laws. So they forbid us to build a new warehouse when we need it. Now do you think that's fair or right or godly? You there, Brother Meyerhoff, do you say the New Mennonites should tell us all how to live, or should our own Church of Holy Thankfulness have something to say about it too?"

Brother Meyerhoff answered, "It hasn't to do with them or with us. It has to do with you, Dulinsky, and you're talking blasphemy!"

A cry of voices, mostly female, seconded him. Len pushed himself to the foot of the stand. Dulinsky was leaning over, looking at Meyerhoff. There were beads of sweat on his forehead.

"Blaspheming, am I?" he demanded. "You tell me where."

"You've been to church. You've read the Book and listened to the sermons. You know how the Almighty cleansed the land of cities, and bade His children that He saved to walk henceforth in the path of righteousness, to love the things of the spirit and not the things of the flesh! In the words of the prophet Nahum—"

"I don't want to build a city," said Dulinsky. "I want to build a warehouse."

There was a nervous tittering, quickly hushed. Meyerhoff's face was crimson above his beard. Len mounted the steps and spoke to Dulinsky, who nodded. Len climbed down again. He wanted to tell Dulinsky to lay off the New Mennonites, but he did not quite dare for fear of giving himself away.

"Who," asked Dulinsky of Meyerhoff, "has been telling you about cities?" He paused, and then he pointed and said, "Is it you, Judge Taylor?"

In the glare of the lanterns, Len saw that Taylor's face was oddly pale and strained. His voice, when he spoke, was quiet but it rang all over the square.

"There is an amendment to the Constitution of the United States that forbids you to do this. No amount of talk will change that, Dulinsky."

"Ah," said Dulinsky, in a satisfied voice as though he had made Judge Taylor fall into some trap, "that's where you're wrong. Talk is exactly what *will* change it. If enough people talk, and talk loud enough and long enough, that amendment will be changed so that a man can build a warehouse if he needs it to shelter flour or hides, or a house if he needs it to shelter his family." He raised his voice in a sudden shout. "You think about that, you people! Your own kids have had to leave Refuge, and more and more of them will have to go, because they can't build any more houses here when they get married. Am I right?"

He got a response on that. Dulinsky grinned. Out on the dark edges of the crowd a man appeared, and then another and another, coming softly from the direction of the river. And Meyerhoff said, in a voice shaking with anger, "Always, in every age, the unbeliever has prepared the way for evil."

"Maybe," said Dulinsky. He was looking out over Meyerhoff's head, to the edges of the crowd. "And I'll admit that I'm an unbeliever." He glanced down at Len, giving him the warning, while the crowd gasped over that. Then he went on, fast and smooth.

"I'm an unbeliever in poverty, in hunger, in misery. I don't know anybody who does believe in those things, except the New Ishmaelites, but I can't recall we ever thought much of them. In fact, we drove 'em out. I'm an unbeliever in taking a healthy growing child and strapping it down with bands so it won't get any taller than somebody thinks it should. I—"

Judge Taylor brushed past Len and mounted the steps. Dulinsky looked surprised and stopped in midsentence. Taylor gave him one burning glance and said, "A man can make anything he wants to out of words." He turned to the crowd. "I'm going to give you a fact, and then we'll see if Dulinsky can talk it away. If you break the township law it won't affect Refuge alone. It will affect all the country around it. Now, the New Mennonites are peaceful folk and their creed forbids them from violence. They will proceed by due process of law, no matter how long it takes. But there are other sects in the countryside, and their beliefs are different. They look on it as their duty to take up the cudgel for the Lord."

He paused, and in the stillness Len could hear the breathing of the people.

"You'd better think twice," said Taylor, "before you provoke them into taking it up against you."

There was a burst of applause from the outer edge of the crowd. Dulinsky asked scornfully, "Who are you afraid of, Judge—the farmers or the Shadwell men?" He leaned out over the rail and beckoned. "Come on up here, you Shads, up where we can see you. You don't have to be afraid, you're brave men. I got a lad here who knows how brave you are. Len, climb up here a minute."

Len did as he was told, avoiding Judge Taylor's eyes. Dulinsky pushed him to the rail.

"Some of you know Len Colter. I sent him to Shadwell this morning on business. Tell us what kind of a welcome you gave him, you Shads, or are you ashamed?"

The crowd began to mutter and turn around.

"What's the matter?" cried a deep, rough voice from the background. "Didn't he like the taste of Shadwell mud?" The Shadwell men all laughed, and then another voice, one that Len remembered only too well, called to him, "Did you give them our message?"

"Yes," said Dulinsky. "Give the people that message, Len. Say it real loud, so they can all hear."

Judge Taylor said suddenly, under his breath, "You'll regret this night." He ran down the steps.

Len glared out into the shadows. "They're going to stop you," he told the people of Refuge. "The Shads

won't let you grow. That's why they're here tonight." His voice went up a notch until it cracked. "I don't care who's afraid of them," he said, "I'm not." He jumped over the rail onto the ground and charged into the crowd. All the helpless rage of the morning was back on him a hundredfold, and he did not care what anybody else did, or what happened to him. He butted his way through until a path was suddenly opened for him and the Shadwell men were standing in a bunch in front of him. Dulinsky's voice was shouting something in which the names of Shadwell and Refuge were coupled together with the word fear. The crowd was beginning to move. A woman was screaming. The Shadwell men were pulling clubs out from under their coats. Len sprang like a panther. A great roar went up from the crowd, and the riot was on.

Len bore his man down and pounded him. Legs churned around them and people fell over them. There was a lot of screaming now, and women were running away out of the square. Clubs, fists, and boots flailed wildly. Somebody hit Len on the back of the head. The world turned upside down for a minute, and when it steadied again he was staggering along in the midst of a little boiling whirlpool of hard-breathing men, hanging onto somebody's coat and punching blindly with his free hand. The whirlpool spun and heaved and threw him up against a shuttered window and passed on. He stayed there, confused and shaking his head, blowing blood out of his nose. The crowd had broken up. The lanterns still burned around the pulpit in the middle of the square, but there was nobody in it now, and nothing left on the grassy space around it but some hats and some gouged-out places in the turf. The fighting had moved off. He could hear it streaming away down the streets and alleys that led to the docks. He grunted and began to run after it. He was glad Pa could not see him now. He felt hot and queer inside, and he liked it. He wanted to fight some more.

By the time he reached the docks the Shadwell men were piling into their boats as fast as they could, shaking their fists and cursing. The Refuge men were all lined up at the water's edge, helping them. Three or four Shads were in the river and being hauled up into the boats. The air rang with hoots and catcalls. Mike Dulinsky was right in the middle of it, his good dark coat torn and his hair on end, and a splatter of blood down his shirt from a cut mouth. "You going to stop us, are you?" he was yelling at the Shadwell men. "You going to tell Refuge what to do?"

The men on either side of Dulinsky caught him suddenly and hoisted him up onto their shoulders and cheered him. The Shadwell men pulled slowly and sullenly out into the dark river. When they were out of sight the crowd turned, still carrying Dulinsky and cheering, to where the fires burned around the framework of the warehouse. They marched round and round, and the guards cheered too. Len watched them, feeling dizzy but triumphant. Then, looking around, he saw a blaze of light in the direction of the traders' compound. He stared at it, frowning, and in the intervals of the noise behind him he could hear the distant voices of men and the whickering of horses. He began to walk toward the compound.

Lanterns and torches burned all around to give light. The men were bringing their teams out of the stables and harnessing them, and going over their gear, and getting the wagons ready to go. Len watched a minute or two, and all the feeling of triumph and excitement left him. He felt tired, and his nose hurt.

He saw Fisher and went up to him, standing by the head of the team while Fisher worked.

"Why is everybody going?" he asked.

Fisher gave him a long, stern look from under the brim of his broad hat.

"The farmers went out of here primed for trouble," he said. "They'll bring it, and we don't aim to wait."

He made sure his reins were clear and climbed up onto the seat. Len stood aside, and Fisher looked down at him, in something the same way Pa had looked so long ago.

"I thought better of you, Len Colter," Fisher said. "But them that picks up a burning brand will get burned by it. The Lord have mercy on you!"

He shook the reins and shouted, and his wagon creaked and moved, and the other wagons rolled, and Len stood looking after them.

TWELVE

Two o'clock of a hot, still day. The men were laying up sheeting boards on the north and east sides of the warehouse, working in the shade. Refuge was quiet, so quiet that the sound of the hammers rang out like bells on a Sabbath morning. Most of the shipping was gone from the docks, and the wharves were empty.

Esau said, "Do you think they'll come?"

"I don't know." Len looked searchingly at the distant roofs of Shadwell across the river, and up and down the wide stretch of water. He didn't know exactly what he was looking for, Hostetter, a friendly face, anything to break the emptiness and the sense of waiting. All morning since before sunup, cartloads of women and children had been leaving the town, and there were some men with them too, and bundles of household goods.

"They won't do anything," said Esau. "They wouldn't dare."

His voice carried no conviction. Len glanced at him and saw that his face was drawn and nervous. They were standing at the door of the office, not doing anything, just feeling the heat and the quietness. Dulinsky had gone up into the town, and Len said, "I wish he'd come back."

"He's got men out on the roads. If there's any news, we'll be the first to know it."

"Yes," said Len. "I reckon."

The hammers rang sharp on the new yellow wood. Along the edges of the warehouse site, well back in the trees, men loitered and watched. There were more of them on the docks, restless, uneasy, gathering in little groups to talk and then breaking up again, moving back and forth. They kept looking sidelong at the office, and at Len and Esau standing in the doorway, and at the men working on the warehouse, but they did not come close or speak to them. Len did not like that. It made him feel alone and conspicuous, and it worried him because he could feel the doubt and uncertainty and apprehension of these men who were up against something new and did not quite know what to do about it. From time to time a jug of corn was pulled out of a hiding place behind a stump or a stack of barrels, passed around, and put away again, but only one or two of them were drunk.

On impulse, Len stepped to the end of the dock and shouted to a group standing under a tree and talking. "What's the news from town?"

One of them shook his head. "Nothing yet." He was one who had shouted the loudest for Dulinsky last night, but today his face showed no enthusiasm. Suddenly he stooped and picked up a stone and threw it at a little gang of boys who were skulking in the background watching hopefully for trouble. "Get out of here!" he yelled at them. "This ain't no game for your amusement. Go on, git!"

They went, but not far. Len returned to the doorway. It was very hot, very still. Esau shuffled, kicking his heel against the doorpost.

"Len."

"What?"

"What'll we do if they do come?"

"How do I know? Fight, I guess. See what happens. How do I know?"

"Well, I know one thing," said Esau defiantly. "I ain't going to get my neck broke for Dulinsky. The hell with that."

"All right, you figure something." There was an anger in Len now, a vague thing as yet, and undirected, but enough to make him irritable and impatient. Perhaps it was because he was afraid, and that made him angry. But he knew the way Esau's thoughts were running, and he didn't want to have to go through every step of it out loud.

"You bet I'll figure something," said Esau. "You bet I will. It's his warehouse, not mine. Let him fight for it. He sure wouldn't risk his skin for anything of mine. I—"

"Shut up," said Len. "Look."

Judge Taylor was coming along the dock. Esau swore nervously and slid back through the door, out of sight. Len waited, conscious that the men were watching, as though what happened might have great significance.

Taylor came up to the door and stopped. "Tell Mike I want to see him," he said.

Len answered, "He isn't here."

The judge looked at him, deciding whether or not he was lying. There was a pinched grayness about the corners of his mouth, and his eyes were curiously hard and bright.

"I've come," he said, "to offer Mike his last chance."

"He's somewhere up in the town," said Len. "Maybe you can find him there."

Taylor shook his head. "It's the Lord's will," he said, and turned and walked away. At the corner of the office he stopped and spoke again. "I warned you, Len. But none are so blind as those who will not see."

"Wait," said Len. He went up to the judge and looked into his eyes, and shivered. "You know something. What is it?"

"The Lord's will," said the judge, "will be made clear to you when it is time."

Len reached out and caught him by the collar of his fine cloth coat and shook him. "Speak for yourself," he said angrily. "The Lord must be sick to death of everybody hiding behind Him. Nothing happens in this town that you don't have a finger in. What is it?"

Some of the fey light went out of Taylor's eyes. He looked down with a kind of shocked surprise at Len's hands laid roughly upon him, and Len let him go.

"I'm sorry," he said. "But I want to know."

"Yes," said Judge Taylor quietly, "you want to know. That was always your trouble. Didn't I tell you to find your limit before it was too late?"

His face softened, became compassionate and full of a genuine sorrow. "It's too bad, Len. I could have loved you like my own son."

"What have you done?" asked Len, moving a step closer, and the judge answered, "There will be no more cities. There is a law, and the law must be obeyed."

"You're scared," said Len, in a slow, astonished voice. "I understand now, you're scared. You think if a city grows up here the bombs will come again, and you'll be under them. Did you tell the farmers you wouldn't try to stop them if—"

"Hush," said the judge, and held up his hand.

Len turned to listen. So did the men under the trees and along the docks. Esau came out from the doorway. And at the warehouse, one by one the hammers stopped.

There was a sound of singing.

It was faint, but that was only because it was still a long way off. It was deep, and sonorous, a masculine sound, martial and somehow terrifying, coming with the solemn inevitability of a storm that does not stop or swerve. Len could not make out any words, but after he had listened for a minute he knew what they were. Mine eyes have seen the glory of the coming of the Lord. "Good-by, Len," said the judge, and was gone, walking with his head up high and his face white and stern in the heat of the July sun.

"We've got to go," whispered Esau. "We've got to get out of here."

He bolted back into the office, and Len could hear his feet clattering up the wooden stairs to the loft. Len hesitated a minute. Then he began to run, up toward the town, toward the distant, oncoming hymn. I have read a fiery gospel writ in burnished rows of steel…Glory! Glory! Hallelujah, His truth is marching on. A tight, cold knot of fear cramped up in Len's belly, and the air turned icy against his skin. The men along the docks and under the trees began to move too, straggling up by other ways, uncertainly at first and then faster, until they were running too. People had come out of their houses. Women, old men, children, listening, shouting at each other and at the men passing in the street, asking what it was, what was going to happen. Len came into the square, and a cart rushed past him so close that the foam from the horse's bit spattered him. There was a whole family in it, the man whipping up the horse and yelling, the women screaming, the kids all clinging together and crying. There was a scattering of people in the square, some heading toward the main north road, some running around aimlessly, women asking if anybody had seen their husbands or their boys, asking, always asking, what is it, what's happening? Len dodged through them and ran out on the north road.

Dulinsky was out on the edge of town, where the wide road ran between fields of wheat almost ripe for the cutting. There were perhaps two hundred men with him, armed with clubs and iron bars, with rifles and duck guns, with picks and frows. They looked grim and anxious. Dulinsky's face, burned brick red by the sun, was only ruddy on the surface. Underneath it was white. He kept wiping his hands on his trousers, one after the other, shifting his grip on the heavy club he held. Len came up beside him. Dulinsky glanced at him but did not speak. His attention was northward, where a solid yellow-brown wall of dust advanced, spreading across the road and into the wheat on either side. The sound of the hymn came out of it, and a rhythmic thud and trample of feet, and across its leading edge there was a pricking here and there of brilliance, as though some bright thing of metal caught the sun.

"It's our town," said Len. "They've got no right in it. We can beat 'em."

Dulinsky wiped his face oil his shirt sleeve. He grunted. It might have been a question or a laugh. Len looked around at the Refuge men.

"They'll fight," he said.

"Will they?" said Dulinsky.

"They were all for you last night."

"That was last night. This is now."

The wall of dust rolled up, and it was full of men. It stopped, and the dust blew away or settled, but the men remained, standing in a great heavy solid blot across the road and in the trampled wheat. The spots of brilliance became scythe blades, and corn knives, and here and there a gun barrel. "Some of them must have walked all night," said Dulinsky. "Look at 'em. Every goddamned dung-head farmer in three counties." He wiped his face again and spoke to the men behind him. "Stand steady, boys. They're not going to do anything." He stepped forward, his expression lofty and impassive, his eyes darting hard little glances this way and that.

A man with white hair and a stern leathery face came forward to meet him. He carried a shotgun in the crook of his arm, and his walk was a farmer's walk, heavy and rolling. But he stretched up his head and yelled out at the Refuge men waiting in the road, and there was something about his harsh strident voice that made Len remember the preaching man.

"Stand aside!" he shouted. "We don't want killing, but we can if we have to, so stand aside, in the name of the Lord!"

"Wait a minute," said Dulinsky. "Just a minute, now. This is our town. May I ask what business you think you have in it?"

The man looked at him and said, "We will have no cities in our midst."

"Cities," said Dulinsky. "Cities!" He laughed. "Now look here, sir. You're Noah Burdette, aren't you? I know you well by sight and reputation. You have quite a name as a preacher in the section around Twin Lakes."

He stepped a little closer, speaking in an easier tone, as a man talks when he knows he is going to turn the argument his way.

"You're a sincere and honest man, Mr. Burdette, and I realize that you're acting on what you believe to be truthful information. So I know you're going to be thankful to learn that your information is wrong, and there's no need for any violence at all. I—"

"Violence," said Burdette, "I don't seek. But I don't run from it, neither, when it's in good cause." He looked Dulinsky up and down, slowly, deliberately, with a face as hard as flint. "I know you, too, by sight and reputation, and you can save your wind. Are you going to stand aside?"

"Listen," said Dulinsky, with a note of desperation coming into his voice. "You've been told that I'm trying to build a city here, and that's crazy. I'm only trying to build a warehouse, and I've got as good a right to it as you've got to a new barn. You can't come here and order me around anymore than I could go to your farm and do it!"

"I'm here," said Burdette.

Dulinsky glanced back over his shoulder. Len moved toward him, as though to say, I'm with you. And then Judge Taylor came up through the loose ranks of the Refuge men, saying, "Disperse, go to your homes, and stay there. No harm will come to you. Lay down your weapons and go home."

They hesitated, looking at one another, looking at Dulinsky and the solid mass of the farmers. And Dulinsky said to the judge in weary scorn, "You sheepfaced coward. You were in on this."

"You've done enough harm, Mike," said the judge, very white and standing very stiff and straight. "No need to make everybody in Refuge suffer for it. Stand aside."

Dulinsky glared at him and then at Burdette. "What are you going to do?"

"Cleanse the evil," said Burdette slowly, "as the Book instructs us to, by burning it with fire."

"In plain English," said Dulinsky, "you're going to burn my warehouses, and anything else that happens to take your fancy. The hell you are." He turned around and shouted to the Refuge men. "Listen, you fools, do you think they're going to stop at my warehouses? They'll have the whole town flaming around your ears. Don't you see this is the time, the act that's going to decide how you live for decades yet to come? Are you going to be free men or a gang of belly-crawling slaves?"

His voice rose up to a howl. "Come on and fight, God damn you, fight!"

He spun around and rushed at Burdette, raising his club high in the air.

Without haste and without pity, Burdette swung the shotgun over and fired.

It made a very loud noise. Dulinsky stopped as though he had struck against a solid wall. He stood for a second or two, and then the club dropped out of his hands and he lowered his arms and folded them over his belly. His knees bent and he sank down onto them in the dust.

Len ran forward.

Dulinsky looked up at him with an expression of stunned surprise. His mouth opened. He seemed to be trying to say something, but only blood came out between his lips. Then suddenly his face became blank and remote, like a window when somebody blows out the candle. He fell forward and was still.

"Mike," said Judge Taylor. "Mike?" He looked at Burdette, his eyes widening. "What have you done?"

"Murderer," said Len, and the word encompassed both Burdette and the judge. His voice broke, rising to a harsh scream. "Goddamned yellow-bellied murderer!" He put up his fists and ran toward Burdette, but the line of farmers had begun to move, as though the death of Dulinsky was a signal they had waited for, and Len was caught up in it as in the forefront of a wave. Burdette was gone, and facing him instead was a burly young farmer with a long neck and sloping shoulders and the kind of a mouth that had cried out the accusation against Soames. He carried a length of peeled wood like those used for fence posts, and he brought it down on Len's head, laughing with a sort of cackling haste, his eyes gleaming with immense excitement. Len fell down. Boots clumped and kicked and stumbled over him and he curled up instinctively with his arms over his head and neck. It had become very dark and the

Refuge men were far off behind a wavering veil, but he could see them going, melting away until the road was empty in front of the farmers and there was nothing between them and the town. They went on into Refuge in the hot afternoon, raising up the dust again as they moved, and when that settled there was only Len, and Dulinsky's body lying three or four feet away from him, and Judge Taylor standing still in the middle of the road, just standing and looking at Dulinsky.

THIRTEEN

Len got slowly to his feet. His head hurt and he felt sick, but his compulsion to get away from there was so great that he forced himself to walk in spite of it. He went carefully around Dulinsky, avoiding the dark stains that were in the dust there, and he passed Judge Taylor. They did not speak, nor look at each other. Len went on toward Refuge until just a little bit before the square, where there was an apple orchard beside the road. He turned off among the trees, and when he felt that he was out of sight he sat down in the long grass and put his head between his knees and vomited. An icy coldness came over him, and a shaking. He waited until they passed, and then he got up again and went on, circling west through the trees.

There was a confused noise in the distance, toward the river. A puff of smoke rose in the clear air, and then another, and suddenly there was a dull booming roar and the whole river front seemed to burst into flame and the smoke poured up black and greasy and very thick, lighted on its underside by the kind of flames that come from stored-up barrels of pitch and lamp oil. The streets of the town were choked with carts and horses and people running. Here and there somebody was helping carry a hurt man. Len avoided them, sticking to the back alleys and the peripheral fields. The smoke came blacker and heavier, rolling over the sky and blotting the sun to an ugly copper color. There were sparks in it now, and bits of flaming stuff tossed up. When he came to a high place, Len could see men on some of the roofs of the houses, and on the church and the town hall, making up bucket lines to wet the buildings

down. He could see the waterfront, too. The new warehouse was burning, and the four others that had belonged to Dulinsky, but things had not stopped there. There was a scurrying, a tossing of weapons and a swaying back and forth of little knots of men, and all along the line of docks and warehouses new fires were springing up.

Across the river Shadwell watched but did not stir.

The stables of the traders' compound were blazing when Len came by them. Sparks had fallen in the straw and the hay piles, and other sparks were smoldering on the roofs of the shelters. Len ran into the one he had been occupying and grabbed up his canvas bag and his blanket. When he came out the door he heard men coming and he fled hastily in among the trees at one side. The green leaves were already crisping, and the boughs were shaken by a strange unhealthy wind. A gang of farmers came up from the river. They paused at the edge of the compound, panting, staring about with bright hard eyes. The auction sheds were untouched. One of them, a huge red-bearded man with inflamed cheeks and a roaring voice, pointed to the sheds and bellowed something about money-changers. They made a hungry breathless sound like a pack of dogs after a coon and ran to the long line of sheds, smashing everything they could smash and piling it together and setting fire to it with a torch that one of them was carrying. Then they passed on, kicking over and trampling and breaking down anything in their path. Len thought of Judge Taylor, standing alone in the middle of the road, looking at Dulinsky's body. He would have a lot of things to look at when this day was over.

He went on cautiously between the trees, edging down to the river through a weird sulphurous twilight. The air was choked with the smells of burning, of pitch and wood and oil and hides. Ash fell like a gray and scorching snow. He could hear the fire bell ringing desperately up in the town, but he could not see much that way because of the smoke and the trees. He came out on the riverbank well below the site of the new warehouse and began to work his way back, looking for Esau.

The whole riverbank as far as he could see ahead of him was a solid mass of flame. The heat had driven everybody away and some of them had come downstream past the wreck of the new warehouse, men with their eyes white and staring in blackened faces, men with burned hands and torn clothing and a look of desperation. Three or four were bent over one who lay on the ground moaning and twisting, and there were others sitting down here and there, as though they had come that far and then quit. Most of them were just standing and watching. One man still carried a bucket half full of water.

Len did not see Esau, and he began to be afraid. He went up to several of the men and asked, but they only shook their heads or did not seem to hear him at all. Finally one of them, a clerk named Watts, who had come to the office frequently on business, said bitterly, "Don't worry about him. He's safe if anybody is."

"What do you mean?"

"I mean nobody's seen him since the trouble began. He took off, him and the girl both."

"Girl?" asked Len, startled out of his resentment at Watts' tone.

"Judge Taylor's girl, who else? And where were you, hiding in a hole somewhere? And where's Dulinsky? I thought that son of a bitch was such a mighty fighter, to hear him tell it."

"I was up on the north road," said Len. "And Dulinsky's dead. So I guess he fought harder than you did."

A man standing nearby had turned around at the sound of Dulinsky's name. Under the grime and the soot, the singed hair and the clothing burned partly off him, it was a minute before Len recognized Ames, the warehouse owner who had come down with Dulinsky and the other man that morning to look at the new warehouse and shake his head at Dulinsky's plea for unity.

"Dead," said Ames. "Dead, is he?"

"They shot him. A farmer named Burdette."

"Dead," said Ames. "I'm sorry. He should have lived. He should have lived long enough for a hanging." He lifted his hands and shook them at the blaze and smoke. "Look what he's done to us!"

"He wasn't alone," said Watts. "The Colter boys were in with him, from the beginning."

"If you'd stuck by him this wouldn't have happened," Len said. "He asked you, Mr. Ames. You and Whinnery and the others. He asked the whole town. And what happened? You all danced around and cheered last night—yes, you too, Watts, I saw you!—and then you all ran like rabbits at the first smell of trouble. There wasn't a man of 'em up in the north road that lifted a hand. They left it up to Mike to get killed."

Len's voice had got loud and harsh without his realizing it. The men within earshot had closed in to listen.

"It seems to me," said Ames, "that for a stranger, you take an almighty interest in what we do. Why? What makes you think it's up to you to try and change things? I worked all my life to build up what I had, and then you come, and Dulinsky—"

He stopped. Tears were running out of his eyes and his mouth trembled like a child's.

"Yeah," said Watts. "Why? Where did you come from? Who sent you to call us cowards because we don't want to break the law?"

Len looked around. There were men on all sides of him now. Their faces were grotesque masks of burns with fury. The smoke rolled in a sooty cloud and the flames roared softly with a purring sound as they ate the wealth of Refuge. Up in the town the fire bell had stopped ringing.

Somebody spoke the name of Bartorstown, and Len began to laugh.

Watts reached out and cuffed him. "Funny, is it? All right, where did you come from?"

"Piper's Run, born and raised."

"Why'd you leave it? Why'd you come here to make trouble?"

"He's lying," said another man. "Sure he comes from Bartorstown. They want the cities back."

"It doesn't matter," said Ames, in a low, still voice. "He was in on it. He helped." He turned around, his hands moving as though they groped for something. "There ought to be one piece of rope left unburned in Refuge."

Instantly an eagerness came over the men. "Rope," said somebody. "Yeah. We'll find some." And somebody else said, "Look for the other bastard. We'll hang them both." Some of them ran off down the riverbank, and others began to beat the bushes looking for Esau. Watts and two others tackled Len and bore him down, savaging him with their fists and knees. Ames stood by and watched, looking alternately from Len to the fire.

The men came back. They had not found Esau, but they had found a rope, the mooring line of a skiff tied to the bank farther down. Watts and the others hauled Len to his feet. One of the men tied a clumsy slipknot in the rope and made a noose and put it over Len's head. The rope was damp. It was old and soft and frayed, and it smelled of fish. Len kicked out violently and tore his arms free. They caught him again and hustled him toward the trees, a close-bunched confusion of men lurching along in short erratic bursts of motion with Len struggling in the center, kicking, clawing, banging them with his knees and elbows. And even so, he sensed dimly that it was not men he was fighting at all, but the whole vast soggy smothering continent from sea to sea and from north to south, millions of houses and people and fields and villages all sleeping comfortably and not wanting to be disturbed. The rope was cold and scratchy around his neck, and he was afraid, and he knew he couldn't fight off the idea, the belief and way of life of which these men were only a tiny, tiny part.

He was very dizzy, from the pounding and the blow on the head he had already had up on the north road, so that he was not sure what happened except that suddenly there seemed to be more men, more bodies around him, more upheaval. He was thrown sharply aside. The hands seemed to have let go of him. He hit a tree trunk and slid down it to the ground. There was a face above him. It had blue eyes and a sandy beard with two wide streaks of gray in it, one at each corner of the mouth. He said to the face, "If there weren't so many of you I could kill you all." And it answered him, "You don't want to kill me, Len. Come on, boy, get up."

Tears came suddenly into Len's eyes. "Mr. Hostetter," he said. "Mr. Hostetter." He put up his hands and caught hold of him, and it seemed like a long time ago, in another hour of darkness and fear. Hostetter gave him a strong pull up to his feet and jerked the rope from around his neck.

"Run," he said. "Run like the devil."

Len ran. There were several other men with Hostetter, and they must have charged in hard with the poles and boat hooks they had, because the Refuge men were pretty well scattered. But they were not going to give Len up without a fight, and the intrusion of Hostetter and his party had convinced them that they were right about Bartorstown. They were determined now to get Hostetter too, shouting and cursing, gathering together again and searching for anything they could use as weapons, stones, fallen branches, clods. Len staggered and stumbled as he went, and Hostetter put a hand under his arm and rushed him along.

"Boat waiting," he said. "Farther down."

Things began to fly through the air around them. A stone bounced off Hostetter's back and he hunched his head down until his broad-brimmed hat seemed to sit flat on his shoulders. They ran in among a grove of trees and out on the other side, and Len stopped suddenly.

"Esau," he said. "Can't go without Esau."

"He's already aboard," said Hostetter. "Come on!"

They ran again, across a pasture sloping down to the water's edge, and the cows went bucketing away with their tails in the air. At the lower end of the pasture was another clump of trees, growing right on the bank, and in their partial concealment a big steam barge was tied up, with a couple of men standing on the deck holding axes, ready to chop the lines free. Smoke began to puff up suddenly from the single low stack, as though a banked fire had been stirred swiftly to life. Len saw Esau hanging over the rail, and there was someone beside him, someone with yellow hair and a long skirt.

There was a board laid from the bank to the rail. They scrambled up over it onto the deck and Hostetter shouted at the men with the axes. Stones were flying again, and Esau caught Amity and hurried her around to the other side of the deckhouse. The axes flashed. There was more shouting, and the Refuge men, with Watts in the lead, rushed right down to the bank and Watts and two others ran out onto the plank. Len did not see Ames among them. The lines parted and went snaking into the water. Hostetter and Len and some others grabbed up long poles and pushed off hard. The plank fell into the water with Watts and the other men that were on it. There was a roar and a clatter from below, the deck shook and sparks burst up through the stack. The barge began to move out into the current. Watts stood waist-deep in the muddy water by the bank and shook his fists at them.

"We know you now!" he shouted, his voice coming thin across the widening gap. "You won't get away!"

The men on the bank behind him shouted too. Their voices grew fainter but the note of hatred remained in them, and the ugliness in the gestures of their hands. Len looked back at Refuge. They were well out in the river now and he could see past the waterfront. Smoke obscured much of the town, but he could see enough. What Burdette's farmers had left untouched the spreading fire was taking for its own.

Len sat down on the deck with his back against the house. He put his arms across his knees and laid his head on them and felt an overwhelming desire to cry like a little boy, but he was too tired even to do that. He just sat and tried to make his mind as blank as the rest of him felt. But he could not do it, and over and over he saw Dulinsky stop and fall down slowly into the hot dust of the north road, and he smelled the smell of a great burning, and Burdette's harsh voice sounded in his ears, saying, "We will have no cities in our midst."

After a while he became aware that somebody was standing over him. He looked up, and it was Hostetter, holding his hat in his hand and wiping his forehead wearily on his coat sleeve.

"Well, boy," he said, "you've got your wish. You're on your way to Bartorstown."

FOURTEEN

It was night, warm and tranquil. There was a moon, lighting the surface of the river and turning the two banks into masses of black shadow. The barge slipped along, chuffing gently as it added a bit to the thrust of the current. There was a lot of cargo on the deck, tied down securely and covered with canvas against the rain. Len had found a place in it. He had slept for a while, and he was sitting now with his back against a bale, watching the river go by.

Hostetter came by, walking slowly along the narrow space left clear on the foredeck, trailing of tobacco smoke from an old pipe. He saw Len sitting up, and stopped. "Feel better?"

"I feel sick," Len said, so viciously that Hostetter knew what he meant. He nodded.

"You know now how I felt the night they killed Bill Soames."

"Murderers," said Len. "Cowards. Bastards." He cursed them until the words choked in his throat. "You should have seen them standing there across the road. And then Burdette shot him. He shot him just the way you'd shoot some vermin you found in the corn."

"Yes," said Hostetter slowly, "we'd have had you out of there sooner if you hadn't gone up after Dulinsky. Poor devil. But I'm not surprised."

"Couldn't you have helped him?"

"Us? You mean Bartorstown?"

"He wanted the same things you want. Growth, progress, intelligence, a future. Couldn't you have helped?"

There was an edge to Len's voice, but Hostetter only took the pipe out of his mouth and asked quietly, "How?"

Len thought about that. After a while he said, "I suppose you couldn't."

"Not without an army. We don't have an army, and if we did have we wouldn't use it. It takes an almighty force to make people change their whole way of thinking and living. We had a force like that just yesterday as time goes for a nation, and we don't want any more of them."

"That's what the judge was afraid of. Change. And he just stood there and watched Dulinsky die." Len shook his head. "He died for nothing. That's what he died for, *nothing.*"

"No," said Hostetter, "I wouldn't say that. But it takes more than one Dulinsky. It takes a lot of them, one after the other, in different places—"

"And more Burdettes, and more burnings."

"Yes. And someday one will come along at the right time, and the change will be made."

"That's a lot to look forward to."

"That's the way it is. And then all the Dulinskys will become martyrs to a great ideal. In the meantime, you're disturbers of the peace. And damn it, Len, you know in a way they're right. They're comfortable and happy. Who are you—or any of us—to tell them it's all got to be torn up and changed?"

Len turned and looked at Hostetter in the moonlight. "Is that why you just stand by and watch?"

Hostetter said, with just the faintest note of impatience in his voice, "I don't think you understand about us yet. We're not supermen. We've got all we can do just to stay alive, without trying to remake a country that doesn't want to be remade."

"But how can you say they're right? Ignorant butchers like Burdette, hypocrites like the judge—"

"Honest men, Len, both of them. Yes, they are. Both of them got up this morning all fired up with nobility and good purpose and went and did the right as they saw it. There's never been an act done since the beginning, from a kid stealing candy to a dictator committing genocide, that the person doing it didn't think he was fully justified. That's a mental trick called rationalizing, and it's done the human race more harm than anything else you can name."

"Burdette, maybe," said Len. "He's another one like the man at the preaching that night. But not the judge. He knew better."

"Not at the time. That's the hell of it. The doubts always come later, and they're usually too late. Take yourself, Len. When you ran away from home, did you have any doubts about it? Did you say to yourself, I am now going to do an evil thing and make my parents very unhappy?"

Len looked down at the gleaming water for a long time without answering. Finally he said, in an oddly quiet voice, "How are they? Are they all right?"

"The last I heard they were fine. I didn't go up this spring myself."

"And Gran?"

"She died, a year ago last December."

"Yes," said Len. "She was terrible old." It was strange how sad he felt about Gran, as though a part of his life had gone. Suddenly, with painful clarity, he saw her again sitting on the stoop in the sunlight, looking at the flaming October trees and talking about the red dress she had had so long ago, when the world was a different place.

He said, "Pa couldn't ever quite make her shut up."

Hostetter nodded. "My own grandmother was much the same way."

Silence again. Len sat and watched the river, and the past lay heavy on him, and he did not want to go to Bartorstown. He wanted to go home.

"Your brother's doing fine," said Hostetter. "Has two boys of his own now."

"That's good."

"Piper's Run hasn't changed much."

"No," said Len. "I reckon not." And then he added, "Oh, shut up!"

Hostetter smiled.

"That's the advantage I have over you. I'm going home. It's been a long time."

"Then you didn't come from Pennsylvania at all."

"My people did, originally. I was born in Bartorstown."

An old anger rose and pricked at Len. "Listen," he said, "you knew why we ran away. You must have known all along where we were and what we were doing."

"I felt sort of responsible," Hostetter admitted. "I kept tabs."

"All right," said Len, "why did you make us wait so long? You knew where we wanted to go."

Hostetter said, "Do you remember Soames?"

"I'll never forget him."

"He trusted a boy."

"But," said Len, "I wouldn't—" Then he remembered how Esau had put Hostetter in a bad place. "I guess I see what you mean."

"We've got one unbreakable law in Bartorstown. That law is Hands Off, and because of it we've been able to keep going all these years when the very name of Bartorstown is enough to hang you. Soames broke it. I'm breaking it now, but I got permission. And believe me, that was the feat of the century. For one solid week I talked myself hoarse to Sherman—"

"Sherman," said Len, straightening up. "Yes, Sherman. Sherman wants to know if you've heard from Byers—"

"What the hell are you talking about?" asked Hostetter, staring.

"Over the radio," said Len, and the old excitement came back on him like a stroke of summer lightning. "The voices talking that night I let the cows out of the barn and we went after them down to the creek, and Esau dropped the radio. The spool thing reeled out, and the voices came—Sherman wants to know. And something about the river. That's why we went down to the Ohio."

"Oh yes," said Hostetter. "The radio. That was the start of the whole thing, wasn't it? I owed Esau something for stealing it. I owed him for the blood I sweated when I found it was gone." Hostetter shivered. "Christ. When I think how close he came to exposing me—I'd never have made it back alive, you know. Your own people would have told me to go and never show my face again, but the word would have spread. I had to throw Esau to the wolves, and I won't say I was sorry. But it was too bad you got dragged into it."

"I never blamed you. I told Esau it wasn't going to be that easy."

"Well, you can thank the farmers, because if it hadn't been for them I'd never have talked Sherman into letting me pick you up. I told him you were sure to get it from one side or the other, and I didn't want your blood on my conscience. He finally gave in, but I'll tell you, Len, the next time somebody gives you a piece of good advice, you take it."

Len rubbed his neck where the rope had scratched it. "Yes, sir. And thanks. I won't forget what you did."

Quite sternly, speaking as Pa had used to speak sometimes, Hostetter said, "Don't. Not for me particularly, or for Sherman, but because of a lot of people and ideas that might just depend on your not forgetting."

Len said slowly, "Are you afraid you can't trust me?"

"It isn't exactly a question of trust."

"What is it, then?"

"You're going to Bartorstown."

Len frowned, trying to understand what he was getting at. "But that's where I want to go. That's why—all this happened."

Hostetter pushed the flat-brimmed hat back from his forehead so that his face showed clear in the moonlight. His eyes rested shrewdly and steadily on Len.

"You're going to Bartorstown," he repeated. "You have a place all dreamed up inside your head, and you call it by that name, but that isn't where you're going. You're going to the real Bartorstown, and it's probably not going to be very much like the place in your head at all. You may not like it. You may come to have pretty strong feelings about it. And that's why I say, don't forget you owe us something."

"Listen," said Len. "Can you learn in Bartorstown? Can you read books and talk about things, and use machines, and really *think?*"

Hostetter nodded.

"Then I'll like it there." Len looked out at the dark still country slipping by in the night, the sleeping, murderous, hateful country. "I never want to see any of this again. Ever."

"For my sake," said Hostetter, "I hope you'll fit in. I'm going to have trouble enough as it is, explaining the girl to Sherman. She wasn't included. But I couldn't see what else to do."

"I was wondering about her," Len said.

"Well, she'd come down there to Esau, to try and help him get away. She said she couldn't go back to her parents. She said she was going to stay with Esau. And it seemed like she pretty well had to."

"Why?" asked Len.

"Don't you know?"

"No."

"Best reason in the world," said Hostetter. "She's got his child."

Len sat staring with his mouth open. Hostetter got up. And a man came out of the deckhouse and said to him, "Sam's talking to Collins on the radio. Maybe you'd better come down, Ed."

"Trouble?"

"Well, it seems like our friend we dumped in the water back there meant what he said. Collins says two towboats went by together just after moonrise. They didn't have any tow, and they were chock full of men. One was from Refuge, the other from Shadwell."

Hostetter scowled, knocking the ashes out of his pipe and crushing them carefully under his boots. He said to Len, "We asked Collins to keep watch, just in case. He's got a shanty-boat and acts as a mobile post. Well, come on. This is all part of being a Bartorstown man. You might as well get used to it."

Continued in Galaxy's Edge #22